DANGEROUS WOMEN PART III

EDITED BY

GEORGE R.R. MARTIN

AND

GARDNER DOZOIS

HARPER
Voyager

HarperCollins*Publishers*
77–85 Fulham Palace Road,
Hammersmith, London W6 8JB

www. harpervoyagerbooks.co.uk

This paperback edition 2014

Published by Harper*Voyager*
An imprint of HarperCollins*Publishers* 2014

Dangerous Women / Edited by George R.R. Martin and Gardner Dozois.

A catalogue record for this book
is available from the British Library

ISBN: 9780007549443

Set in Adobe Caslon Pro

Printed and bound in Great Britain

Find out more about HarperCollins and the environment at
www.harpercollins.co.uk/green

Copyright Acknowledgments

To Jo Playford, my dangerous minion.

[—George R.R. Martin]

Contents

Introduction by Gardner Dozois

Genre fiction has always been divided over the question of just *how* dangerous women are.

In the real world, of course, the question has long been settled. Even if the Amazons are mythological (and almost certainly wouldn't have cut their right breasts off to make it easier to draw a bow if they *weren't*), their legend was inspired by memory of the ferocious warrior women of the Scythians, who were very much *not* mythological. Gladiatrix, women gladiators, fought other women—and sometimes men—to the death in the arenas of Ancient Rome. There were female pirates like Anne Bonny and Mary Read, and even female samurai. Women served as frontline combat troops, feared for their ferocity, in the Russian army during World War II, and serve so in Israel today. Until 2013, women in the U.S. forces were technically restricted to "noncombat" roles, but many brave women gave their lives in Iraq and Afghanistan anyway, since bullets and land mines have never cared whether you're a noncombatant or not. Women who served as Women Airforce Service Pilots for the United States during World War II were also limited to noncombat roles (where many of them were nevertheless killed in the performance of their duties), but Russian women took to the skies as fighter pilots, and sometimes became aces. A Russian female sniper during World War II was credited with more than fifty kills. Queen Boudicca of the Iceni tribe led one of the most fearsome revolts ever against Roman authority, one that was almost successful in driving the Roman invaders from Britain, and a young French peasant girl inspired and led the troops against the enemy so successfully that she became famous forever afterwards as Joan of Arc.

On the dark side, there have been female "highwaymen" like Mary Frith and Lady Katherine Ferrers and Pearl Hart (the last person to ever rob a stagecoach); notorious poisoners like Agrippina and Catherine de Medici, modern female outlaws like Ma Barker and Bonnie Parker, even female serial killers like Aileen Wuornos. Elizabeth Báthory was said to have bathed in the blood of virgins, and even though that has been called into question, there is no doubt that she tortured and killed dozens, perhaps hundreds, of children during her life. Queen Mary I of England had hundreds of Protestants burnt at the stake; Queen Elizabeth of England later responded by executing large numbers of Catholics. Mad Queen Ranavalona of Madagascar had so many people put to death that she wiped out one-third of the entire population of Madagascar during her reign; she would even have you executed if you appeared in her dreams.

Popular fiction, though, has always had a schizophrenic view of the dangerousness of women. In the science fiction of the 1930s, '40s, and '50s, women, if they appeared at all, were largely regulated to the role of the scientist's beautiful daughter, who might scream during the fight scenes but otherwise had little to do except hang adoringly on the arm of the hero afterwards. Legions of women swooned helplessly while waiting to be rescued by the intrepid jut-jawed hero from everything from dragons to the bug-eyed monsters who were always carrying them off for improbable purposes either dietary or romantic on the covers of pulp SF magazines. Hopelessly struggling women were tied to railroad tracks, with nothing to do but squeak in protest and hope that the Good Guy arrived in time to save them.

And yet, at the same time, warrior women like Edgar Rice Burroughs's Dejah Thoris and Thuvia, Maid of Mars, were every bit as good with the blade and every bit as deadly in battle as John Carter and their other male comrades, female adventuresses like C. L. Moore's Jirel of Joiry swashbuckled their way through the pages of *Weird Tales* magazine (and blazed a trail for later female swashbucklers like Joanna Russ's Alyx); James H. Schmitz sent Agents of Vega like Granny Wannatel and fearless teenagers like Telzey Amberdon and Trigger Argee out to battle the sinister menaces and monsters of the spaceways; and Robert A. Heinlein's dangerous women were capable of being the captain of a spaceship or killing enemies in hand-to-hand combat. Arthur Conan Doyle's sly, shady Irene Adler was one of the only people ever to outwit his Sherlock Holmes, and probably one of the inspirations for the legions of tricky, dangerous, seductive, and treacherous "femmes fatale" who featured in the works of Dashiell Hammett and James M. Cain and later went on to appear in dozens of films noir, and who still turn up in the movies and on television to this day. Later television heroines such as Buffy the Vampire Slayer and Xena, Warrior Princess, firmly established women as being formidable and deadly enough to battle hordes of fearsome supernatural menaces, and helped to inspire the whole subgenre of paranormal romance, which is sometimes unofficially known as the "kick-ass heroine" genre.

Like our anthology *Warriors, Dangerous Women* was conceived of as a cross-genre anthology, one that would mingle every kind of fiction, so we asked writers from every genre—science fiction, fantasy, mystery, historical, horror, paranormal romance, men and women alike—to tackle the theme of "dangerous women," and that call was answered by some of the best writers in the business, including both new writers and giants of their fields like Diana Gabaldon, Jim Butcher, Sharon Kay Penman, Joe Abercrombie, Carrie Vaughn, Joe R. Lansdale, Lawrence Block, Cecelia Holland, Brandon Sanderson, Sherilynn Kenyon, S. M. Stirling, Nancy Kress, and George R.R. Martin.

Here you'll find no hapless victims who stand by whimpering in dread while the male hero fights the monster or clashes swords with the villain, and if you want to tie *these* women to the railroad tracks, you'll find you have a real fight on your hands. Instead, you will find sword-wielding women warriors; intrepid women fighter pilots and far-ranging spacewomen; deadly female serial killers; formidable female superheroes; sly and seductive femmes fatale; female wizards; hard-living bad girls; female bandits and rebels; embattled survivors in postapocalyptic futures; female private investigators; stern female hanging judges; haughty queens who rule nations and whose jealousies and ambitions send thousands to grisly deaths; daring dragonriders; and many more.

Enjoy!

Joe Abercrombie

As the sizzlingly fast-paced and action-packed story that follows demonstrates, sometimes chasing a fugitive can be as dangerous for the pursuers as for the pursued—particularly when the quarry has no place left to run . . .

Joe Abercrombie is one of the fastest-rising stars in fantasy today, acclaimed by readers and critics alike for his tough, spare, no-nonsense approach to the genre. He's probably best known for his First Law trilogy, the first novel of which, *The Blade Itself,* was published in 2006; it was followed in subsequent years by *Before They Are Hanged* and *Last Argument of Kings.* He's also written the stand-alone fantasy novels *Best Served Cold* and *The Heroes.* His most recent novel is *Red Country.* In addition to writing, Abercrombie is also a freelance film editor and lives and works in London.

SOME DESPERADO

Shy gave the horse her heels, its forelegs buckled, and, before she had a notion what was happening, she and her saddle had bid each other a sad farewell.

She was given a flailing instant aloft to consider the situation. Not a good one at a brief assay, and the impending earth gave her no time for a longer. She did her best to roll with the fall—as she tried to do with most of her many misfortunes—but the ground soon uncurled her, gave her a fair roughing up, and tossed her, flopping, into a patch of sun-shrivelled scrub.

Dust settled.

She stole a moment just to get some breath in. Then one to groan while the world stopped rolling. Then another to shift gingerly an arm and a leg, waiting for that sick jolt of pain that meant something was broke and her miserable shadow of a life would soon be lost in the dusk. She would've welcomed it, if it meant she could stretch out and not have to run any more. But the pain didn't come. Not outside of the usual compass, least-ways. As far as her miserable shadow of a life went, she was still awaiting judgment.

Shy dragged herself up, scratched and scuffed, caked in dust and spitting out grit. She'd taken too many mouthfuls of sand the last few months but she'd a dismal premonition that there'd be more. Her horse lay a few strides distant, one foamed-up flank heaving, forelegs black with blood. Neary's arrow had snagged it in the shoulder, not deep enough to kill or even slow it right off, but deep enough to make it bleed at a good pace. With her hard riding, that had killed it just as dead as a shaft in the heart.

There'd been a time Shy had got attached to horses. A time—despite reckoning herself hard with people and being mostly right—she'd been uncommon soft about animals. But that time was a long time gone. There wasn't much soft on Shy these days, body or mind. So she left her mount

to its final red-frothed breaths without the solace of her calming hand and
ran for the town, tottering some at first, but quickly warming to the exercise. At running, she'd a heap of practice.

"Town" was perhaps an overstatement. It was six buildings, and calling
them buildings was being generous to two or three. All rough lumber and
an entire stranger to straight angles, sun-baked, rain-peeled, and dust-
blasted, huddled about a dirt square and a crumbling well.

The biggest building had the look of a tavern or brothel or trading post or
more likely all three amalgamated. A rickety sign still clung to the boards
above the doorway but the name had been rubbed by the wind to just a few
pale streaks in the grain. *Nothing, nowhere,* was all its proclamation now. Up
the steps two by two, bare feet making the old boards wheeze, thoughts
boiling away at how she'd play it when she got inside, what truths she'd
season with what lies for the most likely recipe.

There's men chasing me! Gulping breath in the doorway and doing her
best to look beyond desperate—no mighty effort of acting at that moment,
or any occupying the last twelve months, indeed.

Three of the bastards! Then—provided no one recognised her from all the
bills for her arrest—*They tried to rob me!* A fact. No need to add that she'd
robbed the money herself from the new bank in Hommenaw in the company of those three worthies plus another since caught and hung by the
authorities.

They killed my brother! They're drunk on blood! Her brother was safe at
home where she wished she was, and if her pursuers were drunk, it would
likely be on cheap spirits as usual, but she'd shriek it with that little
warble in her throat. Shy could do quite a warble when she needed one,
she'd practiced it 'til it was something to hear. She pictured the patrons
springing to their feet in their eagerness to aid a woman in distress. *They
shot my horse!* She had to admit it didn't seem overpowering likely that
anyone hard-bitten enough to live out here would be getting into a sweat
of chivalry, but maybe fate would deal her a winning hand for once.

It had been known to happen.

She blundered through the tavern's door, opening her mouth to serve
up the tale, and stopped cold.

The place was empty.

Not just no one there, but nothing there, and for damn sure no winning hand. Not a twig of furniture in the bare common room. A narrow

stairway and a balcony running across the left-hand wall, doorways yawning empty upstairs. Chinks of light scattered where the rising sun was seeking out the many gaps in the splitting carpentry. Maybe just a lizard skittering away into the shadows—of which there was no shortage—and a bumper harvest of dust, greying every surface, drifted into every corner. Shy stood there a moment just blinking, then dashed back out along the rickety stoop and to the next building. When she shoved the door, it dropped right off its rusted hinges.

This one hadn't even a roof. Hadn't even a floor. Just bare rafters with the careless, pinking sky above, and bare joists with a stretch of dirt below, every bit as desolate as the miles of dirt outside.

She saw it now as she stepped back into the street with vision unhindered by hope. No glass in the windows, or wax paper, even. No rope by the crumbling well. No animals to be seen—aside from her own dead horse, that was, which only served to prove the point.

It was a dried-out corpse of a town, long since dead.

Shy stood in that forsaken place, up on the balls of her bare feet as though she was about to sprint off somewhere but lacked the destination, hugging herself with one arm while the fingers of the other hand fluttered and twitched at nothing, biting on her lip and sucking air fast and rasping through the little gap between her front teeth.

Even by recent standards, it was a low moment. But if she'd learned anything the last few months, it was that things can always get lower. Looking back the way she'd come, Shy saw the dust rising. Three little grey trails in the shimmer off the grey land.

"Oh, hell," she whispered, and bit her lip harder. She pulled her eating knife from her belt and wiped the little splinter of metal on her dirty shirt, as though cleaning it might somehow settle the odds. Shy had been told she had a fertile imagination, but even so, it was hard to picture a more feeble weapon. She'd have laughed if she hadn't been on the verge of weeping. She'd spent way too much time on the verge of weeping the last few months, now that she thought about it.

How had it come to this?

A question for some jilted girl rather than an outlaw with four thousand marks offered, but still a question she was never done asking. Some desperado! She'd grown expert on the desperate part but the rest remained a mystery. The sorry truth was that she knew full well how it came to this—the same way as always. One disaster following so hard on another that she just bounced between 'em, pinging about like a moth in a lantern. The second usual question followed hard on the first.

What the fuck *now?*

She sucked in her stomach—not that there was much to suck in these days—and dragged the bag out by the drawstrings, coins inside clicking together with that special sound only money makes. Two thousand marks in silver, give or take. You'd think that a bank would hold a lot more—they told depositors they always had fifty thousand on hand—but it turns out you can't trust banks any more than bandits.

She dug her hand in, dragged free a fistful of coins, and tossed the money across the street, leaving it gleaming in the dust. She did it like she did most things these days—hardly knowing why. Maybe she valued her life a lot higher'n two thousand marks, even if no one else did. Maybe she hoped they'd just take the silver and leave her be, though what she'd do once she was left be in this corpse town—no horse, no food, no weapon— she hadn't thought out. Clearly she hadn't fixed up a whole plan, or not one that would hold too much water, leastways. Leaky planning had always been a problem of hers.

She sprinkled silver as if she was tossing seed on her mother's farm, miles and years and a dozen violent deaths away. Whoever would've thought she'd miss the place? Miss the bone-poor house and the broke-down barn and the fences that always needed mending. The stubborn cow that never gave milk and the stubborn well that never gave water and the stubborn soil that only weeds would thrive in. Her stubborn little sister and brother too. Even big, scarred, softheaded Lamb. What Shy would've given now to hear her mother's shrill voice curse her out again. She sniffed hard, her nose hurting, her eyes stinging, and wiped 'em on the back of her frayed cuff. No time for tearful reminiscences. She could see three dark spots of riders now beneath those three inevitable dust trails. She flung the empty bag away, ran back to the tavern, and—

"Ah!" She hopped over the threshold, bare sole of her foot torn on a loose nail head. The world's nothing but a mean bully, that's a fact. Even when you've big misfortunes threatening to drop on your head, small ones still take every chance to prick your toes. How she wished she'd got the chance to grab her boots. Just to keep a shred of dignity. But she had what she had, and neither boots nor dignity were on the list, and a hundred big wishes weren't worth one little fact—as Lamb used to boringly drone at her whenever she cursed him and her mother and her lot in life and swore she'd be gone in the morning.

Shy remembered how she'd been then, and wished she had the chance now to punch her earlier self in the face. But she could punch herself in the face when she got out of this.

She'd a procession of other willing fists to weather first.

She hurried up the stairs, limping a little and cursing a lot. When she reached the top she saw she'd left bloody toe prints on every other one. She was working up to feeling pretty damn low about that glistening trail leading right to the end of her leg, when something like an idea came trickling through the panic.

She paced down the balcony, making sure to press her bloody foot firm to the boards, and turned into an abandoned room at the end. Then she held her foot up, gripping it hard with one hand to stop the bleeding, and hopped back the way she'd come and through the first doorway, near the top of the steps, pressing herself into the shadows inside.

A pitiful effort, doubtless. As pitiful as her bare feet and her eating knife and her two-thousand-mark haul and her big dream of making it back home to the shit-hole she'd had the big dream of leaving. Small chance those three bastards would fall for that, even stupid as they were. But what else could she do?

When you're down to small stakes, you have to play long odds.

Her own breath was her only company, echoing in the emptiness, hard on the out, ragged on the in, almost painful down her throat. The breath of someone scared near the point of an involuntary shitting and all out of ideas. She just couldn't see her way to the other side of this. She ever made it back to that farm she'd jump out of bed every morning she woke alive and do a little dance, and give her mother a kiss for every cuss, and never snap at her sister or mock Lamb again for being a coward. She promised it, then wished she was the sort who kept promises.

She heard horses outside, crept to the one window with half a view of the street, and peered down as gingerly as if she was peering into a bucket of scorpions.

They were here.

Neary wore that dirty old blanket cinched in at the waist with twine, his greasy hair sticking up at all angles, reins in one hand and the bow he'd shot Shy's horse with in the other, the blade of the heavy axe hanging at his belt as carefully cleaned as the rest of his repugnant person was beyond neglect. Dodd had his battered hat pulled low, sitting his saddle with that round-shouldered cringe he always had around his brother, like a puppy expecting a slap. Shy would have liked to give the faithless fool a slap right then. A slap for starters. Then there was Jeg, sitting up tall as a lord in that long red coat of his, dirt-fringed tails spread out over his big horse's rump, hungry sneer on his face as he scanned the buildings, that tall hat which he thought made him look quite the personage poking off his head slightly crooked, like the chimney from a burned-out farmstead.

Dodd pointed to the coins scattered across the dirt around the well, a couple of 'em winking with the sun. "She left the money."

"Seems so," said Jeg, voice hard as his brother's was soft.

She watched them get down and hitch their mounts. No hurry to it. Like they were dusting themselves off after a jaunt of a ride and looking forward to a nice little evening among cultured company. They'd no need to hurry. They knew she was here, and they knew she was going nowhere, and they knew she was getting no help, and so did she.

"Bastards," Shy whispered, cursing the day she ever took up with them. But you have to take up with someone, don't you? And you can only pick from what's on offer.

Jeg stretched his back, took a long sniff and a comfortable spit, then drew his sword. That curved cavalry sword he was so proud of with the clever-arsed basketwork, which he said he'd won in a duel with a Union officer, but that Shy knew he'd stolen, along with the best part of everything else he'd ever owned. How she'd mocked him about that stupid sword. She wouldn't have minded having it to hand now, though, and him with only her eating knife.

"Smoke!" bellowed Jeg, and Shy winced. She'd no idea who'd thought that name up for her. Some wag had lettered it on the bills for her arrest and now everyone used it. On account of her tendency to vanish like smoke, maybe. Though it could also have been on account of her tendencies to stink like it, stick in folks' throats, and drift with the wind.

"Get out here, Smoke!" Jeg's voice clapped off the dead fronts of the buildings, and Shy shrank a little further into the darkness. "Get out here and we won't hurt you too bad when we find you!"

So much for taking the money and going. They wanted the price on her too. She pressed her tongue into the gap between her teeth and mouthed, "Cocksuckers." There's a certain kind of man, the more you give him, the more he'll take.

"We'll have to go and get her," she heard Neary say in the stillness.

"Aye."

"I told you we'd have to go and get her."

"You must be pissing your pants with joy over the outcome, then, eh?"

"Said we'd have to get her."

"So stop pointing it out and get it done."

Dodd's wheedling voice. "Look, the money's here, we could just scrape this up and get off, there ain't no need to—"

"Did you and I really spring from between the same set o' legs?" sneered Jeg at his brother. "You are the stupidest bastard."

"Stupidest," said Neary.

"You think I'm leaving four thousand marks for the crows?" said Jeg. "You scrape that up, Dodd, we'll break the mare."

"Where do you reckon she is?" asked Neary.

"I thought you was the big tracker?"

"Out in the wild, but we ain't in the wild."

Jeg cocked an eyebrow at the empty shacks. "You'd call this the highest extent of civilisation, would you?"

They looked at each other a moment, dust blowing up around their legs, then settling again.

"She's here somewhere," said Neary.

"You think? Good thing I got the self-described sharpest eyes west of the mountains with me, so I don't miss her dead horse ten fucking strides away. Yes, she's here somewhere."

"Where do you reckon?" asked Neary.

"Where would you be?"

Neary looked about the buildings and Shy jerked out of the way as his narrowed eyes darted over the tavern.

"In that one, I reckon, but I ain't her."

"Course you ain't fucking her. You know how I can tell? You got bigger tits and less sense. If you was her, I wouldn't have to fucking look for her now, would I?"

Another silence, another dusty gust. "Guess not," said Neary.

Jeg took his tall hat off, scrubbed at his sweaty hair with his fingernails, and jammed it back on at an angle. "You look in there, I'll try the one next to it, but don't kill the bitch, eh? That'll half the reward."

Shy eased back into the shadows, feeling the sweat tickling under her shirt. To be caught in this worthless arsehole of a place. By these worthless bastards. In bare feet. She didn't deserve this. All she'd wanted was to be somebody worth speaking of. To not be nothing, forgotten on the day of her death. Now she saw that there's a sharp balance between too little excitement and a huge helping too much. But like most of her lame-legged epiphanies, it had dawned a year too late.

She sucked air through the little gap between her teeth as she heard Neary creaking across the boards in the common room, maybe just the metal rattle of that big axe. She was shivering all over. Felt so weak of a sudden she could hardly hold the knife up, let alone imagine swinging it. Maybe it was time to give up. Toss the knife out the door and say, "I'm coming out! I'll be no trouble! You win!" Smile and nod and thank 'em for their betrayal and their kind consideration when they kicked the shit out of her or horsewhipped her or broke her legs and whatever else amused them on the way to her hanging.

She'd seen her share of those and never relished the spectacle. Standing there tied while they read your name and your crime, hoping for some last reprieve that wouldn't come while the noose was drawn tight, sobbing for mercy or hurling your curses and neither making the slightest hair of difference. Kicking at nothing, tongue stuck out while you shat yourself for the amusement of scum no better'n you. She pictured Jeg and Neary, up front in the grinning crowd as they watched her do the thief's dance at rope's end. Probably arrayed in even more ridiculous clothes secured with the reward money.

"*Fuck* them," she mouthed at the darkness, lips curling back in a snarl as she heard Neary's foot on the bottom step.

She had a hell of a contrary streak, did Shy. From when she was a tot, when someone told her how things would be, she immediately started thinking on how she'd make 'em otherwise. Her mother had always called her mule stubborn, and blamed it on her Ghost blood. "That's your damn Ghost blood," as though being quarter savage had been Shy's own choice rather than on account of her mother picking out a half-Ghost wanderer to lie with who turned out—no crashing surprise—to be a no-good drunk.

Shy would be fighting. No doubt she'd be losing, but she'd be fighting.

She'd make those bastards kill her and at least rob 'em of half the reward. Might not expect such thoughts as those to steady your hand, but they did hers. The little knife still shook, but now from how hard she was gripping it.

For a man who proclaimed himself the great tracker, Neary had some trouble keeping quiet. She heard the breath in his nose as he paused at the top of the steps, close enough to touch if it hadn't been for the plank wall between them.

A board groaned as he shifted his weight and Shy's whole body tensed, every hair twitching up. Then she saw him—not darting through the doorway at her, axe in his fist and murder in his eyes, but creeping off down the balcony after the bait of bloody footsteps, drawn bow pointed exactly the wrong way.

When she was given a gift, Shy had always believed in grabbing it with both hands rather than thinking on how to say thank you. She dashed at Neary's back, teeth bared and a low growl ripping at her throat. His head whipped around, the whites of his eyes showing and the bow following after, the head of the arrow glinting with such light as found that abandoned place.

She ducked low and caught him around the legs, shoulder driving hard into his thigh and making him grunt, her hand finding her wrist and clamping tight under Neary's arse, her nose suddenly full of the horse-and-sour sweat stink of him. The bowstring went, but Shy was already straightening, snarling, screaming, bursting up, and—big man though he was—she hoisted Neary right over the rail as neat as she used to hoist a sack of grain on her mother's farm.

He hung in the air a moment, mouth and eyes wide with shock, then he plummeted with a breathy whoop and crashed through the boards down below.

Shy blinked, hardly able to believe it. Her scalp was burning and she touched a finger to it, half expecting to feel the arrow stuck right in her brains, but she turned and saw it was in the wall behind her, a considerably happier outcome from her standpoint. Blood, though, sticky in her hair, tickling at her forehead. Maybe the lath of the bow scratched her. Get that bow, she'd have a chance. She made a step towards the stairs, then stopped dead. Jeg was in the doorway, his sword a long, black curve against the sun-glare of the street.

"Smoke!" he roared, and she was off down the balcony like a rabbit, following her own trail of bloody footprints to nowhere, hearing Jeg's heavy boots clomping towards the stairs. She hit the door at the end full tilt with her shoulder and burst into the light, out onto another balcony behind the building. Up onto the low rail with one bare foot—better to just go with her contrary streak and hope it somehow carried her through than to pause for thought—and she jumped. Flung herself writhing at a ramshackle balcony on the building across the narrow lane, as if flapping her hands and feet like she was having a fit might carry her further.

She caught the rail, wood smashing her in the ribs, slipped down, groaning, clawing for a grip, fought desperately to drag herself up and over, felt something give—

And with a groan of tortured wood the whole weather-blasted thing tore from the side of the building.

Again Shy was given a flailing instant aloft to consider the situation. Again not good, at a brief assay. She was just starting to wail when her old enemy the ground caught up with her—as the ground always will—folded up her left leg, spun her over, then smashed her in the side and drove her wind right out.

Shy coughed, then moaned, then spat more grit. That she had been right about her earlier sandy mouth not being her last was scant comfort. She saw Jeg standing on the balcony where she'd jumped. He pushed his hat back and gave a chuckle, then ducked back inside.

She still had a piece of the rail in her fist, well rotted through. A little like her hopes. She tossed it away as she rolled over, waiting again for that sick pain that told her she was done. Again it didn't come. She could move. She worked her feet around and guessed that she could stand. But she thought that she might leave that for now. Chances were she'd only get to do it one more time.

She floundered clear of the tangle of broken wood against the wall, her shadow stretching out towards the doorway, groaning with pain as she heard Jeg's heavy footsteps inside. She started wriggling back on her arse and her elbows, dragging one leg after, the little knife blade hidden up behind her wrist, her other fist clutching at the dirt.

"Where are you off to?" Jeg ducked under the low lintel and into the lane. He was a big man, but he looked a giant right then. Half a head taller than Shy, even if she'd been standing, and probably not much short of twice her weight, even if she'd eaten that day. He strutted over, tongue wedged into his lower lip so it bulged out, heavy sword loose in his hand, relishing his big moment.

"Pulled a neat trick on Neary, eh?" He pushed the brim of his hat up a little to show the tan mark across his forehead. "You're stronger'n you look. That boy's so dumb he could've fallen without the help, though. You'll be pulling no tricks on me."

They'd see about that, but she'd let her knife say it for her. Even a little knife can be a damned eloquent piece of metal if you stick it in the right place. She scrambled back, kicking up dust, making it look like she was trying to push herself up, then sagging back with a whimper as her left leg took her weight. Looking badly hurt was taking no great effort of acting. She could feel blood creeping from her hair and tickling her forehead. Jeg stepped out of the shadow and the low sun shone in his face, making him squint. Just the way she wanted it.

"Still remember the day I first put eyes on you," he went on, loving the sound of his own bleating. "Dodd come to me, all excited, and said he met Smoke, her whose killer's face is on all them bills up near Rostod, four thousand marks offered for her capture. The tales they tell on you!" He gave a whoop and she scrambled back again, working that left leg underneath her, making sure it would work when she needed it. "You'd think you was a demon with two swords to a hand the way they breathe your name. Picture my fucking *disappointment* when I find you ain't naught but a scared girl with gappy teeth and a powerful smell o' piss about her." As if Jeg smelled of summer meadows! He took another step forward, reaching out for her with one big hand. "Now, don't scratch; you're worth more to me alive. I don't want to—"

She flung the dirt with her left hand as she shoved up hard with her right, coming to her feet. He twisted his head away, snarling as the dust showered across his face. He swung blind as she darted at him low and the sword whipped over her head, wind of it snatching at her hair, weight of it turning him sideways. She caught his flapping coat tail in her left hand and sank her eating knife into his sword shoulder with the other.

He gave a strangled grunt as she pulled the knife clear and stabbed at him again, blade ripping open the arm of his coat and the arm inside it too, almost cutting into her own leg. She was bringing up the knife again when his fist crunched into the side of her mouth and sent her reeling, bare feet wrestling with the dirt. She caught hold of the corner of the building and hung there for a moment, trying to shake the light from her skull. She saw Jeg a pace or two off, bared teeth frothy with spit as he tried to fumble the sword from his dangling right hand into his left, fingers tangled with the fancy brass basketwork.

When things were moving fast, Shy had a knack for just doing, without thoughts of mercy, or thoughts of outcomes, or thoughts of much at all. That was what had kept her alive through all this shit. And what had landed her in it in the first place, for that matter. Ain't many blessings aren't mixed blessings, once you got to live with them, and she'd a curse for thinking too much after the action, but that was another story. If Jeg got a good grip on that sword she was dead, simple as that, so before she'd quite stopped the street spinning she charged at him again. He tried to free an arm but she managed to catch it with her clawing left hand, pressing up against him, holding herself steady by his coat as she punched wildly with the knife—in his gut, in his ribs, in his ribs again—her snarling at him and him grunting at her with every thump of the blade, the grip slippery in her aching hand.

He got hold of her shirt, stitches tearing as the arm half-ripped off, tried to shove her away as she stabbed him again but there was no strength in it, only sent her back a step. Her head was clearing now and she kept her balance, but Jeg stumbled and dropped on one knee. She lifted the knife up high in both hands and drove it right down on that stupid hat, squashing it flat, leaving the blade buried to the handle in the top of Jeg's head.

She staggered back, expecting him just to pitch onto his face. Instead he lurched up suddenly like a camel she'd once seen at a fair, the brim of his hat jammed down over his eyes to the bridge of his nose and the knife handle jutting straight up.

"Where you gone?" The words all mangled as if his mouth was full of gravel. "Smoke?" He lurched one way, then the other. "Smoke?" He shuffled at her, kicking up dust, sword dangling from his bloody right hand, the point scratching grooves in the dust around his feet. He reached up with his left, fingers all stretched out stiff but the wrist all floppy, and started prodding at his hat like he had something in his eye and wanted to wipe it clear.

"Shmoke?" One side of his face was twitching, shuddering, fluttering in a most unnatural way. Or maybe it was natural enough for a man with a knife lodged through his brains. "Thmoke?" There was blood dripping from the bent brim of his hat, leaving red streaks down his cheek, his shirt halfway soaked with it; but he kept coming on, bloody right arm jerking, hilt of his sword rattling against his leg. "Thmoe?" She backed away, staring, her own hands limp and all her skin prickling, until her back hit the wall behind her. "Thoe?"

"Shut your mouth!" And she dived at him with both palms, shoving him over backwards, sword bouncing from his hand, bloody hat still pinned to his head with her knife. He slowly rolled over, onto his face, right arm flopping. He slid his other hand underneath his shoulder as though he'd push himself up.

"Oh," he muttered into the dust. Then he was still.

Shy slowly turned her head and spat blood. Too many mouthfuls of blood the last few months. Her eyes were wet and she wiped them on the back of her trembling hand. Couldn't believe what had happened. Hardly seemed she'd had any part in it. A nightmare she was due to wake from. She pressed her eyes shut, and opened them, and there he still lay.

She snatched in a breath and blew it out hard, dashed spit from her lip, blood from her forehead, caught another breath and forced it free. Then she gathered up Jeg's sword, gritting her teeth against the urge to spew, rising in waves along with the thumping pain in the side of her face. Shit, but she wanted to sit down! Just *stop*. But she made herself turn away. Forced herself up to the back door of the tavern. The one Jeg had come through, still alive, a few moments before. Takes a lifetime of hard work to make a man. Only takes a few moments to end one.

Neary had dragged himself out of the hole his fall had put through the floorboards, clutching at his bloody trouser leg and looking quite put out about it. "Did you catch that fucking bitch?" he asked, squinting towards the doorway.

"Oh, no doubt."

His eyes went wide and he tried to drag himself towards his bow, not far out of reach, whimpering all the way. She hefted Jeg's big sword as she got close, and Neary turned over, eyes wide with terror, holding up one desperate arm. She hit it full-blooded with the flat of the sword and he moaned, clutching it to his chest. Then she hit him across the side of the head and rolled him over, blubbering, into the boards. Then she padded past him, sliding the sword through her belt, picked up the bow, and dragged some arrows from his quiver. She made for the door, stringing one as she went, and peered out into the street.

Dodd was still scraping coins from the dust and into the bag, working his way towards the well. Insensible to the fates of his two companions. Not as surprising as you might suppose. If one word summed up Dodd, it was "insensible."

She padded down the steps of the tavern, near to their edges where they were less likely to give a warning creak, drawing the bow halfway and taking a good aim on Dodd, bent over in the dust with his back to her, a dark sweat patch down the middle of his shirt. She gave some long, hard consideration to making that sweat patch the bull's-eye and shooting him in the back right there. But killing a man isn't easy, especially after hard consideration. She watched him pick up the last coin and drop it in the bag, then stand, pulling the drawstrings, then turn, smiling. "I got the—"

They stayed there awhile. He crouched in the dusty street, bag of silver in one hand, uncertain smile lit up in the sun, but his eyes looking decidedly scared in the shadow of his cheap hat. She on the bottom step of the tavern, bloody bare feet, bloody split mouth, bloody hair plastered across her bloody forehead, but the bow good and steady.

He licked his lips, swallowed, then licked them again. "Where's Neary?"

"In a bad way." She was surprised by the iron in her voice. Sounded like someone she didn't even know. Smoke's voice, maybe.

"Where's my brother?"

"In a worse."

Dodd swallowed, sweaty neck shifting, starting to ease gently backwards. "You kill him?"

"Forget about them two and stop still."

"Look, Shy, you ain't going to shoot me, are you? Not after all we been through. You ain't going to shoot. Not me. Are you?" His voice was rising higher and higher, but still he edged back towards the well. "I didn't want this. It weren't my idea!"

"Course not. You need to think to have an idea, and you ain't up to it. You just went along. Even if it happened to mean me getting hung."

"Now, look, Shy—"

"Stop still, I said." She drew the bow all the way, string cutting tight into her bloody fingers. "You fucking deaf, boy?"

"Look, Shy, let's just talk this out, eh? Just talk." He held his trembly palm up like that might stop an arrow. His pale blue eyes were fixed on her, and suddenly she had a memory rise up of the first time she met him, leaning back against the livery, smiling free and easy, none too clever but plenty of fun. She'd had a profound lack of fun in her life since she'd left home. You'd never have thought she left home to find it.

"I know I done wrong, but . . . I'm an idiot." And he tried out a smile, no steadier than his palm. He'd been worth a smile or two, Dodd, at least to begin with, and though no artist of a lover, had kept the bed warm, which was something, and made her feel as if she weren't on her own on one side with the whole rest of the world on the other, which was something more.

"Stop still," she said, but more softly now.

"You ain't going to shoot me." Still he was edging back towards the well. "It's me, right? Me. Dodd. Just don't shoot me, now." Still going. "What I'm going to do is—"

She shot him.

It's a strange thing about a bow. Stringing it, and drawing it, and nocking the arrow, and taking your aim—all that takes effort, and skill, and a decision. Letting go the string is nothing. You just stop holding it. In fact, once you've got it drawn and aimed, it's easier to let fly than not to.

Dodd was less than a dozen strides distant, and the shaft flitted across the space between them, missed his hand by a whisker and stuck silently into his chest. Surprised her, the lack of a sound. But then, flesh is soft. 'Specially in comparison to an arrowhead. Dodd took one more wobbly pace, like he hadn't quite caught up with being arrow-stuck yet, his eyes going very wide. Then he blinked down at the shaft.

"You shot me," he whispered, and he sank to his knees, blood already spreading out on his shirt in a dark oval.

"Didn't I bloody warn you!" She flung the bow down, suddenly furious with him and with the bow too.

He stared at her. "But I didn't think you'd do it."

She stared back. "Neither did I." A silent moment, and the wind blew up one more time and stirred the dust around them. "Sorry."

"Sorry?" he croaked.

Might've been the stupidest thing she'd ever said, and that with some fierce competition, but what else could she say? No words were going to take that arrow out. She gave half a shrug. "I guess."

Dodd winced, hefting the silver in one hand, turning towards the well. Shy's mouth dropped open, and she took off running as he toppled sideways, hauling the bag into the air. It turned over and over, curving up and starting to fall, drawstrings flapping, Shy's clutching hand straining for it as she sprinted, lunged, fell . . .

She grunted as her sore ribs slammed into the wall around the well, right arm darting down into the darkness. For a moment she thought she was going in after the bag—which would probably have been a fitting conclusion—then her knees came back down on the dirt outside.

She had it by one of the bottom corners, loose canvas clutched by broken nails, drawstrings dangling as dirt and bits of loose stone filtered down around it.

Shy smiled. For the first time that day. That month, maybe.

Then the bag came open.

Coins tumbled into the darkness in a twinkling shower, silver pinging and rattling from the earthy walls, disappearing into the inky nothingness, and silence.

She straightened up, numb.

She backed away slowly from the well, hugging herself with one hand while the empty bag hung from the other.

She looked over at Dodd, lying on his back with the arrow sticking straight up from his chest, his wet eyes fixed on her, his ribs going fast. She heard his shallow breaths slow, then stop.

Shy stood there a moment, then doubled over and blew puke onto the ground. Not much of it, since she'd eaten nothing that day, but her guts clenched up hard and made sure she retched up what there was. She shook so bad she thought she was going to fall, hands on her knees, sniffing bile from her nose and spluttering it out.

Damn, but her ribs hurt. Her arm. Her leg. Her face. So many scrapes, twists, and bruises, she could hardly tell one from another: her whole body was one overpowering fucking throb.

Her eyes crawled over to Dodd's corpse, she felt another wave of sickness and forced them away, over to the horizon, fixing them on that shimmering line of nothing.

Not nothing.

There was dust rising there. She wiped her face on her ripped sleeve one more time, so filthy now that it was as like to make her dirtier as cleaner.

She straightened, squinting into the distance, hardly able to believe it. Riders. No doubt. A good way off, but as many as a dozen.

"Oh, hell," she whispered, and bit her lip. Things kept going this way she'd soon have chewed right through the bloody thing. "Oh, hell!" And Shy put her hands over her eyes and squeezed them shut and hid in self-inflicted darkness in the desperate hope she might have somehow been mistaken. Would hardly have been her first mistake, would it?

But when she took her hands away, the dust was still there. The world's a mean bully, all right, and the lower down you are, the more it delights in kicking you. Shy put her hands on her hips, arched her back, and screamed up at the sky, the word drawn out as long as her sore lungs would allow.

"Fuck!"

The echoes clapped from the buildings and died a quick death. No answer came. Perhaps the faint droning of a fly already showing some interest in Dodd. Neary's horse eyed her for a moment, then looked away, profoundly unimpressed. Now Shy had a sore throat to add to her woes. She was obliged to ask herself the usual questions.

What the fuck now?

She clenched her teeth as she hauled Dodd's boots off and sat in the dust beside him to pull them on. Not the first time they'd stretched out together in the dirt, him and her. First time with him dead, though. His boots were way too loose on her, but a long stride better than no boots at all. She clomped back into the tavern in them.

Neary was making some pitiable groans as he struggled to get up. Shy kicked him in the face and down onto his back, plucked the rest of the arrows from his quiver, and took his heavy belt knife too. Back out into the sun and she picked up the bow, jammed Dodd's hat onto her head, also somewhat on the roomy side but at least offering some shade as the sun got up. Then she dragged the three horses together and roped them into a string—quite a ticklish operation, since Jeg's big stallion was a mean bastard and seemed determined to kick her brains out.

When she'd got it done, she frowned off towards those dust trails. They were headed for the town, all right, and fast. With a better look, she reckoned on about nine or ten, which was two or three better than twelve but still an almighty inconvenience.

Bank agents after the stolen money. Bounty hunters looking to collect her price. Other outlaws who'd got wind of a score. A score that was currently in the bottom of a well, as it happened. Could be anyone. Shy had an uncanny knack for making enemies. She found that she'd looked over at Dodd, facedown in the dust with his bare feet limp behind him. The only thing she had worse luck with was friends.

How had it come to this?

She shook her head, spat through the little gap between her front teeth, and hauled herself up into the saddle of Dodd's horse. She faced it away from those impending dust clouds, towards which quarter of the compass she knew not.

Shy gave the horse her heels.

Diana Rowland

Hell hath no fury like a woman whose city has been scorned. . . .

Diana Rowland has worked as a bartender, a blackjack dealer, a pit boss, a street cop, a detective, a computer forensics specialist, a crime scene investigator, and a morgue assistant. She won the marksmanship award in her police academy class, has a black belt in hapkido, and has handled numerous dead bodies in various states of decomposition. A graduate of Clarion West, her novels include *Mark of the Demon, Blood of the Demon, Secrets of the Demon, Sins of the Demon,* and *My Life as a White Trash Zombie.* Her most recent books are *Touch of the Demon* and *Even White Trash Zombies Get the Blues.* She has lived her entire life below the Mason-Dixon Line and is deeply grateful for the existence of air-conditioning.

CITY LAZARUS

A grey dawn and low tide revealed the body at the water's edge, facedown and partially buried in the silt. One arm drifted in the sluggish current as the river plucked at it. A fetid scent drifted to the people standing on the levee, though the odor likely had more to do with illegal sewage than the corpse.

Rain plopped onto the mud in scattered drops as the flatboat inched out to the body, a thick rope dragging in its wake and doled out by workers on firmer ground. Captain Danny Faciane watched from his vantage on the levee and scowled beneath the hood of his raincoat. He fully understood the necessity for the slow progress across the silt, but he still chafed at it. The tide wouldn't wait for them to complete their business, though at the moment it was more the early hour and the lack of coffee in his system that frustrated him. Yet it paid to be cautious with this river. Since the collapse of the Old River Control Structure, she might not have the teeth she once had, but she still had a few tricks left in her.

Danny's attention drifted to his right, toward the two bridges that spanned the river. The headlights of cars only crossed along one of them. Not enough traffic anymore to warrant having both. Across the river, a grounded ship leaned drunkenly in the mud. Light flickered from a dozen places, the cutting torches of workers fighting to salvage what they could of the trapped heap. Danny wondered if the salvage workers would attack the unused bridge next, like termites drawn to wood.

"I need to learn how to weld," a detective grumbled from behind him. Danny glanced back to see that Farber's attention had also been caught by the crawling lights on the defunct ship.

Danny shook his head. "They'll be gone as soon as they finish. Only a few ships left to cut up. Probably not even a year's worth of work left."

"Maybe so, but in that year those fuckers'll make three times what we do. Besides, I still think the city'll have work for 'em. New Orleans has a way of taking care of itself."

Danny let out a snort. He had little doubt that the welders made more than Farber, but he knew damn well that they didn't come close to matching his own take. And he sure as hell didn't share Farber's bright-eyed optimism about the future of the city. "Filthy work," he said instead. "And dangerous."

"What *we* do is dangerous," Farber protested. Danny cocked an eyebrow at him, let out a low bark of laughter.

"Only if you're doing it wrong," he said, then hunched his shoulders against the gust of wind that sought to drive the sluggish rain into his face. "Like this. Fuck this early morning shit."

The muttered commands and curses of the men in the flatboat drifted to him as they reached the corpse. They fought the pull of the tenacious mud as the river held on to her prize, but finally managed to get the corpse free of its partial grave. It flopped into the bottom of the boat, one mud-covered foot still on the edge as the workers onshore pulled the flatboat back.

Danny walked over as the men pulled the body from the boat and set it on the ground. "Can you wash his face off?" he asked nobody in particular, waited as someone found a bottle of water and dumped it over the victim's face. Danny scowled as he crouched by the body, and only part of it was because of the rank smell of the mud. "It's Jimmy Ernst."

"Jesus," one of the men from the flatboat muttered. "We crawled across the stinking mud for that piece of shit?"

Danny's mouth twisted in sour agreement as he cast a practiced eye over the body. The crime scene tech pulled a pair of gloves out of the side pocket of her pants and held them out for Danny, but he shook his head. He had no intention of touching the corpse and risking getting dirty. Coroner would take care of cleaning the fucking muck off before they did the autopsy.

"Well, that's damn interesting," he said, tilting his head.

"Whatcha got?" Farber asked, crouching beside him.

"He was murdered." Danny pointed to the two scorch marks on the dead guy's neck. Maybe there were more, hiding beneath the filth, but those alone would've been enough. Latest generation of Tasers left that sort of mark, delivering enough punch to paralyze for about half a minute.

Long enough to get cuffs on a perp. Or a few licks in. Whichever they deserved more.

Danny straightened, let his gaze drift over what was left of the Mississippi River. This wasn't the first body to be pulled from the sucking muck and it wouldn't be the last. The banks were a morass of sinkholes and unpredictable currents. Easy enough to die, especially after a couple of jolts from a Taser.

"I've seen enough," he told the crime scene tech as she snapped her pictures in an aimless, desultory fashion. She didn't give a shit about Jimmy Ernst any more than he did.

"See you back at the precinct," Farber said.

Danny nodded, turned away, walked back over the rocks of the now-pointless levee, over the weed-covered train tracks, and up to the street. The rain had paused, and a glance at the sky told him that he had time enough to grab some coffee and finish waking up before the skies opened up again. No pressing need to get back to the precinct station. There sure as hell wasn't any rush to close *this* case. He'd give it a week or so and then suspend it for lack of evidence.

Café Du Monde was open and already catering to a few persistent tourists, but he continued past and up North Peters, his footsteps echoing back at him from the many silent storefronts. Three years ago, before the river changed course, the Quarter would already have been bustling at this hour, with vendors making deliveries and shop owners hosing off sidewalks and garbage men calling out to each other as the trucks rumbled their way through the narrow streets.

Near the French Market, he crossed over to Decatur Street, made his way to the coffee shop on the corner of St. Peters. He flashed his badge to get his coffee and croissant for free, then returned outside to sit at a table under the green-and-white-striped awning.

A scrawny dog reeking of wet and sewage and despair slunk along the sidewalk toward him. Grey with one black ear, hope flickered in its eyes that Danny would throw a piece of the croissant its way, drop a crumb. It had probably been a pet at one time. Lots of animals had been left behind after the Switch, when their owners had abandoned their houses and all ties to the area and rushed away in a desperate flight to find new opportunities elsewhere, as any industry in New Orleans that depended on the river dried up.

The dog whined and sat about a foot from Danny. "Go away," he muttered, shoving the dog carefully away with his foot. To his annoyance, that contact only seemed to encourage the mutt. It came back, and this time put a paw on Danny's knee. He swore and pulled his leg away, pissed to see a broad smear of who-the-fuck-knew-what left behind. "You fucking mutt!" He shot his foot out again. It wasn't a savage blow, but he made sure there was enough force behind it to get his message across. The mutt let out a high-pitched yelp and went sprawling back, then crouched, eyes on Danny. For a brief instant, Danny wondered if the dog would attack him. There were plenty of desperate animals in the city, and a smart person stayed alert. His hand twitched to his gun, more than ready to shoot the thing if it came at him, but after a few seconds, it lowered its head and loped unevenly away, taking its stink with it.

Danny let out a sigh of relief as he snatched up napkins and wiped at the grime on his pants. Shooting the dog here would have drawn all sorts of fucked-up attention. Wouldn't have mattered if the dog had been attacking him; there'd be plenty of people ready to Monday-morning-quarterback the decision, explaining how he should have used less force or found a way to be absolutely certain that the dog intended to cause him harm. There'd even be those who'd insist that, as an officer of the law, he ought to have been willing to suffer a bite or two, and had progressed to lethal force too quickly.

Fuck that, Danny thought grimly. You did what you had to do to survive, especially in this city. You looked out for yourself, because no one else was going to do it for you.

He dropped the soiled napkins onto the table and stood, scowling down at the remaining stain. He picked up his coffee and croissant, began to cross the street, but paused at the sight of a woman on the opposite corner who was holding a folded red umbrella in one hand.

She was beautiful, with dark hair and lighter eyes, and skin a pale brown that made him wonder if she had a touch of Creole blood somewhere down the line. She had on shorts and sandals, paired with a black sleeveless T-shirt that hugged a sleek and toned figure that still held curves in all the right places. Young—early twenties, perhaps. Not rich. That was easy enough to tell. The rich who'd stayed behind were *obscenely* rich, had found ways to make even more profit from the shift in the river, and were far from subtle about flaunting that wealth and influence. A waitress maybe? A stripper? She sure as hell had the body for it.

But it wasn't just her looks that caused her to stand out to Danny. It was more that she didn't have the familiar beat-down look about her, the desperate shift of the eyes, as if seeking any possible escape from this fucked-up shell of a city. She seemed calm, perhaps a touch of worry or sadness in her eyes as they met his. Then she smiled, and he knew it was for him. Daring and coy at the same time, with a whisper of amusement skimming across her features before she broke the gaze, turned away, and continued down the street away from him.

He took a step to follow, then stopped as his phone buzzed in a familiar cadence. He breathed out a curse as he snatched it off his belt, skimmed the text.

Replacing the phone in its holder, he watched the girl continue down the street until she turned a corner. Then he spun and walked the other way to answer the summons.

"You and me, Danny," Peter Bennett said as he looked out over the dregs of the river. Rain pattered against the broad window of the condo, streaking the view of the deserted Riverwalk and the empty wharves. "We're a lot alike." He flicked a glance back at the cop. "We know how to go along with change, find the ways to make it work for us."

Danny leaned up against the back of the black leather couch, hands stuffed into his pockets as he gave the lanky man an agreeable smile. "I'm cool with doing what needs to be done," he replied. After the Old River Control Structure crumbled beneath the weight of spring flooding and insufficient funding, Peter was one of those very rich who'd not only stayed in the city but managed to get even richer. Judicious investments in the Atchafalaya Basin had paid off handsomely when the river changed course, but the real money had come from Peter's uncanny ability to land cleanup contracts. A threefold increase in the amount of water flowing down the Atchafalaya River had, of course, caused a fair amount of destruction, and the man knew there was much to be gained during times of disaster. There'd been plenty of men like Peter who'd made their fortunes after Katrina.

"And that's the key to it all," Peter said with a firm nod. "Too many other people want to clutch their chests and worry about rebuilding, get everything back to how it *used* to be." He let out a snort. "Did you know the city council is still whining to the governor about having the river dredged so that shipping traffic can resume?" He didn't wait for an answer. "Waste of time. Time to let the old New Orleans die. That river is a toothless whore compared to the badass bitch it used to be, but there's still a lot that can be done with this city. Gotta change with the times."

"That's right," Danny replied. He didn't say the first thing that leaped to mind, that even a toothless whore could still shove a knife into you. Jimmy Ernst could testify to that. But Peter didn't want to hear that sort of thing, and Danny was damn good at knowing when to keep his mouth shut. "So, you got something that needs doing?" That's what the text had said. *Got something I need you to do.*

Peter turned away from the dismal view, picked up the cup of coffee from the table by the window, and took a gulp. "Cold." He grimaced. "Get me a new one, will you, Danny? Get one for yourself too." He smiled, magnanimous.

Danny nodded and pushed off the couch, headed to the sleek black and chrome of the kitchen. "Glad to. Your coffee's damn good." He knew where the mugs were, knew how the man took his coffee.

"It's a free enterprise thing, see?" Peter said while Danny poured and stirred. "There's a shop down on Dumaine Street in the Quarter. I bought it about a year ago and rented it out to a guy who sells old books and shit. Dunno how he makes a fucking living with that, but he pays his rent." He scowled at that last bit, took the mug that Danny handed him.

"You want him out?"

Peter took a sip. Smiled down at the coffee. "That's damn good." Looked back up at Danny. "I have plans for that space. Council's going to vote my way about the poker room. I've made sure of that." His smile widened. "*You* made sure of that."

Danny chuckled. Easiest drunk-driving arrest he'd ever made. Helped that he'd been tipped off by Peter that Councilman Walker was leaving the wine tasting to drive the one and a half blocks to his house.

"But there's a little thing in the guy's lease that says I can evict him *if* there's evidence of criminal activity," Peter continued.

Danny nodded, took a sip from his own mug. It was bitter, too dark a roast for his liking, and he preferred it with a lot of cream in it. But Peter took his black and Danny didn't want to nitpick. "I'm sure I can do something about that," he said.

The bedroom door opened. A young woman with sleep-tousled blond hair, wearing only underwear and a tank top, peered out. Her gaze took in Danny and dismissed him, then settled on Peter. A pout formed on her full lips, or at least that's the expression Danny thought that she was trying for. There was a little too much uncertainty and not enough confidence, if any, for her to be able to pull it off, and he couldn't help but think that the girl on the corner would've been able to do it and make it alluring and amusing at the same time.

"Hey, babe," she said to Peter, leaning against the doorframe in what she tried to make a sexy position. "Come back to bed. I need a morning workout."

Danny took a sip of coffee to hide his grin at the sad display. He'd seen it a dozen times before, watched Peter's girl-of-the-month pitch a desperate bid to win back his interest, and seen it fail every time. Peter liked the new and shiny, and got rid of anything with too much wear and tear on it. Didn't matter that he was the one who fucked it up. He was a good-looking man—blue eyed, dark haired, athletic build—as well as being one of the richest men in the city. There was always more new and shiny to be had, more girls convinced that they might become the next Mrs. Peter Bennett.

Peter waved a dismissing hand, eyes on the rain-streaked view. "I'm busy."

Her pout deepened. "But I'm ready now, sweetie. Come give me some."

Now Peter looked her way. He took in her expression and her state of partial undress. Annoyance crawled briefly over his face instead of the lust she was surely hoping for, but then it shifted to amusement as Peter jerked his head toward Danny.

"Let him," he said, eyes on her.

Shock flashed across her face, but only for an instant. Eyes dead, she turned her pouty smile onto Danny. She had nothing to lose, even if it meant buying just a few more days in Peter's care, such as it was. It was worth it to her, Danny knew.

Danny set his mug down, moved to her, gave her a mild push to precede him into the bedroom.

————

When he came back out, he closed the door behind him. She wasn't sniveling, at least. Still, she'd probably be gone by the next day and Peter would be on the prowl for some other chick he could use up and throw away.

"That didn't take long," Peter said, without looking up from his laptop.

"I wasn't trying to make her happy," Danny replied. He looped his tie back around his neck, knotted it quickly.

A smile twitched across Peter's mouth as he tapped an envelope on the table. Danny scooped it up and tucked it into his jacket. He didn't bother counting it.

"I think I'll go visit a bookstore now," he said with a grin.

"Tell me if you find anything dirty."

The aroma of sweat and stale coffee greeted Danny as he entered the station with his arrestee. He kept a hand on the upper arm of the handcuffed man, guided him around the other dregs and the other cops.

"You can't do this!" his guy kept saying, as if hoping that if he said it enough, it would be true, that a cop couldn't simply walk into his bookstore and find drugs that were never there before. "Please. Please! I have a family. You can't do this. Those drugs weren't mine. You—"

Danny gave him a hard yank, pulled him off-balance. His guy let out a yelp as he struggled for footing and went down on one knee. Danny crouched, making a show of helping him back to his feet while he leaned in close to the guy's ear.

"You need to settle the fuck down and be a good boy," he said in a calm, low voice. "This is going to happen whether you behave or not. You want it to be worse?" He met the guy's eyes. "It can be worse."

Sweat tracked down the side of the man's face. Danny watched as a spark of rebellion struggled for life within his eyes.

"There's a lot of paperwork in an arrest like this," Danny continued smoothly. "Some of it might get lost. Maybe it's the part that describes the evidence and the chain of custody. Or maybe it's the part that says you were booked into jail and need to have a bond set. Which one you want lost? You want to have the case thrown out before it goes to trial? Or you want to spend an extra week or so in central lockup?"

The spark of rebellion died. His head dropped.

"That's right," Danny said, helping the unresisting man back up to his feet. "You be a good boy and this'll all be over soon."

Danny booked him in, filed the initial paperwork, and was on his way down the hall to his office when he saw her sitting in an interview room. The girl from the corner. She'd changed into jeans and a deep maroon blouse, but he'd have known her no matter what she was wearing. She looked small and scared in the metal chair, her hands clasped around a paper cup of coffee and her eyes on Detective Farber in the opposite chair.

He stepped into the open doorway, knocked on the jamb. She jerked her eyes up to his. A whisper of a smile touched her mouth and he thought that maybe now she didn't look so scared. "Whatcha got?" he asked Farber without taking his eyes from her.

"She talked to Jimmy Ernst late last night," the detective explained. "Might've been the last one to see him alive. We're just getting started."

"I'll take over," Danny said, moving into the room. He shifted his gaze, caught Farber's eye. The other man hesitated, then flicked a glance back at the girl, hid a grin.

"Yeah, sure thing." He stood and picked up his things. "By the way, Ernst had a gun on him. It's been sent to the lab." Ballistics testing was routine. Maybe they could pin some cold cases on Ernst and improve their stats. Farber's eyes flicked toward the girl, then back to Danny. "Lemme know if you get anything," he added, the double meaning hanging in the air.

Danny waited for him to leave, closed the door, and took a seat in the empty chair. "I'm Captain Danny Faciane," he told her. "I'd like to ask you a few questions."

"Okay." She paused. "I'm Delia," she said, releasing her grip on the paper cup.

"Last name?"

She sat back. "Rochon. Delia Rochon. I talked to Jimmy last night. About midnight or so, I guess. He used to come by the club a lot." Distaste skimmed across her features.

He wrote her name on the pad. "Club?"

"Freddy-Z's." Her eyes dropped to the hands in her lap. "I'm a dancer."

A stripper. Freddy-Z's was one of the best in what was left of the city. Danny jotted the info down. Not because it was important to the case, but because he wanted her to think it was, that it wasn't simply important to him that he knew where to find her again.

He went ahead and asked her about her conversation with Jimmy Ernst, went through the motions the same way they did with most other cases like this. She gave him a clear but sparse tale of the encounter. Jimmy had asked her about a girl who'd used to work at the club, wanted to know where she was now. Delia hadn't told him anything. Nothing too exciting.

She didn't like the victim. She never came out and said so, but it was clear in her manner, the hardening of her eyes when she spoke of him. Then again, Danny knew that he'd be hard pressed to find anyone who did. Jimmy was a pimp, specializing in girls who looked *really* young.

Danny finally set the pen down on the pad. She looked at the pen, then to him. "Am I under arrest?" she asked, voice small but steady.

He let out a snort. "For Jimmy? Nah. We don't give a fuck about him." No one would ever go to jail for that murder. Not unless they came to the station and made a full confession—and that's how it was for most of the murders in this city, not only for scum like Ernst. Danny, and everyone else, did just enough to keep from being indicted for malfeasance.

The cops in this city knew how to survive. And a few smart ones, like him, knew how to prosper.

He walked her out, offered to have an officer drive her home, but she merely smiled and shook her head. It was raining again, a steady downpour that would wash all the trash into the streets and clog the drains, but she simply opened her umbrella and walked out into it without a hitch in her stride. He watched the red umbrella grow smaller in the distance until it was lost in the grey haze of the rain.

Danny talked to the bartender at Freddy-Z's later that day, found out that Delia had started there about a month ago. No one knew much about her. Then again, no one really cared, according to the bartender. They didn't give a shit about the girls' personal lives as long as they showed up on time and kept any trouble they were in away from the club. Delia did both.

She was working that night. He made sure he was there to see her. He didn't even try to convince himself he was checking out a possible witness. He knew damn well that he wanted to see more of her, and not simply the more that happened when she pulled her clothing off.

Neon flashed in tempo to the bass thump of the music. The mingled scents of sweat and sex, money and misery, swirled around the dancers and the men gazing up at them. Delia worked the pole with a lithe grace and sureness that spoke of years of training, and Danny wondered if, in some distant past, she'd been a far different sort of dancer. Yet, despite her obvious strength and control, she exuded a sensuousness, a base sexuality, that he doubted she'd learned in a ballet class.

She only looked at him once, a lingering caress of attention paired with a shy smile, at odds with the sultry glances she bestowed on the other patrons. And because it would have seemed odd or rude for him not to, he held up a fiver and slipped it under her G-string when she paused before him, then felt dirty for doing so with this girl.

"She's a fucking hot piece," said a familiar voice. Danny turned his head, forced a smile for Peter. The other man's eyes were on Delia. Appreciative. Admiring. Hungry.

"She's a witness in one of my cases," Danny found himself saying. Maybe Peter would be scared off by that. He was usually pretty careful about not associating with criminal types. After all, that's what he had Danny for.

But Peter merely smiled, kept his gaze on Delia.

Danny knew what would happen next. Peter would get a lap dance, then pay for a private room. It was possible that he'd invite Danny to come with him, and with any other girl he'd have gone and enjoyed himself.

Danny stood, moved to the bar on a pretense of getting another drink. The envelope crinkled within his jacket and he frowned. He'd been so caught up in thoughts of her that he'd forgotten to take it out and put it someplace safe. But now he felt only relief. He didn't even think before calling the manager over, paying the money for a private room with Delia and another one for Peter with a different dancer. Part of him knew that there was every chance that this wouldn't work. Peter had money and influence and was used to getting what he wanted. But Danny had his own sort of influence. He slid the manager a hundred, along with an agreement to help the man out if he ever got into the sort of trouble that Danny could help with. A few minutes later, the club's second-prettiest dancer made her way over to where Peter sat.

Peter raised an eyebrow as the blonde draped herself around his shoulders, chuckled under his breath as she rubbed her breasts on the back of his neck. He scanned the room for Delia, then asked the blond girl a question. She shrugged and nodded in Danny's direction; he fixed a smile on his face and lifted his drink as Peter looked his way, tried to make it look as if he'd bought the girl for Peter simply because it was a cool thing for one guy to do for another.

The two men locked eyes, gaze broken when the blond dancer took Peter's hand to lead him to the back room. He stood and followed, paused as they neared the bar.

He leaned in to Danny. "I saw what you did there," Peter said, mouth showing amusement that his eyes didn't share. "I think it's cute that you like that girl enough to pull a stunt like that." He paused. "Don't you ever fucking cockblock me like that again."

He turned without waiting for a response and continued through the curtains to the private rooms.

Danny stayed where he was, hands clenched into fists in the pockets of his jacket, telling himself he was controlling himself from going after Peter and beating that smug, superior smile from his face, but knowing that he was actually fighting down the sick knowledge that he and Peter might be cut from the same cloth, but they sure as shit weren't *equals*, weren't partners of any sort. And as much as he hated Peter at this moment, he knew that when the man summoned him he'd go and do what he was told, like a goddamned trained dog. Too much to lose if he didn't.

He also knew that he didn't want to go to a private room with Delia. He turned back to the bartender. "The redheaded kid down by the left stage. Is he a dick to the girls?"

Bartender shook his head. "Nah. Comes in with twenty bucks a coupla times a week. Never caused trouble."

"Give him my room. Tell him happy fucking birthday." He peeled off another hundred to cover a tip. "And tell him if he gets out of line with Delia, I'll break his fucking neck."

He left the club, waited in the bar across the street for her to finish her shift. When he finally saw her step out of the back door, he dropped a twenty to cover his tab and went out to meet her.

She was with two other women. A petite, mousy thing who tried and failed to do "sexy librarian" and a curvy Hispanic with big tits and long legs. As he approached they paused their low conversation. Delia's eyes held a whisper of uncertainty, but the other two watched him with the naked wariness of a rabbit watching a fox.

He wanted to growl to the two rabbits to get lost, watch them skitter off, but instead he merely asked Delia, "Can I buy you a cup of coffee?"

As if she hadn't heard his question, she turned to the other girls. "I'll see y'all tomorrow night," she told them, exchanged quick hugs. Not until the two were halfway down the block did she return her attention to Danny. Her mouth pressed into a tight, thin line.

"I'm not a whore," she said flatly.

Danny found himself smiling. "I know. I promise, I just want to buy you a cup of coffee."

The look she gave him was measuring, doubtful. He wondered if she knew what he'd done in the club and, if so, whether she could possibly understand why. Then again, he didn't completely understand it himself.

"There's a café over on Decatur," she finally said. "It's really good, but I don't like walking there by myself at night."

"I'll protect you," he replied.

She liked her coffee sweet and rich, added enough cream to where it matched the pale mocha color of her skin. Her croissant she tore into small bits before eating it in dainty bites between sips of coffee and conversation.

Like anyone else in the city, they talked first about why they were still there after the Switch, why they hadn't abandoned the city the way that the river had. After all, anyone who could had left, leaving only the very poor, the rich who knew how to profit from disaster, and the few people those rich needed to get richer and stay comfortable.

"Lots of cops left and went over to Morgan City," he told her. "Plenty of work there. But . . . I dunno. I didn't want to leave, and I had enough seniority to avoid the layoffs." And plenty of stroke, too, he added silently. He'd called in a lot of favors to make sure that not only would he stay but those in line ahead of him for promotion would get the ax instead. He'd made captain less than six months later.

"This is my home" was all she said to explain why she stayed. "I love this city."

"Even now?" he asked her, eyebrow cocked in disbelief.

"Especially now," she replied, a soft smile on her lips.

He thought about that for a moment while he drank his café au lait. The night breeze brought the stagnant scent of the river, mingled with the aroma of beer and piss in the street. Even hours before dawn, the muggy air wrapped around them with warm tendrils, promising a brutal summer to come. But this city suited him, suited his personality. The Switch had been the best goddamn thing that had ever happened to him.

"Me too," he finally said, because he knew she expected it, and pushed aside the strange twinge of sadness that came from realizing that he loved it for far different reasons than she did.

Though he never went back inside the club, he waited for her each night and walked her to the café. On the third night, she tucked her arm through his as they walked. On the fifth, she greeted him with a kiss and a smile.

On the seventh, she asked, "Do you have a coffeemaker at home?"

He had an apartment south of the Quarter, a more than decent place where he lived for free, thanks to a desperate landlord who agreed that it was better to have a cop live there than have squatters take up residence. With so many vacant homes and apartments in the city, it was rare for any cop to pay rent.

It was almost a mile from the café, but she insisted that she didn't mind walking.

His place wasn't overly messy, but it sure as hell wasn't set up as a nice place to have company. The curtains had been left behind by the previous tenants, and had likely been old back then. Décor was limited to a pile of magazines with scantily clad women on the covers, a cluster of empty beer bottles on the coffee table, and, by the door, a framed newspaper article from several years back with the headline: *Witness recants testimony. NOPD officers cleared in wrongdoing.*

He never brought girls back here, had never thought what it would look like through a woman's eyes. Oddly ashamed, he started to apologize, but she stopped him with a smile. "It's all right. It's good. You're a good person." Which only made his shame increase, because he knew that he *wasn't,* though it had never mattered to him before.

He snaked his arms around her waist and pulled her tightly to him. She let out a small squeak of surprise. "Nah, I'm a bad boy," he said, trying to be flip, yet feeling it like a confession. He instantly felt silly for saying it and sorry for being rough. He didn't want this girl to think of him like that. He didn't want her to be the kind who was only attracted to the assholes and pricks.

But she simply smiled and laid her hand on his cheek. "You're not fooling me," she said, voice low and husky. "You're my good boy."

Danny knew how to fuck, how to get what he wanted, how not to care. He'd lost count of the number of prostitution "arrests" he'd made—girls who'd paid their fine directly to him with their mouth or cunt. It had been a long time since he'd had any sort of concern for the pleasure of his partner, and he felt like a fumbling virgin as he touched Delia, shamed and horrified when his uncertainty translated into a betrayal of his own physical response.

Yet she neither mocked nor took insult. Lowering her head, she gently coaxed him back, easing him, exciting him. And before he could squander her efforts, he shifted her to her back and returned the attention. She tasted sweet and wild, and as she tightened her hands in the sheet and cried out, he couldn't help but feel a pleasure that nearly matched her own. When she finally lay spent and shaking, only then did he move up and find his own release, thrilled beyond measure when she clasped her arms and legs around him and cried out his name.

He held her close after, stroking her hair as her breath warmed his chest, savoring the almost foreign sensation of feeling whole, secure. Happy.

The next night they walked out to what was left of the Mississippi, made their way upriver, and stood on a dock where, only three years earlier, the Canal Street Ferry had loaded and unloaded thousands of cars and people. The river had a bit more temper here due to the bend in it and the way the silt had settled. The current roiled beyond the mud, but to Danny it felt like an older woman trying to prove she was young and attractive. *Look at me,* he imagined the river saying. *I still got it. I'm still a bad girl.* In a few more years, the silt would build up more and the river would subside, muttering, disgruntled, and hurt to be so unappreciated.

"When I was a kid, my mom would take me out to the levee nearly every Sunday afternoon," Danny told Delia. "We'd sit and watch the ships and barges go up and down the river and we'd make up stories about what they carried and where they were going."

"That sounds nice," she said, tilting her head to look at him.

"Yeah. It was cool. She'd pack sandwiches and chips and we'd make a picnic of it."

She leaned up against him. "Do your parents still live here?"

"Dad left when I was about six," he said. "Mom died about ten years ago. Cancer." He shrugged to show her how much it didn't affect him anymore. He wanted to tell her that he'd scattered his mother's ashes in the river or on the levee or somewhere that would have been meaningful in some way, but the truth was that he'd never even picked them up from the funeral home. He didn't care what happened to the ashes—not because he hadn't loved his mother, but because he felt it was just one more stupid, sentimental detail that people wanted to believe was important.

He looked out toward the bones of a ship that had been stripped nearly clean by the welders. That's what it's like, he thought. No one cared where that metal would end up. That ship would never be rebuilt.

"Do you remember where you were when it happened?" she asked him, and for an instant he thought she was talking about his mother's death.

"You mean the Switch?" he asked, to be certain. She nodded. "Sure," he said, thinking quickly. The truth was he didn't remember exactly. Probably working. Maybe at home. It wasn't until about a week later that it started to sink in to everyone that nothing was ever going to be the same, but even then he didn't remember being upset or worked up over it. The fickle bitch of a river had run off, it wasn't ever coming back, and that's all there was to it. "I was on a domestic violence call," he decided to say. "I'd just put handcuffs on a guy for slapping his wife when my partner told me the spillway had collapsed and the river was changing course."

She looked at him as if expecting him to say more. He wondered if maybe he should make some more crap up, add some details and tell her that the guy worked on a ship and had come home to find out that his wife had been screwing another guy. Maybe tell her that he'd slapped his wife in front of their six-year-old son, and that as soon as he was bailed out, he hopped on another ship and never returned.

No, Danny decided. Best to leave it as it was. One thing he'd learned from the perps he arrested was that most of them tripped themselves up by making their lies too complicated. Keep it simple and short. Less to keep straight that way. "So, where were you?" he asked her.

Delia blinked, pursed her lips. "I was at the emergency room with a neighbor of mine. She . . . fell and broke her wrist. I was playing with her daughter in the waiting room when it came on the TV."

She turned back to the water, rubbing her arms against the light breeze. "I wonder what they'll name it?"

He slipped an arm around her, pulled her close, smiled as she nestled against him. "Seems wrong not to call it the Mississippi."

She shook her head. "But she's gone. Left us behind. Atchafalaya has her now."

"You think the city needs to get over it and move on?" he asked her with an indulgent smile.

A grin touched her mouth. "It's never going to get her back. New Orleans needs to stop being the mopey boyfriend. It needs to take a shower and start dating again. It can be better than it was before."

He chuckled and gave her a squeeze, but his thoughts were on men like Peter and their plans for the city. It wasn't going to be cleaned up. It wouldn't get better, at least not for the people who weren't running the show. The only thing the city had left was tourism, and they had no intention of making the city "family friendly" or any of that shit.

The city council would eventually cave in to pressure. New Orleans would sell itself out, fill up with casinos and even more bars and prostitutes. It made him sad, which surprised him. That kind of place would suit him and his temperament.

"New Orleans will become the whore," he said, more to himself than to her.

"Not if I have anything to say about it," she murmured, then sighed and leaned her head against him. Danny wondered if she knew that there was nothing she could do about it, nothing that could stop the city's slide into total debauchery and corruption. There were too many players lined up against her. His gut twisted with the knowledge that, not only was he was one of them, he wasn't sure that he was capable of doing anything else.

A week later, he met her as usual, but her kiss of greeting seemed distracted and her smile forced. He asked her if something was wrong, but she only shook her head. "It's nothing," she insisted. "Just a guy asking for stuff I don't do." Before he could puff up in righteous defense of his woman, she put her hand on his chest and gave him the smile that always touched the place deep inside him that told him that, to this woman even if no one else, he was special and strong.

"It's all right," she assured him, though a shimmer of doubt touched the corners of her mouth.

The doubt stayed, darkening her eyes and hunching her shoulders. At times he thought she was on the verge of tears. It took several more days for him to coax it out of her, patiently weathering the denials, the false smiles, and the protestations that everything was fine. He wasn't the most honest cop on the beat, but he still knew how to ferret out the truth.

"It's this one guy," she finally confessed while they lay tangled in the sheets of his bed and she rested her head on his chest. A shudder passed through her. "He's rich and powerful, which is why the owners don't toss him out." She lifted her head, met his eyes. "It's not that he's mean or a jerk. But he *wants* me." She swallowed, then managed a chuckle. "Doesn't that sound ridiculously egotistical?"

He smiled, stroked her hair back from her face. "Not to me. I can perfectly understand wanting you."

Delia dropped her head back to his chest, nestled closer to him. "He wants me to be his girlfriend. I told him I wasn't interested." She sighed. "I'm sure it'll all blow over, but right now he's awfully insistent. And, he's . . . ugh."

"Skeevy?"

"No, not that. He's clean-cut, decent looking. But it's . . . it's the way he sees other people. As things to be used. He's not nice."

He wrapped his arms around her, pulled her close, kissed the top of her head while tension curdled his gut. "Who is this guy?" he asked, even though he had a feeling he already knew. "I'll take care of it."

She lifted her head again, a frown puckering her forehead. "I don't want you hurting anyone for me."

"I won't," he lied. He knew damn well how to cover his tracks. As long as it wasn't Peter. Please don't let it be Peter. "Give me his name. I'll make sure that he knows you're off-limits. Nice and friendly."

Peter opened the door of his condo at the knock, an amused smile curving his mouth at the sight of Danny on the doorstep. "What a nice surprise. Come on in."

Danny gave the man a short nod, entered. "Need to talk to you."

"I'm always here for a friend," Peter said, closing the door. "By the way, I never did get to thank you for taking care of that business with the bookstore owner." He moved to the kitchen, pulled down two mugs from the cabinet. "I don't know what you said to him, but he took the eviction with nary a whimper." He poured coffee for himself, then slid a look toward Danny. "So nice when people do as they're told. Makes everyone's life so much more pleasant. Coffee?"

Danny jerked his head in a nod. Peter knew why he was there, Danny realized. He'd been expecting him. He took the mug from the man, forced himself to sip at the bitter liquid.

"I've done a lot of stuff for you," he began, then stopped. None of that made a difference in this situation. He had a speech ready, a chest-pounding "get away from my woman" rant, but one look at Peter's eyes told him that it was the wrong tack, that it would be pointless. He swallowed to try to clear the bitter taste from his mouth, took a deep breath. "Look, there's this girl I really like. Delia. She, uh, says that you've asked her out, and I wanted to talk to you, man-to-man, ask you to leave her be." As soon as the words were out of his mouth, he hated himself. This wasn't man-to-man. This was the dog groveling to his master.

Peter frowned over his mug. "Delia? Is that the stripper chick you've been mooning over?"

"We've been seeing each other," Danny said, jaw tight.

The other man cocked an eyebrow at him. "Is that so? She sure has been friendly with me at the club." The he chuckled, shook his head. "But that's her job, isn't it? I have to say, she's quite good. I could almost believe she really is glad to see me each night."

"Yeah," Danny managed. "She's good. We're good . . . together. I'm asking you to, uh, please back off." He didn't know that Peter had been going to the club so often. How many times had he been in a private room with Delia while Danny waited like an eager puppy in the bar across the street?

"For you, of course," Peter said with a magnanimous nod. "I wish you both the best." Took a sip of coffee, walked over to the window to gaze out at the muddy swath that was more bayou than river now. "Of course, for your sake, I hope she doesn't get a better offer." He glanced back at Danny. "Or rather, if she does get a better offer, that she doesn't take it."

"Right," Danny said. "Appreciate you understanding."

Peter set the mug down on the table by the window. "By the way, the final vote on the poker room is day after tomorrow. I need you to lean on Councilman Nagle. Catch him doing something." His smile widened. "Maybe your Delia can help you out with that." Then he shrugged. "Or not. Best to keep business and pleasure separate, right?"

"Right," Danny repeated. It was a challenge, a power play. Peter wanted to know how much he could trust him. Wanted to know how far Danny would go to keep the influence that had protected him for so long.

Yet Danny knew that it didn't matter. It was already too late. Danny had tried to bare his teeth. From now on, Peter would be watching his back, waiting for the moment when he could throw Danny to the wolves and keep his own hands clean.

Danny simply had to find a way to do the same to Peter first.

He jerked his head in a nod. "Got it. I'll take care of it."

Peter's smile widened. "You're a good friend. Give my best to Delia."

The next week was quiet and calm. Danny readied himself for the next time Peter called on him, ready to record the exchange or whatever else he could do, but his phone remained silent. Delia spent every night at his apartment, only returning to her own place to change clothes and water her plants. She told him that Peter had stopped coming to the club and wanted to know what Danny had done. He merely smiled and said, "Better that you don't know." He couldn't tell her that he'd done nothing except grovel, that the only reason Peter left her alone was because it suited Peter to do so.

And, as Danny had feared, it didn't last.

"He came to my apartment!" she told him after he opened his door to see her standing on his front step. Her lower lip trembled and her eyes were red from weeping. He quickly pulled her inside, took her to the couch, and held her while she poured it all out to him.

Peter had given her an ultimatum—go with him or he'd not only have her evicted but he'd make sure she never found work in this city again.

"I don't know what to do," she told him, looking more defeated and beaten down than he'd ever imagined she could be. "I can't . . . I *won't* leave New Orleans. It's too special to me." Delia's eyes lifted to his. "People like him are destroying this city. I hate it. I hate them all!" Her voice broke on the last word.

Sweat pricked Danny's palms. He could kill Peter. There were a hundred different ways he could do it and stage it like an accident or suicide. Or maybe Danny could go to the feds, tell them everything he knew about Peter's dealings.

"I'll take care of it," he said, kissing her. He stood up, but she caught at his hand.

"I don't want you getting into trouble," she said, eyes wide and frightened.

"It'll be fine. I promise." He gently pulled free of her grasp. "You can count on me."

Danny walked along Chartres Street to Dumaine, headed to Jackson Square and watched pigeons swarm around a bum with a bag of stale bread. A handful of street artists gamely displayed their wares, casting desperate smiles to the sparse trickle of tourists wandering by, and ignoring him, since he was obviously a local and not worth wasting the energy of false friendliness on.

He would kill Peter Bennett, he told himself. That was the only way out. Going to the feds wasn't an option. Anything Danny told them would sink him just as thoroughly as it would Peter, and he didn't have any evidence other than his own testimony.

Late afternoon turned to dusk as he sat on a bench in the park and considered his options, planned out his steps. When full dark came, he headed down Decatur, stopped in a sleazy T-shirt shop full of tourist crap, and bought a cap. After that, he cut over to the Riverwalk, entered Peter's building, and took the elevator to his floor, keeping the cap pulled low over his face to avoid being caught by any cameras.

Peter answered the door, eyebrow lifting in mild surprise at Danny's presence. His gaze flicked to the cap and then back to Danny's face. "You okay? You look upset."

"Yeah," he replied. "A bit. Can I come in?"

"Absolutely." Peter stepped aside, closed the door behind him. Danny swept his gaze around the condo. No one else here. No one else on this floor, for that matter. No one had seen him come in. He had it all planned. Collapsible baton in his pocket to take Peter down, then make it look like an accidental fall in the shower. Doubtful it would be found out as murder even if there was a proper investigation.

Peter leaned up against the counter, watched Danny impassively. Maybe he knew why the cop was here. Probably did, in fact. He had to have known it would come to this.

"I almost forgot," Peter said abruptly, pushing off the counter and moving to his desk. "Forgot to give you that, ah, loan money you asked for."

Sweat prickled Danny's back and his hand eased toward his gun. This was perfect. Peter was going to pull a gun from that drawer and then Danny could shoot him in self-defense.

But it was a thick envelope that Peter retrieved from the drawer. Danny dropped his hand before Peter could see, heart thudding unevenly. The man was paying him for busting Councilman Nagle with a prostitute earlier in the week. Nagle had agreed to vote Peter's way rather than face a humiliating arrest, and the poker room had been approved, no doubt the first of many.

Peter held out the envelope to him. "I think you'll be happy with this. I know I am. Good work with that, by the way."

He didn't move for several seconds, then finally stepped forward and took the envelope. Opened it to see that it held at least ten grand.

Danny closed the envelope and tucked it into the pocket in his jacket. "Appreciate this," he said, voice sounding odd and rough in his ears. He didn't have to kill Peter. He had other options. He could take Delia away from here. He'd convince her to leave. They could start over somewhere else. Away from this fucked-up city. Away from Peter.

"Come by next week," Peter said. "We'll talk." He paused. "You should bring Delia by sometime. Unless you two broke up already?" He lifted a bottle of water, drank without ever taking his eyes from Danny.

"No," Danny replied, feeling the weight of the question, responding to the statements.

The man grinned. "That's real cute. How long you think that'll last?"

He wasn't talking about Delia, Danny knew. Peter was toying with him, wanting to know how long this little flare of defiance would go on before Danny settled down and behaved again.

Like the dog at the café, who'd slunk off instead of attacking. That dog was probably dead now, Danny thought, or at the very least still hungry, slinking through the city, willing to brave a few kicks to get a scrap or two.

No more slinking. No more scraps.

"Forever," he replied. With a practiced move, he pulled the baton from his pocket and snapped it open. Baring his teeth as he stepped toward Peter. Reveling in the shock and fear on the man's face as the dog finally turned on his master.

He called her in the elevator, asked her to meet him at the Canal Street Ferry. He figured he'd beat her there, but when he arrived at the dock, he saw her leaning on the rail down at the end, looking out over the wallowing river and the blinking lights of cars crossing the bridge.

A tension he hadn't even been aware of leached away. A part of him hadn't been sure she'd come, afraid that she'd cut her losses and leave him behind. Yet now he realized that she'd known where he'd gone, had been waiting nearby for him.

She turned at the sound of his hurrying footsteps, watched him as he approached.

"Danny . . . ?" she said, reaching up to touch his face. "What's going on?"

He caught her hand in his, kissed it. "I love you, baby. I'll keep you safe forever, I swear it."

Her breath caught. "Oh God. What did you do?"

"It's cool," he said. "I swear. I . . . I'm good."

She bit her lip, then closed her eyes, wrapped her arms around him. "Yes, you are."

He lowered his head and breathed in the scent of her, feeling all the shit and the muck of his life slipping away. "Let's go," he said. "Let's leave this place forever and start over somewhere else." He didn't want to stay, but he also knew he couldn't leave her behind. She'd end up as beaten and broken as those other girls . . . yet, even as he thought it, he knew that it was an excuse, knew that he wasn't strong enough to leave without her. But maybe if they *both* left, started over . . . maybe *he* could get unbroken.

She pulled back, shock and disappointment flashing across her features. "You want me to leave? I can't!"

"It's just a city, baby," he said, holding her face in his hands. "Nothing but a bunch of buildings and streets and crap and assholes."

"No. It's so much *more* than that." She tried to shake her head. "There's a *soul* to this place, rich and wonderful. We survived Katrina and we'll survive this. We . . . *I* . . . have to stay. Why can't you see it?" She reached up, pulled his hands from her face, but continued to hold them. "Oh, Danny," she breathed. "Peter's gone now. You don't have to be who you were anymore."

She knew, he realized, as the last of his tension dissipated. She *knew* he'd killed Peter, understood the lengths he'd go to for her . . . and didn't hate him for it. "No. I can be better," he insisted. "I *can* be . . . if I'm with you." He squeezed her hands. "But not here. It can't work here. New Orleans died when the river left. There's always gonna be guys like Peter here, looking to cash in on the wreckage. They'll tear this city up and salvage every scrap they can from it, and they won't give a shit who gets crushed in the process."

He couldn't see her expression in the gloom, but he heard a sigh of what sounded like resignation come from her. Maybe she was starting to see things his way? "I have money," he told her. "We can go to Lafayette. Start over. We'll be together." His phone rang and he cursed, pulled it out to see it was Detective Farber. Ice knotted his stomach. Had Peter been found already?

"Think about it," he mouthed to Delia before he stepped back and answered the phone.

"Get this," Farber said without preamble. "Ernst's gun matched the slugs found in Jack-D's body." Jack-D, a pimp even sleazier than Jimmy Ernst, who specialized in girls who didn't just *look* very young but really *were*. He'd been found down on Basin Street the day before Ernst took a swim in the mud. "Betcha one of Jack-D's boys capped Ernst as a get back," the detective continued. "At any rate, we got enough to close both cases."

"Yeah," Danny said. "That's good. Do it." He hung up, looked out at the river and frowned. Didn't make sense that a pussy like Jimmy would go after Jack-D. Didn't make sense that anyone would give enough of a shit to take out Jimmy in revenge. A whisper of unease lifted the hairs on the back of his neck. Delia had known Peter was dead. Had she *wanted* Danny to kill him?

He began to turn back to Delia, felt two prongs of cold metal against his throat an instant before hot lightning flashed through his body. He dropped to the concrete of the dock as pain danced through his nerve endings and he fought for control of his muscles.

She stooped and slipped the Taser back into her purse, pulled him upright, and leaned him against the railing. She was strong—those dancer muscles served her well as she toppled him over the side to the waiting muck below.

He landed flat on his back. The impact knocked his breath from him, but the mud quickly gave way beneath his weight. She leaned over the railing, met his eyes as he sank.

Delia checked her watch, waited as the river slid along its banks with a contented, relieved sigh. In the distance, metal groaned as a ship heeled over with the change in the tide. Moonlight painted the river in a sheet of soft grey, an elegant lady settling into comfortable retirement.

She looked down at the silt below. Barely a ripple to show that anything had disturbed it. A sigh of regret slipped from her. "You were a good boy, Danny," she murmured, a sad smile touching her mouth. "The best one yet."

Delia touched her fingers to her lips, blew a tender good-bye kiss toward the silt below, then turned and headed back to the heart of her city.

Sherrilyn Kenyon

Be careful what you search for—because you just might *find* it.

New York Times bestseller Sherrilyn Kenyon is one of the superstars of the paranormal romance field. She's probably best-known for the twenty-two-volume Dark-Hunter series, including such titles as *Night Embrace, Dance with the Devil, Kiss of the Night,* and *Bad Moon Rising,* and extending to manga and short stories as well as novels, but she also writes the League series, including *Born of Night, Born of Fire, Born of Ice,* and *Born of Shadows,* and the Chronicles of Nick series, which includes *Infinity* and *Invincible.* She's also produced the four-volume B.A.D. (Bureau of American Defense) sequence, three of those written with Dianna Love, including *Silent Truth, Whispered Lies, Phantom in the Night,* and the collection *Born to be BAD,* and the three-volume Belador Code sequence, again written with Dianna Love. Her most recent novels are *Born of Silence,* a League novel, and *Infamous,* part of the Chronicles of Nick series. There's a compendium to the Dark-Hunter series, *The Dark-Hunter Companion,* written by Kenyon and Alethea Kontis, and Kenyon has also written nonfiction such as *The Writer's Guide to Everyday Life in the Middle Ages* and *The Writer's Digest Character Naming Sourcebook.* She lives in Spring Hill, Tennessee, and maintains a website at sherrilynkenyon.com.

HELL HATH NO FURY

Based on a true legend

"I don't think we should be here."

"Oh, c'mon, Cait, calm down. Everything's fine. We have the equipment set up and—"

"I feel like someone's watching me." Cait Irwin turned around slowly, scanning the thick woods, which appeared to be even more sinister now that the sun was setting. The trees spread out in every direction, so thick and numerous that she couldn't even see where they'd parked her car, never mind the highway that was so far back that nothing could be heard from it.

We could die here and no one would know . . .

Anne, her best friend from childhood, cocked her hip as she lowered her thermal-imaging camera to smirk at Cait. "I hope something *is* watching you . . . Which direction should I be shooting?"

Cait shook her head at her friend's joy. There was nothing Anne loved more than a good ghost sighting. "Anne, I'm not joking. There's something here." She pinned her with a caustic glower. "You brought me along because I'm psychic, right?"

"Yeah."

"Then trust me. This"—Cait rubbed the chills from her arms—"isn't right."

"What's going on?" Brandon set his large camera crate down next to Anne's feet as he rejoined them. He and Jamie had gone out to set their DVRs and cameras for the night.

While she and Anne were slight of frame, Brandon and Jamie were well bulked, Brandon more from beer and channel surfing, but Jamie from hours spent in the gym. Even so, with his blond hair and blue eyes,

Brandon was good-looking in a Boy Scout kind of way. But Jamie had that whole dark, brooding, sexy scowl thing that made most women melt and giggle whenever he glanced their way.

Anne indicated her with a jerk of her chin. "Wunderkind over there is already picking up something."

Brandon's eyes widened. "I hope you mean spiritwise and not some backwoods bug we have no immunity to. I left my vitamin C at home."

Cait shivered as another wave of trepidation went through her. This one was even stronger than the previous one. "Whose bright idea was this anyway?"

Anne pointed to Brandon, who grinned proudly.

He winked at her. "C'mon, Cait. It's a ghost town. We don't get to investigate one of these every day. Surely ye of the unflappable constitution isn't wigging out like a little girl at a horror movie."

"Boo!"

Cait shrieked as Jamie grabbed her from behind.

Laughing, he stepped around her, then shrugged his Alienware backpack off his shoulder and set it next to the camera case.

She glared at the walking mountain. "Damn it, Jamie! You're not funny!"

"No, but *you* are. I didn't know you could jump that high. I'm impressed."

Hissing at him like a feral cat, she flicked her nails in his direction. "If I didn't think it'd come back on me, I'd hex you."

He flashed that devilish grin that was flanked by dimples so deep, they cut moons into both of his cheeks. "Ah, baby, you can hex me up any time you want!"

Cait suppressed a need to strangle him. All aggravation aside, a martial arts instructor who was built like Rambo might come in handy one day. And still her Spidey senses tingled, warning her that that day might not be too far in the future.

"We're not supposed to be here." She bit her lip as she glanced around, trying to find what had her so rattled.

"No one is," Brandon said in a spooky tone. "This ground is cursed. Oooo-eeee-oooo . . ."

She ignored him. But he was right. At one time, Randolph County had been the richest in all of Alabama. Until the locals had forced a Native

American business owner to leave her store behind and walk the Trail of Tears.

"Louina . . ."

Cait jerked around as she heard the faint whisper of the woman's name; it was the same name as the ghost town they were standing in. Rather cruel to name the town after the woman who'd been run out of it for no real reason.

"Louina," the voice repeated, even more insistent than before.

"Did you hear that?" she asked the others.

"Hear what?" Jamie checked his DVR. "I'm not picking up anything."

Something struck her hard in the chest, forcing her to take a step back. Her friends and the forest vanished. She suddenly found herself inside an old trading post. The scent of the pine-board walls and floor mixed with that of spices and flour. But it was the soaps on the counter in front of her that smelled the strongest.

An older Native American woman, who wore her hair braided and coiled around her head, straightened the jars on the countertop while a younger, pregnant woman who had similar features, leaned against the opposite end.

But what shocked Cait was how much she looked like the older woman. Right down to the black hair and high eyebrows.

The younger woman—Elizabeth; Cait didn't know how she knew that, but she did—reached into one of the glass jars and pulled out a piece of licorice. "They're going to make you leave, Lou. I overheard them talking about it."

Louina scoffed at her sister's warning before she replaced the lid and pulled the jar away from her. "Our people were here long before them, and we'll be here long after they're gone. Mark my words, Lizzie."

Elizabeth swallowed her piece of licorice. "Have you not heard what they've done to the Cherokee in Georgia?"

"I heard. But the Cherokee aren't the Creek. Our nation is strong."

Elizabeth jerked, then placed her hand over her distended stomach where her baby kicked. "He gets upset every time I think about you being forced to leave."

"Then don't think about it. It won't happen. Not as long as I've been here."

"Cait!"

Cait jumped as Jamie shouted in her face. "W-what?"

"Are you with us? You blanked out for a second."

Blinking, she shook her head to clear it of the images that had seemed so real that she could taste Elizabeth's licorice. "Where was that original trading post you guys mentioned being here?"

Brandon shrugged. "No idea. We couldn't find any information about it, other than it was owned by the Native American woman the town was named for. Why?"

Because she had a bad feeling that they were standing on it. But there was nothing to corroborate that. Nothing other than a bad feeling in the pit of her stomach.

In fact, there was nothing left of this once-thriving town other than rows of crosses in a forgotten cemetery, and a marker that proclaimed it Louina, Alabama.

That thought had barely finished before she saw Louina again in her mind. She was standing a few feet away, to Cait's left, with a wagon filled with as much money and supplies as she could carry. Furious, she spat on the ground and then spoke in Creek to the men who'd come to confiscate her home and store, and force her to leave.

Cait knew it was Creek, a language she knew not at all, and yet the words were as clear to her as if they'd been spoken in English.

"I curse this ground and all who dwell here. For what you've done to me . . . for the cruelty you have shown others, no one will make my business prosper, and when my sister passes from this existence to the next, within ten years of that date, there will be nothing left of this town except gravestones."

The sheriff and his deputies who'd been sent to escort her from her home laughed in her face. "Now, don't be like that, Louina. This ain't personal against you."

"No, but it is personal against *you*." She cast a scathing glare at all of them. "No one will remember any of you as ever having breathed, but they will remember my name, Louina, and the atrocity that you have committed against me."

One of the deputies came from behind the wagon with a stern frown. "Louina? This can't be all you own."

A cruel smile twisted her lips. "I couldn't carry all of my gold."

That piqued the deputies' interest.

"Where'd you leave it?" the sheriff asked.

"The safest place I know. In the arms of my beloved husband."

The sheriff rubbed his thumb along the edge of his lips. "Yeah, but no one knows where you buried him."

"I know and I won't forget . . ." She swept a chilling gaze over all of them. "Anything." And with that, she climbed onto her wagon and started forward without looking back. But there was no missing the smug satisfaction in her eyes.

She was leaving more than her store behind.

Cait could hear Louina's malice as if they were her own thoughts. *They will tear each other apart, questing for the gold my husband will never release . . .*

It was Louina's final revenge.

One paid tribute to by the eerie rows of cross-marked graves in the old Liberty Missionary Baptist Church Cemetery.

The weakness of our enemy is our strength.

Make my enemy brave, smart, and strong, so that if defeated, I will not be ashamed.

Cait felt Louina with her like her own shadow. A part of her that she could only see if the light hit it just right.

Louina whispered in her ear, but this time Cait didn't understand the words. Yet what was unmistakable was the feeling of all-consuming dread that wouldn't go away, no matter what she tried.

She sighed before she implored her group one more time. "We need to leave."

All three of them balked.

"We just got the equipment set out."

"What? Now? We've been here all day!"

"Really, Cait? What are you thinking?"

They spoke at once, but each voice was as clear as Louina's. "We should *not* be here," she insisted. "The land itself is telling me that we need to go. Screw the equipment, it's insured."

"No!" Brandon adamantly refused.

It was then that she understood why they were being stubborn, when Brandon had spent his entire life saying that if you ran into a malevolent haunting, you abandoned that place because nothing was worth the chance of being possessed.

Only one thing would make him and Jamie forget about their own beliefs.

Greed.

"You're not here for the ghosts. You're here for the *treasure*."

Jamie and Brandon exchanged a nervous glance.

"She *is* psychic," Anne reminded them.

Brandon cursed. "Who told you about the treasure?"

"Louina."

"Can she tell you where it is?" Jamie asked hopefully.

Cait screwed her face up at him. "Is that really all you're concerned with?"

"Well . . . not *all*. We *are* here for the science. Natural curiosity being what it is. But let's face it, the equipment's not cheap and a little payback wouldn't be bad."

His choice of words only worsened her apprehension.

"Can you really not feel the anger here?" She gestured in the direction of the cemetery; that had been the first place they'd set up the equipment and it was there that her bad feelings had started. "It's so thick, I can smell it."

"I feel humidity."

Jamie raised his hand. "Sign me up for hunger."

"Annoyed," Brandon chimed in. "Look, it's for one night. Me and Jamie are going to dowse a little and try to find a place to dig."

How could he appear so chipper about what they were planning? "You'll be digging up a grave."

They froze.

"What?" Brandon asked.

Cait nodded. "The treasure is buried with Louina's husband, William, who was one of the Creek leaders during the Red Stick War."

Jamie narrowed his gaze suspiciously. "How do you know all of this?"

"I told you. Louina. She keeps speaking to me."

Brandon snorted. "I'm laying money on Google. Nice try, C. You probably know where the money is and you're trying to scare us off. No deal, sister. I want a cut."

Laughing, Jamie chucked him on the back, then headed to the cooler to grab a beer.

Anne stepped closer to her. "Are you serious about this?"

Cait nodded. "I wish they'd believe me. But yeah. We shouldn't be here. This land is saturated with malevolence. It's like a flowing river under the soil."

And with those words, she lost Anne's support. "Land can't be evil or cursed. You know that." She walked over to the men.

Cait knew better. Part Creek herself, she'd been raised on her mother's belief that if someone hated *enough,* they could transfer that hatred into objects and into the soil. Both were like sponges—they could carry hatred for generations.

Louina was out there, and she was angry.

Most of all, she was vengeful.

And she's coming for us . . .

Cait felt like a leper as she sat alone by the fire, eating her protein bar. The others were off in the woods, trying to summon the very entity that she knew was with her.

"Louina?" Jamie called, his deep voice resonating through the woods. "If you can hear me, give me a sign."

While it was a common phrase, for some reason tonight it bothered her. She mocked him silently as she pulled the protein bar's wrapper down lower.

Suddenly, a scream rang out.

Cait shot to her feet and listened carefully. Who was it, and where were they? Her heart pounded in her ears.

"Brandon!" Anne shouted, her voice echoing through the woods.

Cait ran toward them as fast as she could.

By the time she found them, Brandon was on his back with a twig poking all the way through his arm.

"He said he wanted a cut . . ."

She jerked around, trying to pinpoint the voice that had spoken loud and clear. "Did you hear that?" she asked the others.

"All I hear is Brandon whining like a bitch. Suck it up already, dude. Damn. You keep that up and I'm buying you a bra."

"Fuck you!" he snarled at Jamie. "Let me stab you with a stick and see how you feel. You the bitch. Asshole!"

"Boys!" Cait moved to stand between them. "What happened?"

"I don't know," Brandon hissed as Anne tried to see the wound. "I was walking, going over the thermal scan, when all of a sudden I stumbled and fell into a tree. Next thing I knew . . . this!" He held it up for her to see.

Cringing, Cait averted her eyes from the grisly wound. "We need to get him to the hospital."

"Not on your life," Brandon snarled. "I'll be all right."

"I take it back. You're not a bitch. You're insane. Look at that wound. I hate to agree with Cait, 'cause I doubt there's a hospital anywhere near here, but you need help."

"It's a flesh wound."

Cait shook her head. "Anne, you should have never let him watch Monty Python."

"I should have never left him alone to go to the bathroom," Anne growled at him. "They're right. You need to see a doctor. You could get rabies or something."

Yeah, 'cause rabid trees were a *huge* problem here in Alabama. Cait barely caught herself before she laughed. Anne hated to be laughed at.

"I'm not leaving till I find that treasure!"

Greed, pride, and stupidity. The three most fatal traits any human could possess.

A sudden wind swept around them. This time she wasn't the only one who heard the laughter it carried.

"What was that?" Jamie asked.

"Louina."

"Would you *stop* with that shit?" Brandon snapped through gritted teeth. "You're really getting on my nerves."

And they were getting on hers.

Fine. Whatever. She wasn't going to argue anymore. It was their lives. His wound. Who was she to keep him safe when he obviously had no interest in it?

Arms akimbo, Jamie sighed. "What do you think are the odds that, assuming Cait's right, and Louina's husband has the gold in his grave, that it's in the cemetery? Didn't most of the Native Americans in this area convert over to Baptist?"

Cait shook her head. "He won't be there."

"What makes you say that?"

"If it was that easy to find, it would have been found long ago."

"Yeah, good point. Square one sucks." Jamie glanced back at Brandon. "You sure about the doctor?"

"Positive."

"All right. I'm heading back out. Cait? You coming?"

"You can't go alone." She followed as he switched his flashlight on and went back to his EMF detector and air ion counter.

"You want to take this?" He held his full-spectrum camcorder out to her.

"Sure." She opened it and turned it back on so that she could see the world through the scope of the small screen.

After few minutes, he paused. "Do you really believe any of the bullshit you've been spewing?"

"You know me, James. Have I ever spewed bullshit on site?"

"Nah. That's what has me worried." He narrowed his gaze at her. "Did I ever tell you that my great-grandmother was Cherokee?"

"No, you didn't."

He nodded. "She died when I was six, but I still remember her, and something she'd always say keeps echoing in my head."

"What?"

"'Listen, or your tongue will keep you deaf.'"

Cait was about to compliment her wisdom when she glanced down at the screen.

Holy Mother . . .

Gasping, she dropped the camera and jumped back.

"What?" Jamie turned around to see if there was something near.

Terrified and shaking, Cait couldn't speak. She couldn't get the image out of her mind. She gestured to the camera.

With a stern frown, Jamie picked it up and ran it back. Even in the darkness, she knew the moment he saw what had stolen her tongue. He turned stark white.

Right before he'd spoken about his Cherokee great-grandmother, a huge . . . something with fangs had been about to pounce on him. Soulless eyes of black had stared down as its mouth opened to devour him. Then the moment he'd repeated the quote, it had pulled back and vanished.

Eyes wide, he gulped. "We have to leave."

She nodded, because she still couldn't speak. Jamie took her arm gently and led her through the woods back to where they'd left Anne and Brandon.

They were already gone. Jamie growled in frustration. "Brandon!" he called out. "Anne?"

Only silence answered them.

"All who dwell here will pay . . ." Louina's voice was more insistent now. *"But I hurt those I should not have cursed."*

Cait flinched as she saw an image of Elizabeth as an old woman in a stark hand-built cabin. Her gray hair was pulled back into a bun as she lit a candle and placed it in the window while she whispered a Creek prayer.

Oh, Great Father Spirit, whose voice I hear in the wind–

Whose breath gives life to all the world and with whom I have tried to walk beside throughout my days.

Hear me. I need your strength and wisdom.

Let me walk in beauty, and make my eyes ever behold the glorious sunset you have provided.

Make my hands respect the things you have made and my ears sharp to hear your voice even when it's nothing more than a faint whisper.

Make me wise so that I may understand the things you have taught my people. And why you have taken things from me that have given me pain.

Help me to remain calm and strong in the face of all that comes at me. Against my enemies and those out to do me harm.

Let me learn the lessons you have hidden in every leaf and rock. In the joy of the stream. In the light of the moon and sun.

Help me seek pure thoughts and act with the intention of helping others and never myself.

Help me find compassion without empathy overwhelming me.

I seek strength, not to be greater than my brother, but to fight my greatest enemy . . .

Myself.

Make me always ready to come to you with clean hands and straight eyes. So that when my life fades, as the fading sunset, my spirit may come to you without shame.

And most of all, Great-Grandfather, keep my sons safe and warm wherever they may be.

Elizabeth leaned over and kissed the old photographs of two young men in cavalry uniforms that she had sitting in the window beside the candle she lit every night—just in case they finally found their way home. It was a ritual she'd practiced every single night for the last fifty-two years. Since the war had ended and her boys had failed to return home to tend their crops.

She refused to believe them dead. Just as she refused to die and let her sister's curse harm the town where they had both been born.

Her heart aching, she pulled two brittle letters from her pocket, the last that her boys had written to her, and sat down at the table. Old age had taken her sight so that she could no longer read the words, not even with her spectacles. But it didn't matter. She'd long ago committed their words to her heart.

I dream only of returning home to marry Anabelle. Give her my best, Mother. Soon I will see you both again.

Robert

He'd only been nineteen when he'd left her home with his older brother John, when they'd been conscripted to fight a war that had nothing to do with them. Eighteen months older, John had sworn that he would watch over Robert and return him home.

"On my life, Ecke. I'll bring him back whole and hale."

And I will watch for you every day, and every night I will light a candle to help guide you both to my door.

Tears swam in her eyes, but they didn't fall. She was stronger than that. Instead, she reached for the old hand-carved horn her father had given to her when she'd been a child. "Take this, Lizzie. Should anyone come to our door while your brothers and I are in the field, sound it loud to let us know and then hide with your mother and sisters until we can get to you."

So much had changed. To this day, she didn't regret marrying her husband. She had loved her John more than anything. But he had left her far too soon. She'd laid him to rest on a cold February morning when Robert was barely seven. Since her brothers had been forced to leave along with her sister, Lou, she'd raised the boys on her own, along with her daughter, Mary.

There is no death, only a change of worlds . . .

Soon she would change. She could feel the Great Spirit with her more and more.

Do not grieve for that which is past or for that which you cannot prevent.

"I will see you again soon, my sons." And she would be with her John . . .

Cait flinched as she felt Louina's pain.

You must live your life from beginning to end. No one can do it for you. But be careful when you seek to destroy another. For it is your soul that will be consumed and you are the one who will cry. Never allow anger and hatred to poison you.

"I am poison . . ."

Those words echoed in Cait's head as she followed Jamie in his quest to locate their friends.

"Maybe they went to the hospital, after all." That was her hope until they reached the tents they'd pitched earlier.

Tents that were now shredded and lying strewn across the ground. Jamie ran ahead, then pulled up short. With a curse, he turned and caught her before she could get too close.

"You don't want to know."

"W-what?"

His gaze haunted, he tightened his arms around her. "Trust me, Cait. You don't want to see them. We have to call the authorities."

Tears welled in her eyes. "Anne?"

He shook his head. "It looks like an animal attack of some kind."

"Why!"

"I don't know."

But her question wasn't for Jamie. It was for Louina.

Words spoken in anger have strong power and they cannot be undone. For those who are lucky, they can be forgiven in time. But for others . . .

It is always our own words and deeds than condemn us. Never the ill intent or wishes of our enemies.

Do not dabble with what you don't understand. There are some doors that are blown from their hinges when they are opened. Doors that will never again be sealed.

"Welcome to my hell."

They both jerked at the voice beside them.

There in the darkness stood Louina. Her gray hair fanned out around her shoulders. Her old calico dress was faded against her white apron.

"My sister protects you. For that you should give thanks. Now go and never come here again."

But it wasn't that simple.

"I will not leave and allow you to continue hurting others."

Louina laughed. "You can't stop me."

For the first time in her life, Cait understood the part of her bloodline that had always been mysterious and undefined. She was the great-great-granddaughter of Elizabeth.

It all came together in her mind at once. Her grandmother had told her the story of Elizabeth, who'd died when her cabin caught fire while she was sleeping. Something had knocked the candle that she lit for her sons from her window.

"*You* killed her!" Cait accused.

"She wanted to die. She was tired."

But that wasn't true and she knew it. Yes, Elizabeth had been tired. She'd been almost a hundred and ten years old. Yet she'd been so determined to keep her sister's curse at bay that she'd refused Death every time it tried to claim her.

Until Louina had intervened.

In that moment, Cait felt a connection to Elizabeth. One she embraced.

Jamie released her. "What are you doing?"

Cait looked down to see the glow that enveloped her. Warm and sweet, it smelled like sunshine. It was Elizabeth.

"This ends, Louina. As you said, you are the poison that must be purged."

Shrieking, Louina ran at her.

True to her warrior heritage, Cait stood her ground. She would not back down. Not in this.

Louina's spirit slammed into Cait with enough force to knock her down. She groaned as pain filled her. Still, she stood up again, and closed her eyes. "You will not defeat me. It is time for you to rest. You have not shown respect to those who dwell on this earth."

"They didn't show it to me!"

"And you allowed them to turn you away from the Great Spirit, who loves us all. To do things you knew weren't right!"

"They spat in my face!"

"You returned their hatred with more hatred." Cait reached her hand out to Louina. "Like Elizabeth, you're tired. Nothing is more draining than to keep the fires of hatred burning."

"Nothing is more draining."

"You will not fight me?"

Cait shook her head. "I want to comfort you. It's time to let go, Louina. Release the hatred." And then she heard Elizabeth in her ear, telling her what to say. "Remember the words of Crazy Horse. Upon suffering beyond suffering, the Red Nation shall rise again and it shall be a blessing for a sick world. A world filled with broken promises, selfishness, and separations. A world longing for light again. I see a time of Seven Generations when all the colors of mankind will gather under the Sacred Tree of Life and the whole Earth will become one circle again. In that day, there will be those among the Lakota who will carry knowledge and understanding of unity among all living things and the young white ones will come to those of my people and ask for this wisdom. I salute the light within your eyes where the whole Universe dwells. For when you are at that center within you and I am that place within me, we shall be one."

Louina pulled back as she heard those words. "We are one," she repeated.

Elizabeth pulled away from Cait and held her hand out to Louina. "I have missed my sister."

"I have missed mine."

Jamie placed his hands on Cait's shoulders. "Are you all right?"

She wasn't sure. "Did you see any of that?"

"Yes, but I'm going to deny it if you ever ask me that in public."

Tears filled her eyes as she remembered Anne and Brandon. "Why did we come this weekend?"

"*We* came for greed. You came to help a friend."

Suddenly, a low moan sounded.

"Call for help!" Jamie said. He released her and ran back to their camp.

She dialed 911, hoping it would pick up.

"Anne's still breathing." Jamie pulled his jacket off to drape it over her.

"What about Brandon?"

He went to check while the phone rang.

"It's faint, but yeah . . . I think he's alive too."

Cait prayed for a miracle that she hoped would be granted.

Epilogue

Cait sat next to Anne's bed while the nurse finished checking her vitals. She didn't speak until after the woman had left them alone.

"Sorry we didn't have any readings to show you guys."

Anne shook her head. "Who cares? I'm just glad I'm alive. But . . ."

"But what?"

"Are you and Jamie ever going to tell us what really happened?"

Cait reached up to touch the small gold ring that she'd found on her car seat when she'd gone out to the road to help direct the medics to where Brandon and Anne had been. Inside the band were the names John and Elizabeth. It was the only gold to be found in Louina.

The treasure so many had sought had been used to fund a school and church over a century ago.

Years after her sister had given her the gold to support herself and her children, Elizabeth had taken the last of it and had it melted into this ring.

Smiling, Cait met Anne's gaze. "Maybe one day."

"And what about the treasure?"

"Anne, haven't you learned yet that it's not gold that is precious? It's people. And you are the greatest treasure of my life. I'm glad I still have my best friend."

Anne took her hand and held it. "I'm grateful to be here and I'm truly grateful for you. But—"

"There are no buts."

She nodded. "You're right, Cait. I'd lost sight of what my grandfather used to say."

"And that was?"

"'When all the trees have been cut down and all the animals have been hunted to extinction, when all the waters are polluted and the air is unsafe to breathe, only then will you discover you cannot eat money.'"

Jamie laughed, drawing their attention to the door where he stood with a balloon bouquet for Anne.

"What's so funny?" Cait asked.

"I think we all came away from the weekend with a different lesson."

Cait arched her brow. "And that is?"

"Anne just said hers. You learned that revenge is a path best left alone. Brandon learned to shut up and get help when he's wounded."

"And you?" Anne asked.

"I learned two things. One, the most dangerous place for a man to be is between two fighting women. And two, no matter the species, the deadliest gender is always the female. Men will fight until they die. Women will take it to the grave and then find a way *back*."

Melinda Snodgrass

A writer whose work crosses several mediums and genres, Melinda M. Snodgrass has written scripts for television shows such as *Profiler* and *Star Trek: The Next Generation* (for which she was also a story editor for several years), a number of popular SF novels, and was one of the cocreators of the long-running Wild Card series, for which she has also written and edited. Her novels include *Circuit*, *Circuit Breaker*, *Final Circuit*, *The Edge of Reason*, *Runespear* (with Victor Milán), *High Stakes*, *Santa Fe*, and *Queen's Gambit Declined*. Her most recent novel is *The Edge of Ruin*, the sequel to *The Edge of Reason*. Her media novels include the Wild Cards novel *Double Solitaire* and the Star Trek novel *The Tears of the Singers*. She's also the editor of the anthology *A Very Large Array*. She lives in New Mexico.

Here she takes us to a distant planet to show us that even in a society where spaceships thunder through the night and aliens mingle with humans on crowded city streets, some of the games you might run into go *way* back.

THE HANDS THAT ARE NOT THERE

Glass met glass with dull, tuneless clunks as the human bartender filled orders. A Hajin waitress with a long and tangled red mane running down her bare back clicked on delicate hooves through the bar delivering drinks. The patrons were a surly lot, mere shadows huddled in the dark dive, and carefully seated at tables well away from each other. No one talked. Substituting for conversation were commentators calling the action of a soccer game playing on the wall screen over the bar. Even those voices were growling rumbles because the sound was turned down so low. The odors of spilled beer and rancid cooking oil twisted through the smoke, but they and the tobacco smells were trumped by the scents of despair and simmering anger.

This dank hole was a perfect match for Second Lieutenant Tracy Belmanor's mood. He had picked it because it was well away from the spaceport and he was unlikely to meet any of his shipmates. He should have been happy. He had graduated from the Solar League's military academy only last month and had been assigned to his first posting. Problem was, his fellow classmates had walked out as newly minted first lieutenants, but such was not the case for the lowborn tailor's son who had attended the academy on a scholarship. When he had received his insignia, he'd stared down at the stars and single bar and realized that he was one rung below his aristocratic classmates, even though his grades had been better, his performance in flight the equal of any of them save Mercedes, whose reflexes and ability to withstand high gee had put them all to shame. When he'd looked up at the commandant of the High Ground, Vice Admiral Sergei Arrington Vasquez y Markov, the big man had casually delivered the explanation, totally unaware how insulting it had been.

"You must understand, Belmanor, it wouldn't do for you to be in the position

of issuing orders to your classmates, especially to the Infanta Mercedes. This way you will never hold the bridge solo, and so be spared the embarrassment."

The implication that *he* would be embarrassed to issue an order to high-born assholes, including the Emperor's daughter, had ignited his too-quick temper. *"I'm sure that will be a great comfort to me as I'm dying because one of those idiots wrecked the ship."* But of course he hadn't said that. The unwary words had been at the edge of his teeth, but after four years being drilled in protocol and the chain of command, he managed to swallow the angry retort. Instead he had saluted and managed a simple "Yes, sir." At least he hadn't thanked Markov for the insult.

Later, he wondered why he hadn't spoken up. Cowardice? Was he really intimidated by the FFH? That was a terrible thought, for it implied that he *did* know his place. If he was honest with himself, that was why he hadn't attended the postgraduation ball. He knew that none of Mercedes's ladies-in-waiting would have accepted him as escort. He couldn't bring a woman of his own social strata. And Mercedes was the daughter of the Emperor, and no one could ever know what they had shared, or that Tracy loved her and that she loved him.

So he didn't go to the ball. Instead, he stood on the Crystal Bridge on Ring Central and watched Mercedes, out of uniform and a vision in crimson and gold, enter the ballroom on the arm of Honorius Sinclair Cullen, Knight of the Arches and Shells, Duke de Argento, known casually as Boho, and Tracy's nemesis and rival. It should have been Tracy at her side. But that could never be.

Tracy took a long pull on his whiskey, draining the glass. It was cheap liquor and it etched pain down his throat, and settled like a burning coal in his gut. Unlike the other morose and uncommunicative patrons, Tracy had chosen to sit at the bar. The bartender, a big man, the stripes on his apron imperfectly hiding the grime, nodded at Tracy's empty glass.

"Another?"

"Sure. Why the hell not?"

"You've really been hammering these down, kid." Tracy looked up and was surprised by the kindness in the man's brown eyes. "You gonna be able to find your way back to your ship?" Whiskey gurgled into the glass.

"Maybe it would be better if I didn't."

A rag emerged from the apron pocket and wiped down the steel surface of the bar. "You don't wanna do that. The League hangs deserters."

Tracy downed the drink in one gulp, and fought back nausea. He shook his head. "Not me. They wouldn't look for me. They'd be glad the Embarrassment has been quietly swept under the rug."

"Look, kid, you got troubles. I can see that."

"Wow, you always this perceptive?"

"Cut the attitude," but the words were said mildly and with a faint smile. "Look, if you want feel better about the state of the galaxy and your place in it, you should talk to *that* guy. It may all be bullshit, but Rohan's got one hell of a story."

Tracy looked in the direction of the pointing finger and saw a portly man of medium height seated at a corner table and cuddling an empty glass. His dark hair was streaked with grey, and his forehead overly large due to the receding hairline. The bartender moved to the far end of the bar and started filling the empty glasses on the Hajin's tray. Tracy looked again at the slumped man. On impulse, he snatched up his glass and walked over to the table.

Jerking a thumb over his shoulder at the bartender, Tracy said, "He says you've got a good story that's going to put everything in perspective for me." Tracy kicked out a chair and sat down. He half hoped that the man would object and start a fight. Tracy was in the mood to hit somebody, and here on Wasua, unlike at the High Ground, a fight wouldn't turn into a stupid duel. Tracy touched the scar at his left temple, a gift from Boho. A closer look at the man revealed the unlikeliness of a fight breaking out. There was no muscle beneath the fat, and dark, puffy bags hung beneath his eyes.

"Loren doesn't believe me," Rohan said. "But it's all true." Alcohol slurred the words, but Tracy could hear the aristocratic accent of a member of the Fortune Five Hundred. God knew he could recognize it. He'd been listening to it for four damn years. He even feared he'd begun to ape it.

"Okay, I'll bite: What's all true?"

The tip of the man's tongue licked at his lips. "I could tell the story better with something to wet my throat," he said.

"Okay, fine." Tracy went back to the bar and returned with a bottle of bourbon. He slammed it down between them. "There. Now I've paid for the tale. So go on, amaze me."

Rohan drew himself up, but the haughtiness of the movement was undercut when he began swaying in his chair. A pudgy hand grabbed the edge of the table and he stabilized. "I am more, much more than I seem."

"Okay." Tracy drew out the word.

The man looked around with exaggerated care. "I have to be careful. If they knew I was talking . . ."

"Yes?"

The man drew a finger across his throat. He leaned across the table. His breath was a nauseating mix of booze and halitosis. "What I'm going to tell you could shake the foundations of the League."

The drunk poured himself a drink, tossed it back, and continued. "But it happened—all of it—and it's all true. Listen and learn, young man." Rohan refilled his glass, topped off Tracy's, and saluted with his glass. This time he settled for a sip rather than a gulp. Rohan sighed and no longer seemed focused on the young officer.

"It all started when one of my aides arranged a bachelor party. . . ."

If a strip club could ever be considered tasteful, Rohan assumed that this one fit that bill. Not that he was an expert. This was his first time in such an establishment, where human women flaunted themselves, much to the fury of the Church. So why had he agreed to join his staff at a stag party in honor of Knud's upcoming nuptials? The answer came easily. *Because my wife's latest lover is the same age as my daughter, and this one was just too much.* So his presence in the Cosmos Club was—what? Payback? And how likely was it that Juliana would ever find out? Surpassingly small. And that she would care? Smaller yet.

He blushed as a nearly naked hostess, her breasts and mons outlined with a jeweled harness, took their coats and, with the graceful hand gestures of a trained courtesan, ushered them over to the smiling maître d', a handsome man with a spade beard and sparkling black eyes. He led the group through tall double doors and into the club proper. The lighting in the main room was subdued, but recessed spotlights struck fire from the slowly rotating platforms that held beautiful, naked women. The platforms were shaped like spiral galaxies, the stars formed by faux diamonds. Rohan stared at the rounded buttocks of the girls and wondered what those behinds looked like after a long night seated on the platforms. Between the platforms was a stage made of clear glass. A crystal pole thrust up, an aggressive statement, from the center of the stage.

Waitresses dressed—no, make that accented—with the same kind of jeweled harness worn by the hostess moved between the tables, serving drinks and food. Rohan saw a Brie en croûte garnished with sour cherries go past on a tray, and the aromas from the kitchen were as good as anything he'd smelled in the city's finest restaurants. His belly gave a growl of appreciation. Yes, definitely an upscale establishment, catering to the wealthy and wellborn of the FFH. Another anomaly struck him. There were no aliens present. The waitstaff were all humans, an expensive affectation. Rohan assumed that in the bowels of the kitchen, Hajin and Isanjo labored as dishwashers, but the image presented to the paying customers was aggressively human.

John Fujasaki had reserved a circular booth at the edge of the stage. An ice-filled champagne bucket and the expected bottle were already waiting. As the party arranged themselves, the maître d' opened the bottle with a discreet *pop* and filled their glasses. The upholstery was plush, made from neural fabric that sensed the tension in Rohan's lower back and began to massage the spot. The floating holo table displayed a constantly shifting view of spectacular astronomical phenomenon. Rohan stared, mesmerized, as a blossoming supernova tried to consume his drink.

John Fujasaki, the instigator of this outing, leaned in close to Rohan and murmured, "You're blushing, sir." Laughter hung on the words.

"I'm not accustomed to seeing this much . . . female . . . flesh," he murmured back.

"Pardon my saying so, but you need to get out more" was the response. Then John turned away to respond to another comment.

Rohan watched the bubbles rising in his glass and wondered what the young aide would think if he knew that his boss did frequent less reputable establishments in Pony Town that catered to humans with a taste for the alien and the exotic. Then the hypocrisy of his anger at his wife over her infidelity struck him. He fell back on the age-old defense: whoring was expected of men, and no woman should place a cuckoo in her husband's nest. The excuses rang hollow.

John tapped his glass with a spoon. The young men fell silent and Fujasaki stood up. "Well, here's to Knud. Those of us who've avoided the wedded state think he's mad, and those who have entered the bonds of matrimony also think he's mad. But at least for tonight we'll put aside such worries and concentrate on sending him off in style. So, a toast to Knud on his final night of freedom, and may it be memorable!" John cried.

There were calls of "Here, here!" from around the table; glasses were clinked, drained, and refilled. Knud, smiling but with a hint of worry in the back of his eyes, laid a hand over his glass. "Now, go easy, fellas. I have to be in reasonably good shape tomorrow."

"Not to worry, Knud," Franz said. "You're with *us*."

"And *that's* why I'm worried."

A waitress took their dinner orders. Booze continued to flow. Rohan found himself thinking about the inflation numbers from the Wasua star system. That made him switch from champagne to bourbon. A live band began to play, and girl after girl in various and creative outfits took to the stage. The creative outfits where shed in time to the pulsing music, and the ladies were all very . . . Rohan searched for a word and settled on "flexible." Almost all the tables were filled now, parties of men with sweat gleaming on their faces, stocks and ties loosened, coats removed. Girls settled into laps and ran tapering fingers through their marks' hair. The roar of conversation was basso and primal.

A quintet of five girls was dancing and singing on the stage to an old SpaceCom marching song, but with some interesting new lyrics. The sprightly music had Rohan first humming along and then singing along, but it was frustrating that the girls couldn't get the beat right. They were late. He began to conduct vigorously, and felt his elbow connect with something.

"Whoa!" shouted Fujasaki. There was a large wet stain on the front of his trousers.

"He's drunk," Rohan vaguely heard someone say.

"So what? We're all drunk," Franz replied.

"Yeah, but he's the Chancellor, what if—" Bret, a newly hired aide began.

"Relax. They sweep the place regularly and keep the press out," John replied.

"Yeah, relax, Bret. We're having fun. *I'm* fun. I'm . . . I'm just made of fun!" Rohan shouted.

The five ladies went trooping off the stage, their sassy little buttocks wiggling provocatively. "Where are they going?" Rohan asked. "Where are all the lovely ladies going?" he repeated, and felt a tightness in his chest at the sadness of it all.

"Gone to housewives everyone," Franz said.

"What an awful waste," Rohan groaned. "We need an expert commission— girls keep turning into wives. It's a scandal. We need an investiga—"

A drum roll cut through his slurring words. All the lights in the club went out save for a single stabbing spotlight pinning the stage. Into that cone of light leaped a girl. She seemed to be flying, so high was her *grand jeté*, and the long cloak flowing behind her added to the illusion of flight. The music resumed, a primitive, urgent beat. She stood front and center, her features covered by an elaborate mask and headdress. All that could be seen was an unnaturally pointed chin and the glitter of her eyes. She caught the edges of the cloak with long claws set with light-emitting diodes, and dropped it to reveal an elaborate costume, far more conceal- ing than was usual for a stripper. Rohan wondered if the claws were sewn into gloves?

She began to dance. No harsh gyrating and suggestive posing. She danced with breath-catching grace. Her arms wove patterns, and the diodes left streaks of multicolored fire in the air around her. Layers began to fall away. The crowd shouted its approval as each piece of clothing fell. Another slithered to the stage floor and a long silky tail covered with sleek red and white fur unfolded and wove around her like a dancing snake. The shouts became roars.

The girl danced in close to her sweating admirers. Hands groped for her like blind babies seeing the tit, but she always eluded them. Unless those reaching hands held credit spikes. Those she allowed to be thrust into the credit deck that adorned the low-slung belt that clasped her waist. Rohan sat rigid, fingers gripping the edge of the table, willing her to remove the mask. *Show me . . . show me . . .* She approached their table. The young men leaned across the table, spikes extended like some commercial metaphor for sex. Rohan couldn't move. He just watched as another layer fell away to reveal pale cream and red fur that covered her flanks and belly and rose like a spear point between her breasts. There was a gasp from the audience.

John fell back against the booth. "The Pope's holy whickerbill!" he breathed.

The music quickened in tempo. Fire sparked from the tips of her long claws, the jewels and bells on the mask and headdress set up a hysterical ringing. She spun, faster and faster, then another great leap took her back center stage. Legs widely braced, hands cupping her breasts. She slowly slid them up her chest, across her neck, lifted the mask and headdress and flung them aside. She was alien and yet familiar. Rohan devoured her features. Noting the tiny upturned nose with flaring nostrils, pricked ears thrusting through the wild tumble of cream and red curls. They were tufted on each point. Cat eyes of emerald green.

"An alien," Bret said, and his voice held both disgust and lust.

Blackout.

The lights came up. The stage was empty. Excited conversation danced around the table.

"Cosmetic surgery?"

"No. Gotta be one of those Cara half-breeds."

"Thought we killed all of them."

"Should have. Disgusting."

"Hey, turn out the lights, close your eyes, and think of it as exotic underwear," John said with a laugh.

The room seemed to be ballooning and receding about Rohan. His heart thundered in his chest, and his breath came in short pants. An erection nudged urgently at his fly. He staggered out of the booth.

"Sir?"

"Are you all right?"

"Where are you going?"

He didn't answer.

"Wait," Tracy said. "A Cara/human half-breed? There's no such thing. First off, it's illegal." The young officer pointed at the Hajin waitress. "And second, our equipment might line up, but there's no way we'd produce offspring."

Rohan waved an admonishing finger at him. "Ah, but remember that the Cara were master geneticists. They'd been blending genes from every known alien race long before humans arrived on the scene. They were eager to add us to the mix, and couldn't believe that the League was serious when the ban on alien-human comingling was put in place."

Tracy took a sip of his drink. He knew from his studies that the Cara had no physical norm. They tailored bodies to suit a given situation. They changed sex on a whim. For thousands of years, they had been harvesting, mixing, and manipulating the genetic material from every race they met. A task easily accomplished, since the Cara spent their lives aboard vast trading ships that traveled between systems, or in the shops supplied by those ships. For the Cara, the greatest sin was uniformity. They believed that diversity was the key to survival and advancement. It had all been horrifying to the humans, and human purity became an obsession. Most genetic research and manipulation was outlawed for fear that the Cara might find a way to affect the basic human genome. Tracy said as much to Rohan.

The older man shook his head. "Yes, but that didn't discourage the Cara. They found volunteers, disaffected humans hostile to the League, and produced several thousand half-breeds." He picked up his glass and set it down over and over. Linking the circles formed by condensation into a concentric pattern.

"So, why make this girl look so different?" Tracy asked. "They could have made the offspring look like anything. Even exactly like a human."

Rohan looked up. "And that was their mistake. That's what they should have done. Instead, they tried to temper any backlash by tweaking the genes to make the children attractive to humans. Or at least what they thought would be attractive. They had noticed that we like cats. Hence Sammy." Rohan refilled his glass and took a long pull. "What they didn't realize was that it would make the kids just that much more horrifying."

"But you weren't disgusted by . . . Sammy?"

"Samarith, her full name was Samarith. And no, I wasn't disgusted, but I had a taste for the exotic. They knew that. And used it."

Rohan's stomach was roiling, his head pounding. Swaying, he made his way through the anteroom and out onto the street. The sea-tinged air cleared his head somewhat. He found the corner of the building and went looking for the stage door.

What are you doing? the rational part of his mind wailed.

"I'm going to compliment her on her dancing," he said aloud.

And ask about her life. Explore her thoughts. Share her dreams. Fuck her blind.

He found the side entrance and entered. Inside, the smell of sweat and rancid makeup seeped from the walls and hung in the air. Rohan swallowed hard and tried to find his way past the lighting control panel. He turned down a hall and found himself pressed against the wall as a gaggle of girls came hurrying past, heading for the stage. In the confines of that narrow space, they rubbed against him. He could feel the warmth of their bare skin even through his clothes, and his erection hardened again. He found another hallway, but this one was guarded by a tall man with a pendulous belly. Rohan tried to walk past and was blocked. The bouncer's exposed biceps displayed military tattoos and muscle now overlaid with fat. The overhead lights gleamed on his shaved head.

"Where do you think you're going?"

"I wish to see the young lady who just finished performing."

"You and every other aristo . . ." The man glanced down at Rohan's crotch. "Who stores his brains in his cock."

Rohan gaped at him. "My good man, you can't address me in that way."

"Yeah, I can. And if you want to see Sammy, it'll cost you." He thrust his hips forward, displaying his credit deck. It didn't have the same effect as when the dancers did it. Rohan dithered, remembered that gamine little face, unlimbered his credit spike, and paid.

"Where can I find her?" Rohan asked.

"Follow your prick. It seems to be doing a pretty good job as a dousing rod."

The bouncer stepped aside and Rohan walked down the hall, checking each room as he came to it. Giggles and a couple of lewd invitations were received as he opened and closed doors. Hers was the fifth dressing room he checked. She was dressed in a deep-green robe and seated at a dressing table. The bottom drawer had been pulled out and she rested a bare foot on it. The robe had fallen aside, revealing the shapely leg almost up to the hip. Smoke from the stim she held languidly in one hand swirled like a halo about the tips of her pricked ears. She raked him with a long glance from those amazing green cat eyes.

"How much did you pay?"

"I beg your pardon?"

"To Dal. How much did you pay him to get back here?"

"Three hundred."

"You got taken. He would have let you in for half that."

"I'll remember that next time." Samarith lit a new stim and regarded him. Rohan shifted uncomfortably from foot to foot.

"Don't you want to know why I'm here?" he finally asked.

She let her gaze drift down to his crotch. "You're giving me a moderately sized hint." His erection deflated. "Awww, I broke it," she drawled.

"I wanted to invite you to supper," Rohan said.

"Courtship first? Well, that's a change." She stood and stubbed out her stim. "There's a pretty good place in Pony Town that serves late."

"I was going to take you to the French Bakery." It was the capital's best restaurant. He thought it would impress her.

She laughed. "You're such an idiot. Kind of sweet, but an idiot." He gaped at her. "It's better if I keep a low profile."

"Your profile wasn't very low tonight," Rohan shot back.

"This is a strip joint. It may be frequented by your set, but it's still a strip joint. Waving me around in public wouldn't be good for either of us. And who are you, by the way? Which scion of a decaying noble house are you?"

"How do you even know I'm FFH?"

"Oh, please." Scorn etched the words.

He thought about his job and the stress that it carried. He thought about his cold and distant wife. "Can't I just be Rohan for tonight?"

She cocked her head to the side, an endearing sight, and considered him. Her tone was gentler as she said, "All right. I'll call you Han, and you can call me Sammy, and tonight we'll pretend we aren't who and what we are."

"And after tonight?" Rohan asked.

"That depends on how tonight turns out."

Rohan allowed Sammy to issue directions to his Hajin chauffeur, Hobb. Neither he nor Hobb intimated by word or action that they were familiar with the area. But he knew it well. His favorite massage spa was just a few streets over. It was a place where men with his tastes could feel the touch of the exotic. He liked the way the soft play of fur and the rough pads of an Isanjo masseuse tickled his skin and kneaded his muscles.

That night the summer heat had broken and it was pleasant to be outside. Humans, Hajin, Isanjo, Tiponi Flutes, and Slunkies roamed the streets listening to musicians performing on street corners. They played games of chance or skill—everything from chess, to craps, to a swaying grove of Flutes playing their incomprehensible stick game. Diners lingered in the restaurants. Lovers cuddled on benches in a small park, while the elderly sat and contemplated the ships lifting off from the Cristóbal Colón spaceport. Hobb opened the flitter doors for them. Rohan stepped out and felt the rumble underfoot as another spaceship leaped skyward. The fire from engines was a red-orange scar ripping the darkness. For a brief moment, it almost eclipsed the light from the nebula floating overhead.

The long lines and evident elegance of the flitter drew more than a few looks. "I'll call you when we're ready to be picked up," he said softly to Hobb. The Hajin bowed his long bony head, revealing his golden mane between his collar and hat. Rohan turned to Sammy. She wore slim-legged pants tucked into high boots, and a silk top of varying shades of green and blue that was tied in interesting ways to make it drape and flow. The cream and red hair tumbled over her shoulders. She drew looks. Rohan struggled for breath.

"So, where would you like to eat?" he asked.

"There." She pointed at an Isanjo restaurant. Potted trees dotted the space with webs of rope slung between them. Isanjo, using hands, their prehensile feet, and their tails darted along the woven lines. Somehow none of the items on the trays tilted, slipped, or fell.

They settled into woven rope chairs, and a waiter slithered down the trunk of the tree next to their table. His order pad hung on his neck along with a credit deck. "Drinks?" he asked, the muzzle making him lisp the word.

"Champagne," Rohan said.

"Actually, I don't like champagne," Sammy said.

"Oh. Your pardon. What would you like?"

"Tequila."

The waiter turned dark, wide eyes to Rohan. Their blackness against the gold of his fur made them seem fathomless and terribly alien. "I'll drink what the lady is drinking," Rohan said, making it an act of gallantry. With a bouncing leap, the creature was up the tree, gripping the ropes and racing away.

"You just full of courtesy, aren't you?" Sammy asked. "Do you even like tequila?"

"Well enough."

"What do you drink at home?" she asked, fixing those emerald cat eyes on him.

"Champagne, martinis. In the summer months I'll drink the occasional beer or gin and tonic. Wine with dinner. Why do you ask?"

"How often do you drink?"

"Every night," he blurted before he could help himself. "And why the interrogation? You sound like my doctor."

"Do you drink to relax or to forget? Or both?"

"You make too much of this. I drink because . . . I enjoy a drink in the evenings. That's all." Though he found himself remembering the night five weeks ago when he'd heard Juliana's tinkling laugh as she flirted with the young officer who was currently inhabiting her bed. He had drunk himself into insensibility that night.

Another Isanjo landing next to the table caused Rohan to start and pulled him from his brooding reverie. A bowl of dipping sauce and pieces of bread were slapped down on the table. The pungent scent of the sauce set Rohan's eyes and mouth to watering.

"You were drunk tonight," Sammy said, and popped a piece of bread into her mouth. "Otherwise you would never have come backstage."

"Do you rate your charms so low?"

"I rate your sense of propriety a good deal higher" was the dry reply.

"Well, you're probably right about that," Rohan admitted.

"So, why did you come?"

"Because you're beautiful. . . . And . . . and I'm lonely."

"And do you think two bodies clashing in the dark will alleviate that?" she asked.

He was embarrassed to discover that his throat had gone tight. He swallowed past the lump, coughed, and said, "Are you propositioning me, young woman?" He hoped his tone was as light as the words.

"No. You have to do that. I still have some pride left. Not a lot, but some."

"You find your . . . er . . . profession to be demeaning?" The look of contempt and incredulity almost cut. He looked away from those blazing green eyes. "Well, I think you answered that question."

Sammy shrugged. "It's this state religion of yours. Women are either Madonnas or whores."

"And which are you?" he asked, deciding to hit back.

It was the right move. She gave him an approving smile. "Whichever you want."

"Oh, I doubt that. I think you're not at all accommodating," Rohan said.

Their drinks arrived. She lifted hers and smiled at him over the rim of her glass. "For an aristo, you're not at all stupid."

"Thank you. And for a stripper you're not at all common."

They clinked glasses. She sipped. Suddenly nervous, he threw his back in a single gulp. "Whoa, slow down there, *caballero*. Otherwise I'll be carrying you out of here."

"My driver would handle that," Rohan said.

"Yes, but he can't handle propositioning me," Sammy retorted. She picked up her menu. "Shall we order? I'm famished."

She made love as well as she stripped.

Rohan rolled off her with a gasp and a groan. Shudders still shook his body. She sat up, straddled him, and raked her mane of hair back off her face. She drew a forefinger down his nose, traced the line of his lips, stroked his neck, and then rubbed his paunch. Futilely, Rohan tried to suck in his gut. She chuckled deep in her throat, and Rohan felt his penis try to respond, then collapse in defeat.

He had wanted her so badly by the time they reached her apartment deep in Stick Town, where the Flutes congregated. He had ripped off her clothes and shoved her down on the bed. Then, with clumsy fingers, he'd freed the clasps on his shirt, ripped loose his belt, pulled down the zipper, skinned his trousers over his hips, and fallen onto her. There had been little foreplay.

He reached up and gently touched that gamine little face. "I'm sorry. That probably wasn't very good for you."

"I'm sure there will be an opportunity for you to make it up to me," she said softly, and bent forward to kiss his lips. She tasted of vanilla with a hint of tequila on the back of her tongue.

He rubbed his hands across her groin, and stopped when his fingers hit deep, twisting scars beneath the silken fur. How had he not felt them earlier? Too absorbed in his own pleasure and the sensations sweeping through his body. She froze and stared down at him.

"What—?" he began.

"I was on Insham." He yanked back his hands as if he's been the one who had applied the knife and cut away her ovaries. "Of course, I'm one of the lucky ones. Neutered beats dead." The words were flat, matter-of-fact.

He found himself making excuses, offering the party line. "It was the actions of one overzealous admiral. The government never . . . we stopped it as soon as word reached us."

"But not before three thousand seven hundred and sixty-two children were killed. Do you know how many are left?" He stared up at her, at the glitter in her eyes, and shook his head. "Two hundred and thirty-eight."

"You know the exact count?" It was inane, but he couldn't think of anything else to say.

"Oh yes."

"How did you . . . ?"

"One of your soldiers saved me. Me and a few other children. He guarded the nursery, shot and killed other SpaceCom troops who weren't so . . . squeamish."

"You think that's the only reason he acted?" Rohan asked. "Maybe he knew it was barbaric and immoral. Can't you give us humans that much credit?"

"You humans started it." She pressed her lips together, as if holding back more words. "But perhaps you're right." She paused, lost in some memory. "I always wonder what happened to him. Did your government court-martial and execute him for refusing an order?"

Rohan couldn't continue to meet her gaze. He turned his head on the pillow, catching a scent of lilac as his stubbled cheek rasped across the silky material of the pillowcase. "No. All the troops, and there were a number of them who refused the order," he added defensively, "were allowed to resign from the service without prejudice."

"I'm glad. I would hate to think he died for an act of mercy."

They were both silent for a long time. "None of you would have suffered if the Cara had just obeyed the law."

Sammy smiled and drew her finger down the bridge of his nose. "And if they had, I wouldn't be here, and you wouldn't be lying, sated, in my bed."

There was no answer to that. He struggled to sit up past the curve of his belly and kiss her. She made it easy by lying down next to him and cradling his dick in her hands. Her head was on his shoulder, hair tickling his chin, breath warm against his neck. Tentatively he asked, "Do you hate us?"

"What a silly question." She paused. "Of course I hate you." The words landed like a blow. "Oh, not 'you' as in *you*. Humans in general, yes. You personally, no. Humans are mean, violent monkeys, and the galaxy would be better off if you'd never crawled off your rock, but *you* seem to be all right."

"You're half human."

"Which means that I'm at least half as mean. You should keep that in mind," she said, her voice catching on a little chuckle.

"I'll keep that in mind," Rohan mumbled as sleep fell on his eyelids as soft as snowflakes. He drowsily thought back over the evening, the quick steps of her tiny, arched feet, the play of muscles in her belly. The memories and the heat of her skin pressed against his had his dick hardening again. He remembered the flash of light from her claws. Unease banished torpor. "Those were gloves, right? The claws, I mean. They were sewn onto gloves."

There was a sharp pricking against the soft skin of his penis. His eyes snapped open, and he tried to peer past the bulge of his gut, but to no avail. He pushed up on his elbows, the pinpricks becoming stabs of pain. "Shit!" he yelled as he saw the extruded claws inset with the diodes. The razor-sharp tips pressed against the pink, wrinkled skin of his rapidly deflating dick.

"No. They're real."

He stared up at her, now deeply frightened. She retracted the claws, then she fell onto his chest, hair spread like a cloak across them both. He took her hand in his and inspected her fingers, trying to see how the claws were sheathed. He noticed that the pads on the tips of her fingers were completely smooth, but then she kissed him hard, her tongue demanding, forcing past his teeth. His erection returned, and all thought about her odd hands was driven from his head.

"I won't hurt you, Han," she murmured against his mouth. "That much I promise."

Tracy stared, stricken. "We . . . SpaceCom . . . killed . . . children?"

"Yes. All but a handful." Rohan refilled his glass. "I wasn't lying to Sammy, it really did start with an overly pious and deeply bigoted admiral." He shrugged. "And some good came from the revulsion that shook the League once word of the butchery got out. The laws on aliens were relaxed somewhat."

"Was this why the Cara vanished?" Tracy asked.

"Yes. Within days of the slaughter, the Cara were gone. Their shops standing empty, the freighters drifting abandoned and stripped in space or laying derelict on various moons and asteroids, as if a great storm had swept through and tossed them aground." Rohan looked around the bar with the exaggerated care of the profoundly drunk. He leaned in across the table and whispered, the words carried on alcohol-laden breath, "They could still be all around us, and we wouldn't even know it."

There was a prickling between Tracy's shoulder blades, as if hostile eyes or something more lethal were being leveled at him. "That's stupid. Space is big. They probably just went someplace else. Got away from us. Went back to their home world. We never found it."

"In what? They abandoned their ships."

Tracy found himself reevaluating the sullen drinkers, the jovial bartender, the waitress. Did each face hide a murderous hatred?

Rohan resumed his story.

For their two-month anniversary, Rohan gave Sammy an emerald-and-gold necklace. It was a massive thing, reminiscent of an Egyptian torque from Old Earth, and it seemed to bend her slender neck beneath its weight. He had bought it originally for Juliana, but she had never worn it, disparaging it as gaudy and more what she would have expected from some jumped-up, nouveau riche trader than a member of the FFH.

"So, I get your wife's castoffs?" Sammy asked with a crooked little smile.

"No . . . that's not . . . I never—"

Sammy stopped the stammered words with a soft hand across his mouth. "I don't mind. It's beautiful, and it's rather appropriate. I got her cast-off husband."

They were at his small hunting lodge in the mountains, enjoying a rare snowfall. The only light in the bedroom was provided by the dancing flames in the stone fireplace. Outside, the wind sighed in the trees like a woman's sad cries.

Sammy sat up and twined her fingers through his. "Why did you marry her? Was it arranged? Did you ever care for her?"

"I was a replacement. Her fiancé was lost along with his ship. No bodies, no debris, just a ship and her complement of spacers gone. After an appropriate period of mourning, her father approached my father. I was the dull number cruncher. I was never going to equal Juliana's dashing SpaceCom captain."

"Tell me about your father. Is he still alive?"

Hours passed. He told her about his family, the estate in the Grenadine star system. His sisters. His younger brother. His hobbies, favorite books, taste in music. Occasionally she asked a question, but mostly she listened, head resting on his shoulder, hand stroking his chest. He talked of his daughter, Rohiesa, the one good thing that had come from his marriage.

He poured himself out to her. His hopes and dreams, his secret shames and deepest desires. She never judged, just listened. Only the fire seemed to object with an occasional sharp snap as flame met resin.

Over the next month, his need for Sammy rose to the level of an addiction. He left work early, returned home at dawn, if at all. The conversations continued. Unlike Juliana, Sammy seemed genuinely interested in his economic theories as well as the name of his old fencing master.

Some nights he couldn't see her. He had to escort Juliana and Rohiesa to various soirees. The final night had began that way, at the first grand ball of the season.

The walls and ceiling of the enormous ballroom of Lord Palani's mansion seemed to have vanished and been replaced with the glitter of stars and the varicolored swirl of nebulas. The effect was spectacular and utterly terrifying. Guests clustered near the center of the room, avoiding the seeming emptiness all around them. It made it difficult for those who did wish to dance to actually dance. Lady Palani was in a rage, as evidenced by her pinched nostrils and compressed lips. One of the young Misses Palani was in tears. Tomorrow's gossip would be filled with talk of the Palani disaster. Rohan handed his empty plate to a passing Hajin servant and snagged a glass of champagne from yet another. His host approached, his long face had drooped into even more lugubrious lines.

Rohan gestured at the holographic effect. "It's quite . . . stunning."

Palani took a long pull of champagne. "Stunning price tag, too, and everyone's terrified. But they insisted." He gave a sad shake of his head. "There's no accounting for what mad notion will seize them."

Rohan correctly interpreted this as a reference to Lady Palani and the couple's five daughters. It also brought back the memory of a conversation he'd had with Sammy only three day before.

They had been walking in the Royal Botanical Garden, Sammy pausing frequently to touch and sniff the flowers. He loved to watch her: each gesture was a sonnet, each step a song. She had gently stroked the petals on a rose and turned back to him. He had tucked her arm through his and as they strolled he had casually mentioned how a friend's daughter was at a discreet clinic after a very public and embarrassing breakdown at a Founder's Day picnic.

She had glanced up at him, the glitter back in those strange eyes. "Are you surprised? You keep your women mewed up and deny them any kind of meaningful activity. I'm surprised more of them don't go nuts. You give them nothing to think about or talk about beyond family and gossip. You never let them do anything but plan parties or attend parties, run households and raise children."

"That's a schedule that would kill most men," Rohan said with a ponderous attempt at humor. "Thus proving you are the stronger sex, Sammy."

"On Earth, before the Expansion, woman were lawyers, doctors, soldiers, presidents, and captains of industry."

"And space is hostile, and most planets difficult and dangerous to colonize. Women are our most precious possession. Men can produce a million sperm, but it requires a woman to gestate and deliver a child." Rohan's voice had risen and his breath had gone short. He wondered at his own vehemence and defense of the system. And why had he brought up De Varga's daughter? Because he feared for his own Rohiesa?

"And those days are gone. Your conservatism will be the death of the League, Han. The Cara were right about one thing. Adapt and change . . . or die."

"Rohan?"

"What? Ah, beg pardon. I was drifting."

"I was just asking about the inflation figures," Palani repeated.

"Ugly, but let's not mar the evening with such talk," Rohan said, and moved away.

He risked a surreptitious glance at the chrono set in the sleeve of his evening jacket. *Forty minutes.* It seemed like he'd been here for an eternity. Just a few more and he should be able to slip away and join Sammy at the street festival in Pony Town. He imagined the pungent scents of chile and roasting meats, passionate music from the street musicians, bodies moving in wild abandon to the primal beat and thrum of guitars. The imagined music clashed with the lovely but formal dance music provided by the orchestra hidden in an overhead alcove. Rohan deposited his champagne flute and moved toward the doors. To hell with it, he couldn't wait any longer.

Juliana intercepted him. The hand-sewn sequins on her formfitting dress flashed as she moved, echoing the glitter from the diamonds tucked into her dark curls. "You're not leaving, are you?"

"Umm . . . yes."

"You abandon me for your whore?" Her voice was rising, the words starting to penetrate through the stately measures of the music.

"What are you talking about?" He knew it wouldn't work. He was a terrible liar. He resorted to pleading. "For God's sake, don't make a scene."

"And why not? You're making a spectacle of yourself with this alien *puta.*"

"How—"

"Bret's wife had it from Bret. She told her mother. It's all over Campo Royale and you're a laughingstock."

"You had already assured that with your parade of lovers!" he spat back, finally saying aloud what had lain between them and rubbed like sand in his craw.

"At least mine are *human.*"

People were starting to stare. Rohan looked around at the gawking faces, the soft-footed servants, the elaborate clothes. Steel bands seemed to close around him, penning him in, holding him fast. The cry of the guitars in the streets of the Old City seemed faint and far away.

"No," he said, not certain what he was rejecting, but rejecting it all the same.

He heard Juliana screaming imprecations after him as he trod down the curving crystal staircase.

He found her in the streets among the beribboned stalls that sold jewelry and pottery, perfumes and scarves. The roar of voices mingled with the music; fat sizzled as it fell from roasting meats onto the wood beneath. He clung to Sammy and buried his head against her shoulder.

She brushed his hair back with a gentle hand. "What's happened?"

"Juliana knows. They all know. They'll make me give you up." He choked. "And I can't. I can't."

"Come," she said, and, taking his hand, she led him through the rollicking crowds where humans and aliens could dance and feast together, and perhaps even fall in love.

She took him back to her apartment. She prepared him a drink. He slammed it down, only realizing after that there was an odd taste. The room began ballooning and receding around him.

"I'm sorry, Han, I wish we could have had a little more time together." Her voice seemed to echo and be coming from a vast distance. Then there was darkness.

The first return to consciousness brought with it an awareness of the chill of a metal surface against bare back, buttocks, and legs. He knew he was naked and cold, and that nausea roiled his gut. He felt gloved hands pressing against his arms and the bite of a needle, then Sammy's voice murmured soothing words and her hand stroked his hair. He dropped back into darkness.

A bright pinpoint of light glaring directly into his eye was the next memory. The light shifted from his right eye to his left and was snapped off. Concentric circles of blue and red obscured his vision as he tried to focus after being nearly blinded. This was followed by hard pressure against the tips of his fingers. Another needle prick and he slipped away again.

When he awoke he was in Sammy's apartment, lying on a bed frame without mattress, sheets, or cover. He staggered out of bed and stood swaying in the middle of the bedroom. His eyes felt crusty; slowly the disjointed memories returned. He looked down at the crook of his elbow. There was a small red dot like the bite of a steel insect. His clothes were dumped on a chair in the corner of the room. He searched the pockets and found them empty. His keys, wallet, and comm were gone. Even his comb and mono-grammed handkerchief had been taken.

"Just a thieving whore," he said, testing out the words, and then recoiled at the unfamiliar sounds issuing from his throat. He had gone from a light baritone to a deep bass. His throat felt sore and his mouth was desert dry. That's why he sounded so strange.

Pressure on his bladder sent him into the bathroom. As he relieved himself it started to penetrate: every vestige of Sammy was gone. No toothbrush, no hairbrush, no makeup, even the delicate perfume bottle he'd bought her—all gone. But if it had been nothing more than a con, why had she waited so many months and through so many encounters before robbing him? He staggered to the sink to wash his hands and splash his face, and recoiled from the image in the mirror.

A stranger looked back at him.

The frightened eyes staring out at him were now a pale grey. His hair was dark and straight rather than reddish and curly. His forehead was much higher because this alien hair seemed to be rapidly retreating toward the back of his neck. His skin tone was decidedly darker. Nose larger and bulbous on the tip. Ears clipped closer to his skull. His real ears had been rather protuberant. He looked down. His belly was larger, and the birth-mark on his left hip was gone. He stumbled back to the toilet and vomited until he was reduced to dry heaves.

Whimpering, he returned to the sink, rinsed out his mouth, and gulped down water. Then stared at his hands. His wedding ring and the heavy signet ring with the family crest were missing. His gut twisted again, but he managed to keep from hurling. Back in the bedroom, he snatched up his clothes with trembling hands and started to dress. Because of his weight gain, he couldn't close the top clasp on his trousers, and the straining but-tons on his shirt gapped open enough to reveal skin.

He left the bedroom and found the living room to be equally void of any trace of the occupant. On an impulse, he checked the kitchen. All the dishes, utensils, and food were gone. In this room he was more aware of a faint disinfectant smell, as if every surface had been washed down with bleach.

He made his way down the stairs and out into the street, where he stood blinking in the sunlight. He had lost a night. Then he realized that heat and humidity pounded at his head and shoulders. Sweat bloomed in his armpits and went rolling down his sides. It was high summer. When he'd come looking for Sammy the night of the ball it had been a cool fall night. Dear God, he had lost *months*!

He needed to get home. But how to accomplish that journey loomed monumental. No money, no comm, no proof that he was who he claimed to be. Not even a face. He guessed it was about twenty miles from Pony Town to the Cascades and his mansion. He didn't think he could walk one mile, much less twenty. Still, he wouldn't know until he tried. He walked away from the building. He tried not to, but he looked back several times until its salmon-colored stucco was hidden by other structures.

Two hours later his feet were a mass of stabbing pain, and he felt the wetness of a burst blister. He saw the glowing shield that indicated a police station and realized that he was an idiot. He had been kidnapped, assaulted, surgically altered. The police would help him. They would call his home, Hobb would arrive with the flitter, and he would be whisked away from all this. And the hue and cry would be raised for Sammy. Rohan swallowed bile. It was unfortunate but necessary. The creature deserved nothing less. He walked into the precinct house.

"I need to report a crime," he announced to the desk sergeant.

The man didn't even look up, just pushed over an etablet. "Write it up. Bring it back when you're done."

When he presented his name and title in his aristocratic accent, the man became a good deal more attentive. His eyes did narrow with suspicion as he studied the ill-fitting clothing, but the sergeant offered coffee and water. It would never do to offend if Rohan really was a member of the FFH.

Mollified, Rohan settled into a chair and typed up his experiences. The beverages were supplied and the desk sergeant sent the report up to his superiors. A few minutes later a captain arrived. He walked up to stand in front of Rohan and called over his shoulder to the desk clerk.

"Don't follow politics, do you, Johnson? This is not the Chancellor."

"As I indicated in my report, my appearance has been altered," Rohan said.

"And I just talked to the Chancellor's office. According to John Fujasaki, the Chancellor's aide, the Conde is in a meeting with the Prime Minister. Now, get out of here and try your con someplace else."

Rohan just kept staring up at the officer, trying to process the words. His removal was then expedited by the arrival of two burly officers, who frog-marched him out of the building.

Panic lay like a stone on his chest. Rohan gasped for breath. He stood on the sidewalk, blocking the flow of humanity and staring back at the police station. Eventually he resumed his slow march toward home.

He was getting odd looks because of his formal, too-small evening attire in the middle of the day, and his limping progress wasn't helping. A Hajin message runner gave him a somewhat sympathetic look. Rohan gathered his nerve and approached the alien.

"Excuse me. I've been robbed, and I need to make a call. May I borrow your comm? If you'll give me your name, I'll see that you're compensated once I have access to my funds."

The Hajin handed over his comm. "Of course." The creature ducked his head, his forelock veiling his eyes. "And you don't have to pay me."

The sudden kindness in the midst of the nightmare had tears stinging his eyes. "Thank you." Rohan forced the words past the lump in his throat. He took the offered comm and called his private line at the Exchequer. John answered.

"Chancellor's office, Fujasaki speaking."

"John," Rohan said. "John, listen. I'm in a nightmare. I think—"

"Who is this?"

"It's Rohan. I know it sounds incredible—"

The line went dead. Numbly, Rohan handed back the comm to the Hajin. "Thank you," he said automatically. One should always show respect to one's inferiors.

He turned and continued walking.

At the house, he didn't even attempt to explain the situation to the butler. Instead he shoved the elderly Hajin aside and ran, panting, up the long, curving staircase. Behind him were rising cries of alarm. He raced through Juliana's mirrored and gold-inlaid dressing room. Her Isanjo maid clutched a discarded ball gown against her chest and gazed at Rohan from wide, frightened eyes.

"Where is she? Where's my wife?"

The creature reverted to her alien nature and went swarming up the drapes to cower on the rod. The large golden eyes shifted toward the bedroom door.

Rohan stormed through. He was met with the sight of an expanse of bare white back, a few freckles on the shoulders. The man propped himself on his forearms, his doughy behind pumping in an age-old dance. A woman's soft cries emerged from among the tumbled pillows.

Juliana opened her eyes, looked at Rohan, and let out a piercing scream. The man who had been plowing her gave a grunt and pulled out.

"What in the hell?" he roared, and now Rohan finally saw his face.

It was him.

"The authorities arrived and took away the *madman*. I kept trying to make them understand. To realize that the Cara had placed an agent at the very heart of government. No one would listen. I would show them articles that proved what the impostor was doing, sending money to companies that I knew were fronts for the aliens. An audit would have revealed that funds were missing, redirected, but they wouldn't listen. Eventually, I realized if I ever wanted to be released I had to end my accusations. I also knew that in the sanatorium I was at greater risk of being assassinated. I needed to get free. Once I was released, I headed to the outer worlds. Here I tell the story to people like you." He rose to his feet, swaying. "I am Rohan Danilo Marcus Aubrey, Conde de Vargas, and I adjure you to act! Inform your superiors. Alert them to the danger!"

He seemed to have expended all his strength in the ringing call to arms. The drunk dropped heavily into his chair and his head nodded toward his chest.

Disgusted by his gullibility, and out the cost of a bottle, Tracy pushed back violently from the table. The shriek of the chair legs on the floor brought Rohan, or whatever his name might be, out of his stupor. The drunk belched and raised his head.

"Wha . . . ?"

"Nice. What a scam. He"—Tracy jerked a thumb at the bartender—"sells more booze, and you get to drink for free."

"Wha . . . ?" the grifter repeated.

"The Conde de Vargas is Prime Minister. Second only to the Emperor in power." Tracy tapped the name into the comm set in his jacket sleeve. "*This* is the *real* Rohan." Tracy thrust his arm under the man's nose, showing him the photos.

He waved a pudgy hand in a vague circle, indicating his visage. "I told you. They stole my face, my life . . . my wife . . . he made her love him again, or maybe love him for the first time."

Tracy shook his head and headed for the door.

"Wait!" the drunk called. The young officer looked back, and the drunken Scheherazade gave Tracy a desperate look. "Your duties will take you all over League space. If you see her tell her . . . tell her . . ." His voice was thick with unshed tears and an excess of booze. "I never saw Sammy again, and I need to . . . need to . . ." The man began to sob. "I love her," Rohan said brokenly. "Love her so much."

Embarrassment, pity, and fury warred for primacy. Tracy embraced the anger. Clapping slowly, Tracy said, "Nice touch."

The young officer stepped out into the darkness. The cold air cleared his head a bit, but he was still very drunk. He stared at the distant glow of the spaceport. Follow through on his threat? Go AWOL? He was only twenty-one. Was it worth risking a noose to walk away from casual insults and petty condescension? He realized that he could far too easily become that pathetic drunk in the bar, telling fantastic stories for the price of a drink.

I saved the heir to the throne from a scandal that might have rocked the League. We shared a secret love. I know that Mercedes de Arango, the Infanta, loves me, the tailor's son.

But his story was *true*, not like that bit of farrago to which he'd just been treated.

And your story is any less fantastic?

No, Rohan's—or whatever his name was—his story couldn't be true. If it was, then he, Tracy Belmanor, second lieutenant in the Imperial Fleet, was privy to a secret that would not just rock the League but destroy it. He peered suspiciously into the shadowy depths of the alley to his left and saw nothing beyond the hulking shadow of a garbage container. But what if they were there, hiding among them, watching, waiting, listening? What if they decided they needed to silence him?

Tracy broke into a run and didn't stop until he reached the ship. The outer hatch cycled closed and he leaned, panting, against the bulkhead. Inside the steel-and-resin bulwark of the warship, his panic receded. How foolish. The whole thing had been a scam. Sammy didn't exist. The Cara weren't hiding among them. Human males were still at the apex of power.

It had just been a story.

Pat Cadigan

Everyone knows what that road to hell is paved with, don't they?

Pat Cadigan was born in Schenectady, New York, and now lives in London with her family. She made her first professional sale in 1980, and has subsequently come to be regarded as one of the best new writers of her generation. Her story "Pretty Boy Crossover" has appeared on several critic's lists as among the best science fiction stories of the 1980s, and her story "Angel" was a finalist for the Hugo Award, the Nebula Award, *and* the World Fantasy Award (one of the few stories ever to earn that rather unusual distinction). Her short fiction—which has appeared in most of the major markets, including *Asimov's Science Fiction* and *The Magazine of Fantasy & Science Fiction*—has been gathered in the collections *Patterns* and *Dirty Work*. Her first novel, *Mindplayers,* was released in 1987 to excellent critical response, and her second novel, *Synners,* released in 1991, won the Arthur C. Clarke Award as the year's best science fiction novel, as did her third novel, *Fools,* making her the only writer ever to win the Clarke Award twice. Her other books include the novels *Dervish Is Digital, Tea from an Empty Cup,* and *Reality Used to Be a Friend of Mine,* and, as editor, the anthology *The Ultimate Cyberpunk,* as well as two making-of movie books and four media tie-in novels. Her most recent book was a novel, *Cellular.*

CARETAKERS

"Hey, Val," said my sister Gloria, "you ever wonder why there aren't any female serial killers?"

We were watching yet another documentary on the Prime Crime Network. We'd been watching a lot of those in the month since she had moved in. Along with two suitcases, one stuffed with products especially formulated for curly brown hair, and a trash bag containing two sets of expensive, high-thread-count bed linens, my little sister had also brought her fascination with the lurid and sensational disguised as an interest in current events—the inverse of expensive sheets in a trash bag, you might say.

"What about Aileen What's-Her-Name?" I said.

"One. And they executed her pretty fast. So fast you can't remember her last name."

"I can remember it," I said. "I just can't pronounce it. And it wasn't *that* fast—at least ten years after they caught her. They executed Bundy pretty quickly, too, didn't they? In Florida. Her, too, now that I think of it."

Gloria gave a surprised laugh. "I had no idea you were such an expert on serial killers."

"We've watched enough TV shows about them," I said as I went into the kitchen for more iced tea. "I could probably make one on my iPad." An exaggeration but not much; the shows were so formulaic that sometimes I wasn't sure which ones were repeats. But I didn't really mind indulging Gloria. She was fifteen years younger, so I was used to making allowances, and as vices went, true-crime TV was pretty minor. More to the point, Gloria had been visiting Mom in the care home every day without fail. I'd expected the frequency to drop after the first two weeks but she was still spending every afternoon playing cards with Mom or reading to her or just hanging (unquote). I had to give her credit for that, even though I was fairly sure she felt this made her exempt from having to look for paid employment.

When I returned, Gloria was busy with my iPad. "Don't tell me there's an app for serial killers?" I said, a little nervous.

"I Googled them and you're right—Aileen Wuornos and Ted Bundy both died in the Florida State Prison. Over twenty years apart—he got the chair, she got lethal injection. But still." She looked up at me. "Think it's something about Florida?"

"Dunno but I *really* wish you hadn't done that on my iPad," I said, relieving her of it. "Google can't keep anything to themselves. Now I'll probably get a flood of gory crime scene photo spam."

I could practically see her ears prick up, like a terrier's. "You can get that stuff?"

"No." I moved the iPad out of her reach. "I forbid it. Make do with the crime porn on cable."

"Party pooper."

"I get that a lot." I chuckled. On TV, credits were scrolling upward too fast to read over a sepia photograph of a stiff-looking man, probably a serial killer. Abruptly, it changed to a different set of credits rolling even more quickly against a red background. At the bottom of the screen was the legend, *NEXT: Deadlier Than the Male—Killer Ladies.*

I grimaced at my sister, who brandished the remote control, grinning like a mad thing, or maybe a killer lady. "Come on, isn't one of the movie channels showing *Red Dawn*?" I pumped my fist. "Wolverines?"

Gloria rolled her eyes. "How about something we *haven't* seen a bajillion times already?"

"How much *is* a bajillion?" I asked.

"Like the exact size or the universe or how many times you've seen *Red Dawn*, nobody knows." She nodded at the iPad on my lap. "Not worried about crime scene spam anymore?"

My face grew warm. "I was surfing on automatic pilot," I said, which was either half-true or half a lie, depending.

"Yeah, *you're* not really interested in any of that gory stuff."

"The least you could do is microwave us some popcorn," I said. "There's at least one bag left in the cupboard."

She cringed in pretend horror. "This stuff *doesn't* kill your appetite?"

"If I pick up some pointers, I might kill *you*."

As usual, the ad break was long enough that Gloria was back with a big bowl of movie-style buttered before the end of the opening credits.

According to the listings, this was a *Killer Ladies* marathon, back-to-back episodes into the wee hours. After a teleshopping break from 4 to 6 a.m., early risers could breakfast with *Deadly Duos—Killer Couples*.

Killer Ladies followed the usual formula but ratcheted up the melodrama. The Ladies in question were all abnormal, evil, twisted, unnatural, cold, devious, and unrepentant, while most of their victims were warm, easygoing, trusting, generous, open, honest, well-liked, down-to-earth, and the best friend anyone could ever ask for. Except for a few misfits who were uneducated, foolish, immature, troubled, reckless, self-destructive, or habitually unlucky, and the occasional ex-con with a long criminal record (no one ever had a short criminal record).

Between bursts of urgent narration and detectives who spoke only in monotone, there were some nuggets of real information, much of it new to me. Of course, I hadn't known a lot to begin with—the only other notorious Killer Lady I could think of besides Aileen Wuornos was Lizzie Borden. Killer Ladies were a hell of a lot more interesting than their male counterparts. Unlike men, who seemed mainly to gratify themselves by asserting power, Killer Ladies were all about getting away with it. They planned carefully, sizing up their victims and their situations, and waited for the right time.

They were also masters—or mistresses—of camouflage, with the unwitting help of a society that even in these parlous times still sees women as nurturers, not murderers. When not killing someone, many of the Killer Ladies were nurses, therapists, babysitters, assistants, even teachers (remembering some I'd had, I could believe it).

Eventually I dozed off and woke to see a repeat of the first episode we'd watched. Gloria was absolutely unrouseable, so I threw one of Mom's hand-crocheted afghans over her. Then the devil got into me—I tucked a pillow under her arm with a note saying, *This is the pillow I didn't smother you with. Good morning!* before I staggered off to bed.

The note I found on my own pillow when I woke later said, *Still alive? (One answer only) [__]Yes (we need more cereal) [__]No (we don't)*

The expression on Gloria's face as I sat down to breakfast made me wince. "Oh, no, not *another* bench warrant for parking tickets."

"No, of course not. I took care of that. *You* took care of that," she added quickly. "I didn't sleep very well."

"I tried to wake you so you could sleep in a real bed. You didn't stay up all night, did you?" Staying up all night and then sleeping all day was something Gloria was prone to when life handed her lemons without water, sugar, or glasses; I'd warned her that wouldn't fly with me.

"No. All those Killer Ladies gave me bad dreams."

For a moment I thought she was kidding, but she had the slightly haunted look of a person who had found something very unpleasant in her own head and hadn't quite stopped seeing it yet. "Jeez, Glow-bug, I'm sorry. I shouldn't have left that note."

"Oh, no, *that* was funny," Gloria said with a small laugh. "Did you find mine?"

"Yeah. Yours is funnier, because it's true."

"I'll remember you said that." She looked down at the bowl in front of her. "You can have this," she said, pushing it toward me. "I'm not hungry. All night, I kept dreaming about Angels of Death. You know, the sneaky ones."

"They were all sneaky," I said through a yawn. "Women are better at staying under the radar, remember?"

"Yeah, but the ones who took care of people, like nurses and aides, they were the sneakiest." Pause. "I can't stop thinking about Mom. How much do you know about that place she's in?"

I shook my head. "Trash TV's got you jumping at shadows. Better swear off the crime channels for a while."

"Come on, Val, didn't all that stuff about Angels of Death creep *you* out?"

"You're the crime buff," I said evenly. "*I* want my MTV. Or, failing that, wolverines."

"You didn't last night," she said with a short, humorless laugh.

"Touché. But enough is enough. Tonight is box-set DVD night. One of those bizarro things where even the cast didn't know what was happening—*Lost Heroes of Alcatraz* or *4400 Events in 24 Hours*. What do you say?"

My bad mash-ups didn't rate even an eye roll so I checked out the morning news on the iPad while I ate her cereal. Maybe getting her own iPad would put her in a better frame of mind, I thought. She'd love the games. Not to mention the camera—although I'd have to make her promise in writing not to upload any sneaky candids to the web.

"Val?" she said after a bit. "Even if I *am* jumping at shadows, humor me for a minute. How *did* you find that home?"

The only way to kill shadows was to turn on all the lights, I thought resignedly. That was what big sisters were for, although I'd never imagined I'd still be doing it at fifty-three. "It's a nice place, isn't it?" She nodded. "Doesn't have that institutional smell, residents aren't wandering around confused or tied to their beds, lying in their own—"

"*Val.*" She gave me the Eyebrow. "You're not answering the question."

"Okay, okay. I didn't find it—Mom did. She and Dad had an insurance plan through Stillman Saw and Steel—"

"But Stillman went under twenty years ago!"

"Lemme finish, will ya? Stillman went under, but the insurance company didn't. Mom and Dad maintained the policy and Mom kept it up after Dad died. She knew she didn't want us to have to go through what she did with Grandma, which was the same thing Grandma had been through with *her* mother. You were only a baby when Grandma died, so you missed it. But I didn't."

Gloria looked skeptical. "I have friends whose parents spent a fortune on policies that never paid them a nickel."

"Mom showed me everything some years back. Obviously it's all aboveboard and legit—otherwise, she wouldn't be able to afford that place." I decided not to mention that although Mom had seemed perfectly all right to me at the time, she had already felt herself starting to slip. "The policy pays about half the cost, her pension and the proceeds from the sale of her house cover the rest."

"And when the money from the house is gone?"

"We step up, little sister. What else?"

Her eyes got huge. "But I'm broke. I don't even have anything I can sell."

"Well, if you don't win the lottery, you'll have to go to Plan B and get a job," I said cheerfully. Gloria looked so dismayed, I wasn't sure whether I wanted to laugh or smack her one. "But we'll cross that bridge when we come to it. *If* we come to it."

"What do you mean by that?"

This was something I'd hoped to avoid until such time as it became moot. "Mom made a living will. She's DNR—Do Not Resuscitate. No defibrillator, no tubes, no ventilator, no extraordinary measures. Her body, minus useful organs or parts, goes to the local med school. *Her* decision," I added in response to Gloria's half-horrified, half-grossed-out expression. "You know Mom—waste not, someone else would be glad to have that liver."

Gloria gave a short laugh in spite of herself. "Okay, but *Mom's* liver? She's eighty-four. Do they take *anything* from people that old?"

I shrugged. "No idea. If they don't, that's more for the med students."

"It doesn't sound very respectful."

"On the contrary, Glow-bug—they actually hold memorial services twice a year for all the people who willed their remains to the school. They invite the families and they read out the names of all the deceased, thanking them for their contribution to the future of medicine."

She looked a little less grossed-out, but no happier. "What happens after, uh, you know, when they . . . when they're done?"

"They offer cremation. Although Mom said she'd prefer compost. There's an organization that plants trees and flowering bushes—"

"Stop it!"

"I'm sorry, Sis, maybe I shouldn't have told you about that part. But it *is* what Mom wants."

"Yeah, but she's got Alzheimer's."

"She was clear as a bell when she set this up."

We went back and forth. Gloria just couldn't seem to get her mind around our mother's rather alternative approach to death. A Viking funeral would probably have been easier for her to accept. From the various things she said, I wasn't sure whether she felt guilty for being the ever-absent daughter or hurt that no one had thought it necessary to consult her. Maybe it was a little of both.

Or a lot of both. The age difference had always made it hard for me to see things from her perspective. I'd thought it would get easier as we got older, but it hadn't, probably because Gloria was still where she'd been at twenty-five, trying to decide what she wanted to be when she grew up.

"Sorry, Glow-bug," I said finally, collecting the breakfast things. "This debate is called on account of my job."

"I don't know how you do it," she said, watching me rinse the bowls and put them in the dishwasher.

"Do what—make a living?"

"Stay awake looking at spreadsheets."

"It helps to see all the little numbers with dollar signs," I told her. "I'm sure you can find something to keep your eyes open." But probably not Plan B yet, I thought as I shut myself in my office and woke the computer.

Doing other people's taxes isn't the most exciting work I've ever done, but it's virtually recession-proof and less physically demanding than cleaning toilets. It's not even really that hard once you know how—although knowing how can be tricky. Every third change in regulations, I added another hard drive to back up my backups. There wasn't as much paper as there used to be, which was a relief. But I couldn't bring myself to rely completely on cloud storage—there's tempting Fate and then there's teasing it so unmercifully that Fate has to make an example of you. I stuck with CD-ROMs—not enough room on USB drives for sticky notes. One of my younger colleagues had a system using stickers with symbols—a clever idea but I thought I was a little too old for such an extreme administrative make-over. Especially after my recent lifestyle makeover.

In the ten years since Lee and I had come to our senses and called it quits, I'd discovered that living alone agreed with me. But that was over now. At first, Gloria had made vague noises about looking for a place of her own when she got back on her feet—whatever that meant—but I didn't kid myself. My sister was here for the duration. Even a boyfriend was unlikely to change things. The kind of men Gloria attracted invariably wanted to move in with *her* rather than vice versa, usually because they needed to.

I heard the car pull out of the driveway just as I stopped for lunch; the usual time Gloria headed out to see Mom. Mom's appetite was poor these days, but Gloria could usually get a few extra bites into her. It was one of the reasons the staff was so fond of her.

"I wish everyone's family was like her," a young nurse named Jill Franklyn had confided on my last visit. "She doesn't treat the staff like servants and she isn't texting or talking on the phone the whole time she's here. And even if most people had the time to come every day, they probably wouldn't."

I couldn't help feeling slightly defensive. Two visits a week was my self-imposed minimum, although I tried to make it three more often than not. I didn't always succeed, something I was usually too tired to feel guilty about. Which was what I felt guilty about instead. Meanwhile, Mom kept saying that I should think less about twice-weekly visits and more about a week or two in the Caribbean.

Tempting, but the web meant that my work could follow me and probably would. The last time I'd gone away, a five-day stay in a forest lodge had become half a day when I got a panicky text from a client whose house had burned to the ground just before he'd been called in for an audit. Well, I've since heard mosquitoes in the Maine woods grow to the size of eagles and sometimes carry off small children.

Of course, a mosquito with a seven-foot wing span might pale next to work that had been piling up for two weeks. Or not. There was only one way to find out.

Funny how I'd started thinking about taking time off again now that Gloria was here. So she didn't have a job and probably wouldn't get one except at gunpoint—she had lightened my load from the start. If she kept it up, I might even be able to revive my all-but-dormant social life—call friends, go shopping. Eat out. See a new movie in a theater. Just thinking about it gave me a lift.

Gloria was still out at five, so I spent another hour at my desk finishing work I'd have otherwise left for the next morning. When she hadn't come back by six, however, I started getting nervous. For all her faults, my sister was an excellent driver, but that didn't make her immune to bad drivers or, worse, bad intentions. Was there a fee to trace a LoJack, I wondered, or did the car have to be reported stolen first? Or could I do it myself? I vaguely remembered registering the navigation software; was there a Find My Car app, like Find My iPad?

Fortunately, I heard her pull into the driveway before I tried something stupid. "Anybody home?" Gloria called, coming in through the kitchen. "If you're a burglar, clear out."

"No burglars, just me," I called back.

She bustled in, curls bouncing with happy excitement, and held up a bag from Wok On the Wild Side. "You'll never guess what I did."

"You're right," I said, making room on the coffee table. "So you'd better just tell me."

"*I* got a *job*."

My jaw dropped; all hope of taking even a long weekend out of town evaporated as my social life rolled over and went back to sleep. "You . . . got . . . a job?"

She was busy taking little white cartons out of the bag and putting them on the table. "What, you didn't think that was possible?"

"No, it's just—I didn't know you were looking for a job."

"Relax, big sister," she laughed. "It's not a *real* job."

I blinked at her. "You got an *imaginary* job?"

"What? No, of course not. I am now an official volunteer aide at Mom's home!"

"Official—seriously?" I wasn't sure I'd heard her right. "Are you qualified?"

"As a matter of fact, big sister, I am."

This was probably the most startling thing she'd said in the last two minutes. Or maybe ever—*qualified* was not a word I associated with my sister. "How?" I asked weakly.

"Did you *actually* forget that I was a lifeguard almost every summer when I was in high school?" she said with a superior smile. I'd already been living away from home then, so I hadn't forgotten as much as I'd barely known in the first place. Mostly what I remembered was how Gloria practically lived in a swimsuit from May till September. And how even when I'd still looked good in one myself, I'd never looked *that* good. "After graduation, I taught swimming at the Y and for the Red Cross," she was saying, "and I've been lifeguarding and teaching swim classes on and off for years."

I still didn't get it. "The people at the care home go swimming a lot?"

She rolled her eyes. "I know CPR, you idiot."

Heat rushed into my face; I felt like *two* idiots.

Gloria laughed again. "Guess you won't faint after all. For a minute there, I wasn't too sure." She went into the kitchen for some plates while I sat on the couch feeling like a bad person as well as an idiot.

"I can also teach water aerobics," she said chattily, plopping a dish on my lap. "Well, actually, I'd have to update my aqua-aerobics certificate, but I've kept my CPR current. It's such a pain in the ass if a pool needs someone but can't hire you because your CPR's out-of-date." She served me from three different cartons and then held up a pair of chopsticks. "Want me to break these apart for you? Or would you like a fork?"

"I'm still *qualified* for sticks, thank you," I said. She handed them over, grinning; I wasn't quite there yet. "So . . . what? You got up this morning and decided to be an official volunteer? Or one of the nurses heard you talking about your summers as a lifeguard and said, 'Hey, you must know CPR, want to volunteer?'"

Her grin turned faintly sly as she served me and then herself. "Actually, I did the paperwork a couple of weeks ago."

Another surprise. "You never mentioned it to me," I said.

"There was no reason to, till now. I mean, if I ended up not volunteering, there'd be nothing to talk about anyway. Besides, do *you* tell *me* every single thought that crosses your mind?" Now her bright smile was so innocent that I actually wasn't sure whether that had been a jab or not. "Of course not," she went on. "Who would?"

I ate in silence, musing on the concept of my sister the qualified volunteer with the mad CPR skillz. I had none myself, which now that I thought of it was rather shortsighted. Even if none of my clients had ever had a heart attack after seeing what they owed the government, it wasn't impossible; many of them were already in heart-attack country. Meanwhile Gloria rattled on about recognizing the signs of a stroke, the right way to perform the Heimlich maneuver, and how CPR classes were good for meeting handsome firemen.

At last, the Gloria I knew and loved, I thought, relieved. "You know, I don't think you'll be meeting many handsome firemen at the home," I said when she paused for breath.

"Unless it burns down. *Kidding!*" she added, then sobered almost as quickly. "That's what I'm there to prevent."

I was baffled again. "Only you can prevent nursing home fires?"

"I'll make sure no Angel of Death tries anything."

I waited for her to laugh; she didn't. "You're serious."

"As a heart attack, sister." She impaled a shrimp that had been eluding her and popped it into her mouth.

Another reason to be glad she was qualified, I thought, feeling surreal. "I didn't realize you'd be there twenty-four hours a day."

She gave me the Eyebrow. "What are you talking about?"

"Most Angels of Death do their thing when everyone's asleep," I said. "Remember? Or did you sleep through that part of the *Killer Ladies* marathon?"

"No, I remember. Obviously I can't be there 24/7, but I'll make it obvious I'm watching closely. Every day as soon as I come in, I'll make the rounds, talk to everybody, see how they're doing. Make sure they're getting the right meds in the right amounts—"

"Don't the doctors and nurses do that?" I asked.

"I'll only double-check if something doesn't seem right," Gloria replied. "Volunteers don't give meds. We're not even supposed to have our own stuff when we're on duty. Like, not even an aspirin."

I barely heard her; something else occurred to me. "Doesn't being an official volunteer mean less time to visit with Mom?"

"She'll still know that I'm around."

This was going to be interesting, I thought, and probably not in a good way.

A fat lot I knew—it already was.

In the days that followed, my mother improved visibly. She was happier and more alert for longer; even her appetite was better. I was glad, but at the same time I knew from talking with her doctor that it wasn't permanent and the inevitable deterioration could be gradual or sudden. Not to mention cruel.

"Thanks to TV and movies, a lot of people think of dementia patients as daffy old folks who smile at things that aren't there and don't know what day it is," Dr. Li had told me, her normally friendly face a bit troubled. "People with dementia become frightened and angry and they lash out in unexpected and uncharacteristic ways. People who have never raised a hand in anger suddenly punch a nurse—or a relative. Or they bite—and unlike the old days, most still have enough teeth to draw blood. Or they get amorous and grabby. I treated a nun once, former professor of classical studies who spoke six languages. Swore like a biker in all of them and had a passion for—well, never mind."

There was a lot more that was even harder to listen to, but I came away feeling—well, not exactly prepared, because I didn't think I'd ever be truly prepared for certain behaviors no matter how realistic I tried to be, but maybe just a little less unprepared. So far, my mother was very much like herself, even when she couldn't remember why she wasn't in the old house or how old I was. And there had been fewer of those with Gloria around.

Mom's good streak held for about a month and a half. Every visit, she'd tell me to go on vacation; before long, I was looking at travel websites with real intent and work be damned. There was a nagging concern in the back of my mind, however, as to how a change like my absence would affect Mom's stability.

I decided to talk it over with her before I did anything, or didn't. She'd probably just tell me to fly to Jamaica for lunch—Jamaica was her latest idea of a dream destination—but what the hell, I thought as I arrived on my usual Thursday afternoon. My mother was outside on the patio, enjoying the lovely weather, an aide told me, and would I mind bringing her a glass of cranberry juice, thanks.

I found her parked at one of the umbrella tables in her wheelchair, away from the handful of other residents also outside. The lovely weather was lost on her. She sat glaring at a book of sudoku puzzles and holding a thick mechanical pencil in one fist like a dagger. The wheelchair meant that she was having dizzy spells, no doubt because she had swimmer's ear again. It could be chronic for people who needed two hearing aids. As I got closer, I saw that she was only wearing one today. Hence the sudoku, which she did only when she wanted to be alone.

"Well, *you* took your sweet time," she said as I sat down next to her and put the cranberry juice on the table. "I asked for that hours ago."

"Mom, it's me, Valerie," I said, hoping I didn't sound like my heart was sinking.

"Oh, for chrissakes, I *know* who you are." My mother looked as if she couldn't believe how stupid I was. "You *said* you'd bring me some cranberry juice and I've been waiting *forever.* S'matter, they make you pick the cranberries yourself?"

"I'm sorry you had to wait, Mom," I said gently, "but I just got here. This is Thursday. My last visit was Sunday."

She started to say something, then stopped. She set the pencil on the table and looked around—at the patio, at the umbrella overhead, at the aide and the elderly man in a bright blue sweat suit coming slowly up the path from the garden in front of us, at me, at herself—searching for what Dr. Li referred to as *mental true north,* some single thing that hasn't suddenly changed like the rest of the traitor world. Her face went from bewildered to fearful to suspicious, until finally she sat back heavily, covering her eyes with one hand.

"It's okay, Mom," I said, putting an arm around her. She was little more than skin and bones now, but in three days she seemed to have diminished even more.

"*There* you are!" Gloria materialized on Mom's other side. "Why didn't you tell me you were here?" Her too-bright smile vanished as Mom looked her over with a critical frown, tsk-ing at a food stain on her navy blue smock. "What's wrong? What did you say to her?"

"Nothing, I've only been here two minutes.

Gloria was about to answer when Mom put both hands up. "Don't *fight*," she said. "I can't *stand* when women fight. The hectoring—*hector, hector, hector*! Like crows arguing with seagulls. Is today Thursday?"

The fast change of subject was not, in fact, unusual; my mother thought segues were for politicians and game-show hosts. "All day," I said.

She pushed the book and pencil away. "I don't like writing outdoors. I told them that but they always forget. Maybe Alzheimer's is catching. Take me inside."

I moved to obey but Gloria beat me to it in a rush that seemed oddly desperate. "That's what I'm here for," she told me, as if it explained something, or everything.

My mother wanted a nap, so Gloria and I helped her into bed, fluffed her pillows, and promised not to *hector-hector-hector* even if she couldn't hear us. I settled into the chair by her bed, intending to dip into one of the novels on my iPad. But as soon as Mom fell asleep, Gloria insisted that I go back outside with her.

"Is this going to take long?" I said.

"It's *important*."

I followed Gloria away from the now empty patio, down the walk to a bench under a large maple tree. "Make it fast," I said. "I'd like to be back before Mom wakes up."

"Not so loud." She leaned forward and spoke in a half whisper. "As an aide, I see and hear a lot more than when I was a visitor. I think there's something funny going on. And I don't mean funny ha-ha."

At last, the Gloria I knew and loved. "Why? Did something in particular happen?" When she didn't answer right away, I added, "Or did someone just give you a dirty look?"

She drew back, looking stony as she folded her arms. "I should have known you wouldn't take me seriously. You never have."

"That's not true," I said promptly, but I could hear the lie in my own voice.

"You think it's just my imagination, because I'm the little sister. *Baby* sister. I'll never be more than a child to you. You have no idea what it was like, growing up with you three adults. Dad, Mom, and Mom, Jr. You all knew better about everything. When you weren't all *tolerating* me—ho-hum, another Christmas, we have to do *Santa* again; you all acted like you didn't want me to grow up. Like Mom trying to make me sit on Santa's lap when I was *eight*."

"Just for the photo," I said, which was true. "I know, I was there. She wanted me to sit on his other knee but the guy said he'd quit if I tried it." Also true; the bastard.

Gloria almost smiled at the memory, then caught herself. "You're doing it *again*—trying to pacify me. Just listen to me for once, will you? Something's not right here."

"I'm only asking why you think that," I said, trying to sound utterly reasonable and not at all like I might be smarting (a *very* tiny bit) from certain (*very* minor) points she'd scored. "It's a fair question. If it was the other way round, you'd ask me the same thing. Especially if this was the first you'd heard about anything being the slightest bit wrong even though I'd been coming here every day for weeks."

"I *told* you, this isn't like just visiting," she said. "You don't know, you haven't done both." A movement behind Gloria caught my eye, an aide looking around the patio. She picked up my mother's forgotten sudoku book and dropped it in the large front pocket of her smock, then paused when she noticed us. I smiled and waved. Gloria twisted around to look; when she turned back to me, she was pissed off again.

"Fine. *Don't* believe me. I'll *prove* it. Then you can't say I'm *jumping at shadows*." She got up and walked off. Unbidden, the memory came to me of her doing the same thing as a toddler during what Mom called one of her bossy episodes. I suppressed a smile, just in case she looked back, but she didn't. She hadn't back then, either.

Things were strained between us after that. My tries at initiating a conversation fell flat; if she answered at all, it was usually just a wordless grunt that let me know she hadn't gone deaf. She thawed a bit by Monday, occasionally even speaking to me first. Encouraged, I suggested we go shopping and see a movie, in an actual movie theater, my treat, including popcorn dripping with artery-hardening butter-flavored goop. She declined politely, saying her feet hurt. Considering she always went straight into the tub as soon as she came home, they probably hurt all the way up to her hips.

Maybe finding a bath all ready and waiting when she got home would soften her up even more, I thought. The first time surprised the hell out of her; she sounded awkward when she thanked me, and spent the whole evening watching movies with me in the living room, even making a bowl of popcorn without being asked. She wasn't quite as surprised the second time; the third time, she asked me what I wanted.

"What do you think I want?" I said, holding half a pastrami on pumpernickel; I'd splurged at the deli counter that morning, a treat for the extra work I had to put in on a new account. "I want us to be friends again. I want us to be *sisters* again. You're acting like I owe you money *and* I slept with your boyfriend."

She stared down at me, expressionless. "You just don't take *anything* seriously, do you?"

"Oh, for chrissakes." I sighed. "I'm trying to break the ice between us before it turns into permafrost." Her mouth curled briefly and I felt a surge of irritation. "I'm sorry—still not serious enough?"

"Don't bother running any more baths," she told me. "I keep a swimsuit at the home so I can use the Jacuzzi. Sometimes Mom and I go in together."

I bit back a smart remark about being a lifeguard in a whirlpool and then felt ashamed for even thinking it. Maybe I *had* been making her feel small all her life and never realized it.

"I was just trying to do something nice for you," I said. "I've seen how much work you do—"

"How kind of you to notice," she said stiffly. "But, being a grown-up, I can run my own baths." She actually turned on her heel and walked out.

"Fine," I said at her back, my sympathy evaporating. If my sister wanted to be taken seriously—as a grown-up, no less—she could damned well act like one instead of a thirteen-year-old girl with her period.

Oh, no, you didn't, said my brain.

My face burned, even though I was alone. Okay, maybe Gloria did have her period. Back in the day, I hadn't exactly been a ray of sunshine during Shark Week. Now I was coping with the onset of menopause and doing fairly well thanks to hormones, but every day wasn't a picnic and neither was I.

My thoughts chased each other round and round. Had I really been horrible to Gloria all her life? Or were we just doomed to be permanently out of step no matter what? We were from different generations, after all; we practically spoke a different language. Still, if I had acted like that after she had run a bath for me, my conscience would have tortured me for *years*. Of course, that was me-the-older-sister. Could I see things as if I were the younger sister? Etc., etc., and so on, and so forth. When I finally remembered to eat the sandwich I'd been looking forward to all day, it sat in my stomach like a hockey puck.

My indigestion subsided later when I heard her go out again instead of putting her sore feet up. Gloria wasn't letting the problems between us affect her relationship with my car.

Gloria continued volunteering with a wholeheartedness she'd never shown for paid employment, or at least none that hadn't involved wearing a bathing suit. I did wonder occasionally if her apparent dedication might really be an unhealthy obsession with finding evidence that didn't exist to prove something that wasn't true.

Except that when I saw her during my visits, she didn't look obsessed. She looked cheerfully busy, the way people do when they're happy in their work. Maybe in trying to prove something to me, Gloria had found herself, discovered that caregiving was lifeguarding in street clothes— unlikely but not impossible. Her being too embarrassed to say so wasn't impossible, either, and even less unlikely.

Unless she still believed that something wasn't right and she was playing a role more Method than anything Brando had ever done while she watched and waited for something to happen. I really couldn't tell. While she wasn't openly hostile, she was still distant and had little to say beyond updates on Mom.

Maybe *I* was jumping at shadows now. After a lifetime as the grasshopper in a family of ants, Gloria was now up close and personal with the reality of Mom's decline. Coming to terms with that would shake anyone up. I wished like anything she'd talk about it with me, but if she really felt that I'd always patronized her, I could hardly be surprised that she was keeping her distance. Nor could I blame her.

Eventually, she warmed up enough that we occasionally saw a movie or went out to eat together, but the wall between us remained. Much as I wanted to, I didn't push her. Partly because I was afraid she'd get angry and shut me out again. But I'd also developed this rather weird, superstitious idea that looking too closely at her newfound self-discipline would somehow jinx it. She'd stop volunteering or even visiting more than once a month, if that. Eventually, despite rules I'd laid down, she'd drift into sleeping all day and staying up all night. I'd seen it happen before. Regardless of what had inspired her sense of purpose, I didn't want her to lose it. Even if it meant we'd never say anything deeper than *It's gonna rain* or *Guess what's on TV? Hint: wolverines!* to each other for the rest of our lives.

Gloria held still for *Red Dawn* and even made popcorn. But she never suggested any more true-crime programs. That was fine with me, although I wasn't sure what it meant, if it meant anything at all.

A month and a half after Gloria's initial blowup, Mr. Santos and his daughter Lola sought me out to tell me my sister was a hero. Mr. Santos was a wiry little man in his late seventies who shared my mother's fondness for puzzles and card games. I knew Lola to nod to, but she and her father had made Gloria's acquaintance in a big way.

"I've never seen anything like that in real life," Lola Santos said, looking at me through wide, dark eyes, as if my being Gloria's older sister was an accomplishment in itself. "I was in the bathroom for maybe two minutes. Gloria had brought him some juice—"

"And if she hadn't, I wouldn't be here right now." Mr. Santos thumped his chest twice with one bony fist before his daughter caught his hand.

"Don't, Popi, you're still bruised!"

"Good. The bruises remind me of the heroine with the curly brown hair and the dimple in her cheek who saved my life." He shook his index finger at me. "She's a wonderful girl, your sister. I don't know what we'd do without her. She's our heroine. She's *my* personal heroine."

"And mine," Lola added.

I had no idea what to say to that, so I just smiled and thanked them for telling me. I tried to talk to Gloria about it at home later, but she wasn't very forthcoming; when she started to look annoyed, I let it go. The next day I rearranged my work schedule and went back to see if I could find out anything else, but I might as well not have bothered. I couldn't get any more out of Mr. Santos than what he had already told me. My mother alternately claimed to have been taking a nap or sitting in the garden. The few other residents I spoke to had nothing new or useful to add. Even the usually chatty Jill Franklyn was reticent on the subject; after praising Gloria's mad CPR skillz and her ability to stay calm in a crisis, she made a very pointed comment about patient privacy and the confidentiality of medical records. I took the hint and spent the rest of the time with Mom, who was slightly confused by my consecutive visits.

I went back to three visits a week, on the grounds that it made Mom happy and not because I was still trying to find out more about Gloria's big heroic moment. Because that would have been pointless, considering that I'd gotten a full account from Mr. Santos and Lola themselves. Happy ending, smiles all round—what more could there possibly be to the story? If I were jumping at shadows now, they were shadows I couldn't even name. Maybe all the *she's a heroine* business was getting on my nerves; weeks after the fact, it had yet to die down.

Jealous much? said that still small voice in my brain.

I was pretty sure I hadn't become that neurotic. Practically certain. But if I *were*—I *wasn't*, but if I *were*—I told myself, there was still only one way to kill the shadows. Mom would benefit from the extra visits and so would I—no one knew how much longer she'd be herself. If good things sometimes got done for stupid reasons, it didn't make them any less good. Did it?

"Weren't you here yesterday?" my mother asked as I sat down next to her at the umbrella table. To my surprise, she seemed vaguely annoyed.

"No, I came on Thursday and today's Saturday. What's the matter, you sick of me hanging around?"

"I don't understand why you won't take advantage of Gloria's being here," she said, "and go away, even just for a long weekend. Instead, you come here more. What's the matter with you? Don't you have a life?"

"No," I said honestly.

"What about your friends?"

"They don't have lives, either. It's rough out there. I was thinking about moving in with you."

My mother gave a grim laugh. "You better win the lottery first. They don't let you split expenses." She looked around. "Where's that thing? You know, with all the books inside and the screen. I coulda sworn I had it. See if I left it in my room, will ya? Since you're here anyway."

My mother's door was open; inside, an aide stood with her back to me, doing something on the tray table next to the bed. On her left was a cart, both shelves crowded with water pitchers.

"Oh, hi," I said cheerfully, and she jumped. The pitcher she'd been holding sprang out of her hands, spilling water over the bed before it fell to the floor. "Oh, damn, I'm so sorry!" I rushed to help.

"Don't, it's okay, I can take care of this, it's fine—" The aide sounded almost desperate as she tried to wave me away, grab the pitcher, and pick up several small white pills all at once. "It's only water, not plutonium, I can manage, really, I can."

"I'm sure, but let me help anyway," I said guiltily as I got down on my knees. The pitcher had come apart and the lid had gone under the bed. I used it to sweep up several small white pills.

"I was just taking something for a headache," the aide said, grabbing up the pills and dumping them into the front pocket of her smock, ignoring the minor dust bunnies attached. "I have cluster headaches, they're murder."

"How awful." I had no idea what cluster headaches were, but judging by how stricken she looked, she wasn't exaggerating much. Her olive complexion had gone almost ashy. I made another sweep with the pitcher lid in case I'd missed any pills before I got to my feet. "I really am sorry, I didn't meant to sneak up on you. I should change the bed—"

"*No,* absolutely *not,* you don't come here to do the housekeeping, I'll take care of it." She spoke so quickly she was almost babbling. "I'll take care of this, you don't have to worry, *please* don't take any time away from your visit, but if—" she cut off suddenly. Her color had improved slightly but now she looked like she was going to cry.

"What's wrong? Is it your headache?" I asked.

I was about to suggest she sit down and drink some water when she said, "It's nothing. Please, just go on with your visit, I'll be all right."

"Look, you won't even let me help you change the bed, so *anything* I can do to make up for scaring the bejeebus out of you, just tell me."

She looked down, embarrassed. "It's kind of stupid."

"Kind of stupid—that's definitely in my wheelhouse," I said. That got me a smile.

"Okay, it's that—I just—" All at once, she was stripping the bed. "No, I can't. I *was* going to ask if you'd mind not mentioning this to your mother, but forget it." She dropped a bundle of wet linens on the floor and started to pull off the padded mattress cover. "It's only because I feel like *such* an *idiot*. But I have no business asking you someth—"

"It's done," I said, holding up one hand. "I can't think of a good reason why I'd have to mention it anyway."

"But—"

"Forget it. I'm not talkin' and you can't make me."

She gave a small, nervous laugh.

"I really only came in here to get her e-reader—" I spotted it on the nightstand and pointed. The aide handed it to me somehow looking grateful, sheepish, and relieved all at once. Her name tag said she was Lily R. "Thanks. What's the *R* for?"

She stared, baffled.

"Lily R." I nodded at her name tag. "*R* for . . . ?"

"Romano," she said, and rolled her eyes. "You must think I'm a real clown."

"Hardly." As I went back outside to my mother, I couldn't help feeling a bit guilty for leaving Lily *R*-for-Romano to remake the bed by herself. Then Mom asked me to read to her and I put it out of my mind. I might never have given it another thought if I hadn't found a pill in the sole of one of my very expensive athletic shoes.

I wore them not because I was particularly sporty but because walking in them felt so good. Plus, they came in bright, jazzy colors, which I had a new fondness for in my old age. And what the hell—if I ever decided to defy my old age and run a marathon, I was ready.

Running a marathon was probably the only thing that could have been farther from my mind than Lily R. when I felt something stuck to the sole of my shoe. Pausing at the kitchen door, I took it off before I scarred the tile flooring for life. A tiny rock—I used an ice pick to flip it out the open door, then checked the other shoe, just in case. The pill was about the same size as the rock but wedged in more deeply. Maybe that was why it was still intact, I thought, carefully working it free. Although I had no idea why I was bothering—I was hardly going to give it to Lily Romano next time I saw her. *Hey, girlfriend, found this on the bottom of my shoe, thought you'd want it back anyway.* Now *who's kind of stupid?*

I put it in an empty ring box on my bureau. As Mom always said, waste not; in a cluster-headache emergency, I'd be glad I'd saved it. Stranger things had happened; were happening now.

A week later, Jill Franklyn called in the middle of the afternoon, apologizing so much I couldn't get a word in edgewise. The I heard her say something about death being harder for some people, especially the first death.

"The *first* death?" I interrupted. "Are you talking about my mother?"

"Oh, no, no, no, your mother is fine!" she said quickly. "It's your sister—"

"My *sister?*" Suddenly the pit of my stomach was filling with ice water. "Something happened to *Gloria?*"

"No, no, no, she's fine," Jill Franklyn said. "Well, not *fine,* exactly—"

"Is she still alive?" I demanded.

"Yes, of *course* she's still *alive.*" Bewilderment crept into her apologetic tone. "But—well—you need to come and get her, she shouldn't drive home."

I said I was on my way and hung up without telling her that would be a bit longer than either of us would have liked, because I'd have to take a cab, and although this wasn't the middle of nowhere or darkest suburbia, it wasn't Manhattan, either. I got there in half an hour, which was actually sooner than I'd expected.

Jill Franklyn was waiting for me at the reception desk, looking a bit flustered. "I'm so glad you're here," she told me, smiling, but I could hear the admonition in her voice. The receptionist pretended not to eavesdrop by studying something intently on her desk.

"Sorry, I had to get a cab." I tried to look contrite or at least sheepish. "I'm not sure I understand what's going on. You said my mother's all right—"

"Yes, just fine." Jill Franklyn nodded vigorously as she ushered me through the entry gate and down the corridor leading directly to my mother's room. "Gloria's with her right now."

I found the two of them sitting side by side on Mom's bed. Mom had her arm around my sister, who had obviously been crying. Lily Romano was there as well, looking concerned and fidgeting. She left as soon as I came in, nodding a silent hello as she rushed past. I frowned, wishing she'd stay, but I had no chance to ask and no good reason to do so.

"What kept you?" my mother was saying, a bit impatient.

"There's only one car between us," I said, "and Gloria has it. I don't usually need it. What's up, Glow-bug?"

Gloria looked up at me and I thought she was furious at my using her childhood nickname so publicly. Then she got up, flung her arms around me, and sobbed.

By the time we got to the car, she had quieted down and stayed quiet all the way home, for which I was grateful. Rush hour had started and I didn't want to fight the traffic to the soundtrack of Gloria's heartbroken sobs. A dozen years ago, never driving in rush hour again had been one more good reason to leave the local tax-preparation firm in favor of a home business; now I decided that it had been the best reason.

We made it home alive; in lieu of kissing the ground in thanksgiving, I put a pizza in the oven and joined Gloria in the living room. I found her wedged into the far corner of the sofa, hugging her knees to her chest as if to make herself as small as possible. A joke about never having a white-knuckle ride on the couch crossed my mind, but for once I actually thought before speaking.

"I don't know what happened today," I said after a bit. "Jill Franklyn didn't have a chance to tell me and I thought I'd better just get you home rather than hang around."

She flicked a glance at me but neither spoke nor moved. I waited a little longer, then went into the kitchen to check on the pizza. I was taking it out of the oven when I heard Gloria say, "I couldn't save her."

I turned to see her sitting at the table. I cut the pizza into eight slices, grabbed a couple of plates, and put the platter on a heat pad within easy reach before taking the chair on her right.

"They gave me coffee with, like, six sugars." She frowned at the plate in front of her as if she were seeing something other than a Currier-and-Ives style winter scene in blue and white. We'd grown up with these dishes; in thirty or more years, we'd only lost two. "They said it was good for shock. I didn't think I was in shock but I guess I was." She raised her face to me. "I never, ever, *ever* imagined what it would be like to do CPR on someone and not . . . not w—" She swallowed hard. "Not have it work."

"Oh, sis, I'm so sorry." I got up and put my arms around her. She sat passively for a little while; then I felt her slowly move to hug me back. "I can't even imagine."

"It's not how it should've happened. Mrs. Boudreau should be playing bridge with her son and her friends right now. Watching a movie tonight. Getting up for breakfast tomorrow morning and then . . . just . . . having a few more years to be happy. Like Mr. Santos and the others."

The last three words clunked in my ear, but I was too busy trying to remember the dead woman. Still keeping hold of both her hands, I sat down again after a bit and said, "I'm sorry, Gloria, but I can't place her. The lady who died. Mrs. Boudreau?"

My sister nodded sadly. "She only moved in a couple of weeks ago; I don't think you ever even saw her." She took a shuddery breath. "I promised her son I'd look after her. I promised *her* I'd take care of her. And then her son had to watch while I broke that promise."

"You're a good person, sis." My thoughts shifted around like puzzle pieces trying to fit themselves together. "You *did* take care of her, as best you could. But no matter how well you do it, CPR isn't a get-out-of-death-free card."

As soon as the words were out of my mouth, I wanted to kick myself. Gloria frowned and I waited for her to tear me a new one for making stupid jokes again. Instead she said, "You don't understand. Mrs. Boudreau *really shouldn't be dead*. She wasn't even long-term. She was only there till the end of the month," she added in response to my questioning look. "Then she was gonna live with her son and his family. They're adding another room to their house for her. It isn't ready yet. And now they'll just have an extra room with nobody in it."

It was on the tip of my tongue to say that no extra space in any home ever went unused under any circumstances, but then I didn't. Having grown up in a decidedly uncrowded house, Gloria's experience was limited, and it was beside the point anyway.

Little by little, I got the story out of her; it was pretty much Mr. Santos all over again, with a slightly different cast and an unhappy ending that even a portable defibrillator couldn't change. "The defib's the last of the last resorts," Gloria said as she started on a slice of pizza. That had to be a good sign, I thought. "It's too easy to screw it up even if you're trained. I'm trained to defib, but I've never done it." She paused, head tilted to one side. "Jesus, I just heard myself. 'I'm trained to defib but I've never done it.' Like it's routine. Until I started volunteering, I'd never done any CPR for real. Not even once."

I was trying to think of something to say when she dropped the slice of pizza she'd been holding and put a hand to her mouth. "And I never even thought anyone would actually *die*. Mr. Santos and his daughter were calling me a heroine, the head nurse put a letter in my file, I got my name in the newsletter as this month's MVV—Most Valuable Volunteer. I didn't think, *What if somebody dies?* because nobody did. So I didn't think for one second that Mrs. Boudreau might die. I just waited for the nurses to say she had a pulse."

I frowned. Had Gloria performed CPR on someone else besides Mr. Santos? "Gloria, how many times—"

She didn't hear me. "Even after they shocked her, I was still waiting for someone to say she was back." She put her hand to mouth again. "Omigod, deep down I'm *still* waiting for Jill to call and say someone at the hospital decided to give it one last try and brought Mrs. Boudreau back after all."

And I was waiting for her to burst into tears again or even get sick all over the table. Instead, Gloria finished the slice and reached for another. Good to see she was recovering from the experience, I thought. My own appetite was history.

The head nurse who called the next morning to check on Gloria was new. Celeste Akintola had that friendly but no-nonsense voice all RNs above a certain level of experience seem to have. Jill Franklyn didn't have it, and I couldn't imagine that she ever would. I shook the thought away and focused on getting acquainted with the new head nurse. More specifically, on trying to find out how often Gloria had used her mad CPR skillz, but without sounding like I was prying. Or like I had to.

Celeste Akintola made friendly but no-nonsense noises about patient confidentiality, adding that she expected all staff, including volunteers, to respect the privacy of the residents. I gave up, handed the phone to Gloria, and stood by, blatantly eavesdropping; all I heard was *yes* and *okay*. After hanging up, Gloria said she had strict orders to take a full two weeks off before she even considered coming back. Even then, it would be for no more than three days a week, at least to begin with. My sister didn't mind going along with that, which was a relief. Also a little amazing—or perhaps not. She was subdued, obviously deep in thought.

If I were honest, I had to do some thinking of my own about taking Gloria seriously. As the older, supposedly wiser sister, I'd never saved a life or seen a person die right in front of me. Gloria had saved one person and had another die practically in her arms just in the space of a few weeks. Life and death—it didn't get any more serious than that.

I wanted to tell her as much, but I couldn't figure out how to begin. Whatever I said came out trite, if not weaselish. Gloria by contrast had a new eloquence. Or maybe it was only new to me.

"I was scared of what you'd say," she told me later. "I was doing so good, you know? Everybody needed me—*me*, personally. Me *specifically*. And then *this* happened. I needed you to come and be Mom, Jr., so much, but at the same time I was thinking how pathetic it was to be such a mess at thirty-eight. Then you came in and just—" She shrugged. "All you cared about was me. And I realized there's only one person in the whole world who'll always show up, no matter how pathetic I am. You didn't go all smarter or older or wiser on my ass and you didn't act like it was all a big joke." She paused. "Although the get-out-of-death-free-card thing was kinda cool."

"Some people make jokes when they're nervous," I said.

"Yeah, I get that now," she said. "See? I'm growing up."

But, I hoped, not so much that she'd ever realize how utterly and completely she'd pwned her big sister.

It was a nice two weeks. I took some time off and let Gloria introduce me to the quirky world of hard-core flea-market shopping, including lessons in haggling for the reserved soul. She even got me to admit it was fun, which it was, although I didn't see myself doing it without her. She said she felt the same way about *Red Dawn*.

I visited Mom alone and quickly learned to come in the mornings, when she was sharper, upbeat, and much more like her old self. After mid-day, her energy flagged and she had a hard time concentrating, whether she'd had a nap after lunch or not. Jill Franklyn said this was called *sundowning*. Her sympathetic expression wasn't perfunctory, but there was something *professional* about it, almost rehearsed. Maybe it was all the training she'd had in how to discuss these things with the family.

Or maybe, I thought, suddenly ashamed, it was repetition. How many times had she explained this to anxious relatives? I really had to work on giving credit where credit was due, I thought, or I'd end up yelling *Get off my lawn!* at everyone under sixty.

After her two-week break, Gloria was ready to go back to work—or "work"—and I was happy to let her, despite being tempted to drop hints about looking for a paying job. Then I thought of Mom; having Gloria around again would probably be good for her, even if it wasn't as often as before.

After the first week, however, Gloria announced she'd be going every day again. "Akintola said I can only *volunteer* three days a week," she said when I questioned her. "So, fine. The rest of the time, I'll just visit Mom." She smiled like she'd just cut the Gordian knot with blunt-end scissors.

"I'm not trying to go all older, wiser, or smarter on your ass," I said, wincing, "but I'm pretty sure that violates the spirit of the order."

"She doesn't want me to volunteer, I won't volunteer," Gloria said stubbornly. "Four days out of seven, I'll sit around like a lady of leisure."

"I don't think you should go seven days in a row—"

Gloria huffed impatiently. "Have you seen Mom lately?"

My heart sank. "I know what you—"

"You always go in the morning, right? Who told you about sundowning—was it Jill?" I tried to say something but she talked over me. "It's code for Mom gets worse as the day goes on. They use *sundowning* with the families because the word makes them think of things like pretty sunsets after a nice day—as if the person started out good in the morning. But they don't. They're *better* in the morning—that's not the same as *good*."

I stared at her, slightly awestruck, then tried to cover it by saying the first thing that came into my head. "I thought you weren't volunteering today."

She frowned. "I'm not."

"So if Mr. Santos has another heart attack—or someone else has a coronary—you'd stand back and let the pros handle it?"

"Are you insane?" she demanded. "You think I'd just watch someone die just because it's my day off?"

"No, only if they were DNR. Like Mom."

She looked so stricken, I wanted to bite my tongue off and let her throw it away. "When you don't know for sure, you assume they want to live until you know otherwise for sure," she said in a stiff little voice, and I could have sworn she was trying to do Celeste Akintola's no-nonsense voice.

"And if it *is* otherwise?" I asked, trying not to sound argumentative.

She didn't answer.

"You know you can get into big trouble for doing CPR when you're not supposed to? Not just you, but the doctors and nurses and everyone else who works there, including all the other volunteers." I wasn't sure exactly how true that was, but it wasn't a complete lie. "*You* could even get arrested for assault, and I don't think the family has to wait till you're out of jail to sue you."

Gloria gave me the most severe Eyebrow I'd ever seen. "The box set of *Law & Order* doesn't come with a law degree. I do what I know is right."

"I just asked what if you knew for sure—"

"Like *Mom*?" she said, almost spitting the word. "Go ahead, say it: *Mom*. What's the matter, can't say who you really mean? Why? Things get too cold-blooded for you all of a sudden? Or are you really afraid Mom would sue me? Press charges? Both?" Gloria gave a single, short laugh. "Have I asked you for bail money? *Lately?*" she added. "No, I haven't. Case closed."

"So, what—you always guessed right?" I frowned. "Just how many times *was* that?"

She hesitated. "Counting Mr. Santos and Mrs. Boudreau? Five."

My jaw dropped. "Why didn't you tell me?"

"I was mad at you."

"Then why didn't *Mom*—no, scratch that. Why didn't *anybody* tell me?"

"Maybe they thought you knew." She shrugged. "I mean, they kept calling me a heroine."

I wanted a desk to pound my head on. "Don't you think I'd have said something if I *had* known?"

"I was mad at you," she said again. "Remember?"

"Yeah. I also remember why: I asked you why you thought there was something wrong at the home." I gave her a sideways look. "Does this mean you've changed your mind about that?"

She shifted her weight from one foot to the other and huffed. "Do you *really* have to make a big deal out of it?"

"Hey, it was *your* idea," I called after her as she left.

If Gloria had changed her mind, so had I, although I didn't realize it right away. It crept up on me in chilly slow motion. My visits went from three a week to daily. I thought it was intimations of mortality—specifically, my mother's—brought on by the revelation of how many times Gloria had used her mad CPR skillz. No, I corrected myself: *how many times Gloria had performed CPR in an emergency situation.* Taking her seriously meant swearing off funny terms for matters of life and death.

I was even ready to confess that I had a case of the jitters—not eager but willing—except that she didn't ask. Baffling—surely she was wondering why I'd rearranged my schedule so drastically . . . wasn't she? I waited, but she didn't try to talk to me during visits or at home, where I was now working through evening hours we had previously spent together.

After a week, I couldn't stand it anymore and called in one of my temps. Gloria raised her eyebrows—it wasn't the first half of April—but didn't ask. In fact, she didn't say a word on the drive in.

"Are you picking me up or should I get a ride with Lily?" she asked as I pulled into an empty space in the visitor's lot.

I made an exasperated noise. "You're gaslighting me, aren't you?"

"What is that?" Gloria looked genuinely baffled.

"Okay, not a fan of old movies. You're trying to drive me crazy," I said.

"And what happened to make you think that?" she asked politely. The strong urge I had to smack her must have been obvious. "Come on, seriously," she added. "You're the one who's gotten all weird, working all night so you can be here every day—"

"And you've never asked me why. Aren't you even a little bit curious?"

"Well, yeah," she said, like she'd never heard a stupider question. "But I figured I'd just be wasting my breath. You don't tell me a goddam thing till you feel like it. If you ever do."

I felt my face getting hot again.

"What's the matter?" she said, a little impatient now. "It's true, isn't it?"

I gave up. "Okay, okay. I'm nervous about Mom. Finding out how many times you'd done CPR kinda . . ." I shrugged. "It kinda freaked me out, I guess."

"Really." My sister gave me the skeptical Eyebrow. "When? After you considered the legal ramifications of my possibly keeping Mom alive?"

"I never did CPR on anyone—I don't even know how—so it took a while for the reality to sink in, that Mom could . . . you know. Die." I barely managed not to choke on the word.

My sister let out a long breath, staring through the windshield at nothing in particular. Then: "If it makes you feel any better, Mom isn't too likely to have a coronary anytime real soon. Her heart's in pretty good shape. To be honest, I worried more about her falling—the dizzy spells. Fortunately, she doesn't fight using the wheelchair as much as she did, so it's less of a worry than it was. But if you want to keep coming every day, I'm not gonna stop you," she added with a sudden smile. "Because it really seems to help her stay clear."

"What about the sundowning?"

"That's what I mean." Gloria's smile grew even brighter. "Some days, I can barely tell it's happening."

"New medication?" I asked.

"Nope, same stuff, same dose. Some of the other residents take a lot more and don't do as well."

"Maybe it's because she's eating better?" I said.

Gloria shrugged. "It doesn't hurt. Now, are we going in, or do you want to sit here and, as Mom says when she thinks no one's listening, fret like a motherfucker all day?"

She was right—Mom *was* better. But Dr. Li had warned me that these periods of near recovery, when patients somehow seemed to shake off the fog that had been rolling in, weren't signs of genuine improvement, only the erratic nature of the disease showing itself—one of dementia's special cruelties.

But it didn't make Mom any less lucid. She started telling me to go on vacation again and was annoyed when I refused, occasionally getting so agitated with me that I had to leave so she'd calm down.

"You want to know the truth," Lily Romano said as she walked me out one afternoon, "she's kinda scared that you're coming every day. She's afraid maybe it means that she's dying and the doctor won't tell her."

"Really?" I was shocked. "I'd never have thought of that. Gloria never said anything."

Lily Romano shrugged. "She doesn't know. Residents don't always tell their families everything. Sometimes it's easier for them to confide in someone they aren't so close to, especially when—"

"When . . . ?" I prodded after a moment.

She winced. "When it's something where they think their family will, like, just say they're being silly or paranoid."

When the family doesn't take them seriously, I thought, wincing a little myself. "So does my mother confide in you a lot?" She looked so uncomfortable, I went on quickly, "Forget I asked, it's not important. How're your headaches?"

She looked blank for a moment. "Oh, yeah, fine—I haven't had any in a while."

I might have mentioned finding the pill in my shoe just for the hell of it, but we were nearly at the entry gate and she was making gotta-get-back-to-work noises. I made a mental note to talk to Gloria later about Mom's possible anxieties. Then the day got busy; Gloria was getting a lift home with another aide, so I did the grocery shopping, and somewhere between the deli counter and the perennial choice between paper or plastic, a gust of tedium blew all the mental notes off the front of my mental refrigerator.

Only much later, after several hours into another night at the computer, did it come back to me. My work ethic said it could wait; my procrastinator said it was a golden opportunity. For once, I went with the latter.

I opened the door to find Gloria standing there with one hand raised, about to knock. "I'm sorry, I know I'm not supposed to interrupt you—"

"It's okay," I said. "I think I'm off tonight. What's up?"

"I've got a dilemma," she said, her face troubled, "and I need some advice."

"I'll get the Shiraz, you save me a seat on the couch."

"You'll probably think it's silly," she said as I poured wine into her glass.

"Apparently that's going around. Never mind," I added when she looked bewildered. "Just tell me. We'll decide if it's silly later."

She hesitated, gazing at me with uncertainty. Then she took a deep breath. "Okay, there are certain things that everybody at Brightside has to do—certain rules, I mean, that everybody has to obey, no matter what, or get terminated. Even the nurses. Even the janitorial staff. Even the gardening service people."

I nodded.

"Those are the strictest rules, and if you see an *infraction*"—she made a face at the word—"you're supposed to report it. Which is, like"—she rolled her eyes—"who wants to be a snitch? I mean, if I ever saw someone *hurt* a resident, I'd yell at the top of my lungs. But—"

"Did you see something?" I asked gently.

She nodded. "It was one of those things you can actually get away with if you're careful. And probably everyone there's done it at least once, but they'll fire you on the spot for it, even if nothing bad happens."

I shook my head. "What is this incredibly evil thing?"

"Having any unauthorized medication on you during your shift." She frowned. "I thought I told you that. We can't even have aspirin in our pants pocket."

"Why not?" I asked.

"Because it's a hazard to the residents."

"Only if they get into your pants pockets," I said, laughing a little.

"They don't care." Gloria was shaking her head. "Zero tolerance. The only way to be absolutely certain a resident doesn't take anything they're not supposed to is if there *isn't* anything."

"That's even stricter than a hospital, isn't it?" I said, thinking out loud.

"Beats me. And it doesn't matter anyway—it's their policy."

"So you saw someone—" I cut off, already knowing who it would be.

"Lily Romano," she said with a mournful sigh. "I caught her so red-handed, I couldn't even pretend that I didn't see anything. She was doing the rounds with water pitchers–"

I put up a hand. "Been there, sis."

"What are you talking about?" she asked, unsure again and about to get angry.

"I caught Lily Romano with pills," I said sadly. I gave her a quick rundown of our encounter in Mom's room, adding, "I can't remember if you told me about the no-drugs rule. If you did, I forgot it that day."

"Did she beg you not to tell?" Gloria asked, still unhappy.

"Yes, but not about that." I told her the rest.

"That's weird. Why would she ask you to keep quiet about her having to change the bed but not about the pills?"

I thought for a moment. "Because she realized that I didn't know the rule and she didn't want to tip me off. Making me think I was just saving her some embarrassment was pretty clever. Really clever."

"She kind of took a chance, though," Gloria said.

I shook my head. "I didn't even tell *you*, did I?"

Gloria sighed again. "She made me go with her to her locker and watch her put the pills in her purse, all the time begging me not to tell and promising she'd never do it again. I feel bad for her—cluster headaches really are murder—"

"Yeah, that's what she told me," I said. "But when I asked her this afternoon, she said she hadn't had any lately." I fetched the pill from my room. "It got stuck in my shoe," I explained, holding it out to her on a fingertip. "Is it the same as what you saw?"

"I didn't actually see the pills, just the bottle," she said, picking it up between thumb and forefinger. "This isn't a headache pill. It's methylphenidate."

I frowned. "Is that meth as in *meth*?" I asked, uneasy now.

"Methylphenidate as in Ritalin," she said. "You know, ADHD? No, you don't. Pardon me for saying so, Val, but you're too old. You grew up before they started trying to cure childhood. At least half the kids I went to school with were on Ritalin or Adderall or whatever."

I was aghast. "Did Mom and Dad—"

"Oh, hell, no." Gloria laughed. "But plenty of kids supplemented their allowance by selling anything they didn't need to kids without prescriptions. They'd buy it to lose weight or study all night before a test, and I heard that a sixth-grader was supplying a couple of teachers." She frowned. "You'd never take this for a headache. It would *give* you one."

"Okay, pointing out the obvious now: Lily Romano isn't a schoolkid. So why would she take it?" I asked.

"Adult ADHD, I guess?"

"Never mind, I think we'd better go back to the home right now and talk to whoever's on duty."

Gloria caught my arm as I stood up. "Okay, but what do we tell them?"

"We'll start with what we know and let them figure it out."

———

Gloria was as surprised as I was to find Jill Franklyn in charge of the graveyard shift. I supposed it figured: unremarkable but competent enough that no one would lose any sleep. Jill Franklyn was a hell of a lot more surprised to see us. We were heading down the main corridor in the residential area toward the nurses' station when a door on the left opened suddenly but very quietly and she stepped into the dim, shadowy hallway. She had her back to us but I knew that thin silhouette and ballerinaesque posture. She paused with her back to us. Gloria and I stopped dead in our tracks and looked at each other. I shrugged, then cleared my throat.

Jill Franklyn whirled and snapped on her flashlight, blinding both of us. "Omigod!" The word came out in a screechy whisper. The light went off again, leaving me and Gloria no less blind as Jill came toward us, her shoes making tiny squeak-squeak-squeak sounds. "What are you two *doing* here at this hour? It must be after midnight. Are you out of your minds?"

"Which question should we answer first?" I gave a nervous laugh and Jill Franklyn shushed me. She herded us down the hall toward the nurses' station, I thought, but before we reached it, she shoved us through a door on the right, hurriedly and with a strength I'd never imagined she had in those skinny ballerina arms. Gloria seemed equally taken aback; she was rubbing her upper arm.

"Sorry about that," Jill Franklyn said, not sounding very apologetic. "If anyone else sees you, they'll call Akintola and we'll all be in trouble. What are you doing here?"

I blinked rapidly, trying to clear my vision, and saw we were in Celeste Akintola's office. Jill Franklyn surprised me by sitting down behind her desk and motioned for us to take the chairs on the other side. Gloria and I traded looks as we sat down; she gave me a *you-first* nod.

Jill Franklyn sat straight up in the high-backed chair, listening to me with a troubled expression, nodding from time to time but saying nothing. I finished and turned to Gloria, who hesitated, waiting for some kind of response, but the nurse remained silent, not even looking at my sister.

Gloria spoke in a small, uncertain voice, occasionally pausing to look at me. Each time I made a small, keep-going gesture. She did, but any confidence she'd had had deserted her, and I had no idea why. Maybe she was having trouble with the whole snitching thing, I thought. Except this wasn't just tattling to teacher—Lily Romano was carrying around more pills than she needed. A *lot* more.

When Gloria was done, I sat forward in my chair and said, "What would happen if someone gave that stuff to a patient here?"

Jill Franklyn finally lifted her gaze to meet mine. "It would depend on the patient," she said, sounding calm and logical, like we were discussing the amount of caffeine in a cup of coffee. "And the dosage. And, of course, what other medications they might be on at the time. Someone taking vasopressin, for example, might be less drowsy. Depending on the dosage. It would probably have to be twenty or thirty milligrams, I think.

"Dementia patients respond best, though. Early dementia, I mean. Dexedrine's a lot better than methylphenidate but you have to work with what you've got." She sighed. "I don't suppose either of you have access to Dexedrine? It's practically impossible to get nowadays."

Gloria and I looked at each other. "Did you hear anything we just told you?" I asked.

Jill Franklyn wrinkled her nose. "Yeah, Lily Romano's screwed. And so am I, right?" She sat forward, putting her arms on the desk. "Or instead of being Girl Scouts, you could be part of advancing medicine and making life better for dementia patients everywhere."

"How?" I asked, wondering why her eyes weren't crazy.

"By going home and catching up on your sleep, and when you get up tomorrow, we'll all just have business as usual. You"—she pointed at Gloria with one hand—"can volunteer as much as you want, whenever you want; I'll get Akintola to sign off on it. I don't see why she wouldn't, considering you're four for five. That was pretty nice, wasn't it—getting to be a hero? Heroine, whatever. It was too bad about Mrs. Boudreau, but that'll happen—every so often, one of them won't come back for you, no matter how healthy they look. And you"—she pointed at me and frowned—"I can't remember what you do, but I remember your mother's always talking about how you never take a vacation. So take one. She won't lose much ground while you're away. Maybe none."

"How many people are in on this?" I asked incredulously.

Jill Franklyn looked up for a moment. "Hard to say. Here, it's just me and Lily."

"Are you saying this is a—a conspiracy?" My sister practically squeaked on the last word.

"What conspiracy?" Jill Franklyn looked at us like we were crazy. "You're on the Internet, does that mean you're in a conspiracy?" She looked from me to Gloria and back again, then stood up abruptly. "I should have known you wouldn't go for it." She began edging toward the door. "You two Girl Scouts're probably like most middle-aged women—not too physical. I know I don't look like much, but I've got nurse muscles—I can lift almost any resident here unassisted. Or subdue them if they get violent. So I'll just fold my tent now and you can call the—"

I never even saw Gloria move. One moment Jill Franklyn was opening the door; I felt something brush past me. A framed picture of Celeste Akintola's children skidded off the top of the desk into my lap. I barely had time to register that Gloria was crouched on the desk before she sprang forward, landing on top of Jill Franklyn as they fell through the open door into the hallway.

The next minute or so was chaos. Jill Franklyn was on her belly, screaming in outrage and calling for help while Gloria sat on her back, holding her arm so that she couldn't move without breaking it. I stood in the doorway, blinking down at them.

"I'm calling the police!" yelled a woman, presumably Deirdre, from the nurses' station.

"Tell them to hurry," Gloria yelled back. "No security guard?"

"Cost-cutting," Jill Franklyn grunted. "See how safe your mother is? No on-site security guard—"

"Shut up," Gloria said and twisted her arm slightly. "I'll show you who's middle-aged, bitch."

Now, I would like to say that Gloria kept Jill Franklyn subdued until the police arrived, and after hearing what we had to tell them, they immediately sent a car to pick up Lily Romano and they were prosecuted and got long prison sentences and so on and so forth. But Deirdre—yes, it was Deirdre—only saw my sister assaulting another nurse and, after summoning more staff via the PA, did something about it. Deirdre was closer to my age but her nurse muscles were more well developed and more experienced. She knocked me flat on my ass when I tried to get in her way. I still might have had a chance, except, of course, we woke everyone up and they all came out to see what was going on.

Except that it wasn't just a lot of half-asleep people opening their doors to see what all the noise was about—it was a lot of very disoriented elderly people who couldn't see or hear properly, all bumping into each other, stepping on me, falling over Gloria and Jill Franklyn, and crying out in pain or panic or both. In all the confusion, Jill Franklyn managed to get away several minutes before the police arrived.

They arrested me and Gloria, of course.

We didn't end up going to jail, but it was a very near thing. Fortunately, Celeste Akintola believed us.

There was little evidence—methylphenidate leaves the body relatively quickly. Metabolizes efficiently was how Celeste Akintola put it, I think. By the time she got a doctor to order blood tests, it was too late. I turned Lily Romano's pill over to the police but I couldn't prove it was hers; when I told the cop taking my statement how I had come by it, she just shook her head. Needless to say, both Lily and Jill were long gone. Celeste Akintola resigned.

I had to take a second mortgage on the house to cover our legal expenses, and yet I still felt funny about telling Gloria that she had to get a job. She started looking, which, in her case, meant uploading her somewhat padded résumé to a few job-hunters' websites and checking her e-mail before she went to see Mom. There was no more volunteering, but she still went to see our mother every day.

Interestingly enough, the firm that owned the nursing home saw fit to give me a nice break on the bill—apparently, their legal department advised that, despite the lack of hard evidence, the disappearance of both alleged wrongdoers might be enough for civil proceedings. I signed all the papers happily, including the confidentiality agreement and the waiver of responsibility (theirs, of course). With a second mortgage to feed, I was short on resources.

The change in Mom was undeniable, though not as dramatic as I'd feared it would be. She complained about not having any energy, of feeling slow. A number of other residents seemed to feel something similar, including some whom I knew weren't dementia patients.

I asked Gloria one night if there were any new heroes or heroines at the home, now that she was a civilian again. She said she hadn't heard anything. "But then, I probably wouldn't," she added. "They replaced most of the staff and all the volunteers. I'm out of the loop."

Gloria found a health club that needed an aqua-aerobics teacher, but still found a way to squeeze in a visit to Mom almost daily. Apparently aerobics in water was less exhausting than the dry-land variety. Or maybe exercise really was energizing—I didn't remember being able to maintain such a high level of activity in my late thirties.

And even then, it was six months after the fact before I really began to wonder. Mom's decline had come to another of its periodic plateaus, but she was still having slightly more good days than bad, or so I thought. Or so I wanted to think. And then I finally started thinking about Gloria and her energetic lifestyle.

It was a stupid idea, I decided, which was why it hadn't occurred to me before. But still, a small voice in my mind insisted that it actually had occurred to me and I'd deliberately refused to consider it. So it had simmered on the back-most of back burners in the back-most area of my mind until I was ready to jump at shadows.

Which made me think of how Gloria had leaped up onto Celeste Akintola's desk and from there across half the room to land on Jill Franklyn. With my own eyes, I'd seen her sitting on Jill Franklyn's back with her arm in a bone-breaker hold. We had both suffered through everything that followed. How could I think that Gloria would go through all of that with me only to turn around and do the same thing?

Not *the same,* nagged that mental voice. *Gloria's messiah complex is strictly limited—just her and Mom, no one else, not even you. Not yet anyway.*

The only way to kill shadows was to turn on all the lights. I got as far as opening the door to her room, but I couldn't go any farther. I'm not sure what I was more afraid of—that I *would* find Ritalin or Adderall or even Dexedrine, or that I wouldn't. If I did, I'd know what to do—I just didn't know if I could.

But if I didn't, no one would ever have to know . . . except *me,* of course. Because that's what I would find instead. I decided I would rather wonder about my sister than know for sure about myself, and closed the door.

It's been the same every night since for the past year and a half. Intellectually, I know I might as well stop, because I'm not going to do anything different. But on a gut level, I don't dare. I'm afraid of what could happen if I don't stand there and deliberately choose not to be a bad, sneaky, dangerous woman.

Cecelia Holland

Cecelia Holland is one of the world's most highly acclaimed and respected historical novelists, ranked by many alongside other giants in that field such as Mary Renault and Larry McMurtry. Over the span of her thirty-year career, she's written more than thirty historical novels, including *The Firedrake, Rakóssy, Two Ravens, Ghost on the Steppe, The Death of Attila, Hammer for Princes, The King's Road, Pillar of the Sky, The Lords of Vaumartin, Pacific Street, The Sea Beggars, The Earl, The Kings in Winter, The Belt of Gold*, and more than a dozen others. She also wrote the well-known science fiction novel *Floating Worlds*, which was nominated for a Locus Award in 1975, and of late has been working on a series of fantasy novels, including *The Soul Thief, The Witches' Kitchen, The Serpent Dreamer, Varanger*, and *The King's Witch*. Her most recent books are the novels *The High City, Kings of the North*, and *The Secret Eleanor*.

In the high drama that follows, she introduces us to the ultimate dysfunctional family, whose ruthless, clashing ambitions threw England into bloody civil war again and again over many long years: King Henry II, his queen, Eleanor of Aquitaine, and their eight squabbling children. All deadly as cobras. Even the littlest one.

NORA'S SONG

Nora looked quickly around, saw no one was watching, and slipped away between the trees and down the bank to the little stream. She knew there would be no frogs to hunt; her brother had told her that when the trees had no leaves, the streams had no frogs. But the water glittered over bright stones and she saw tracks printed into the damp sand. She squatted down to pick a shiny bit from the stream. It wouldn't be pretty when it dried out. Behind her, her little sister Johanna slid down the bank in a rush.

"Nora! What do you have?"

She held out the pebble to her sister and went on a little way along the trickle of water. Those tracks were bird feet, like crosses in the damp sand. She squatted down again, to poke at the rocks, and then saw, in the yellow gritty stream bank, like a little round doorway, a hole.

She brushed aside a veil of hairy roots, trying to see in; did something live there? She could reach her hand in to find out, and in a quick tumble of her thoughts she imagined something furry, something furry with teeth, the teeth snapping on her hand, and tucked her fist against her skirt.

From up past the trees, a voice called, "Nora?"

That was her new nurse. She paid no attention, looking for a stick to probe the hole with; Johanna, beside her, went softly, "Ooooh," and on all fours leaned toward the burrow. Her skirt was soaked from the stream.

"Nora!" Another voice.

She leapt up. "Richard," she said, and scrambled up the bank, nearly losing a shoe. On the grassy edge, she pulled the shoe back on, turned and helped Johanna up behind her, and ran out through the bare trees, onto the broad open ground.

Her brother was striding toward her, smiling, his arms out, and she ran to him. She had not seen him since Christmas, the last time they had all been together. He was twelve years old, a lot older than she was, almost grown up. He bundled her into his arms and hugged her. He smelled like horses. Johanna came whooping up and he hugged her too. The two nurses, red in the face, were panting along behind them, their skirts clutched up in their hands. Richard straightened, his blue eyes blazing, and pointed across the field.

"See? Where Mother comes."

Nora shaded her eyes, looking out across the broad field. At first she saw only the crowded people, stirring and swaying all around the edges of the field, but then a murmur swept through them, and on all sides rose into a roar. Far down there, a horse loped up onto the field and stopped, and the rider raised one hand in salute.

"Mama!" Johanna cried, and clapped.

Now the whole crowd was yelling and cheering, and, on her dark grey horse, Nora's Mama was cantering along the sideline, toward the wooden stand under the plane trees, where they would all sit. Nora swelled, full to bursting; she yelled, "Hooray! Hooray, Mama!"

Up there, by the stand, a dozen men on foot went forward to meet the woman on the horse. She wheeled in among them, cast her reins down, and dismounted. Swiftly she climbed onto the platform, where two chairs waited, and stood there, and lifted her arm, turning slowly from one side to the other to greet the cheering crowd. She stood straight as a tree, her skirts furling around her.

Above the stand, suddenly, her pennant flapped open like a great wing, the Eagle of Aquitaine, and the thunderous shouting doubled.

"Eleanor! Eleanor!"

She gave one last wave to the crowd, but she had seen her children running toward her, and all her interest turned to them. She stooped, holding her arms out toward them, and Richard scooped Johanna into his arms and ran toward the platform. Nora went up the steps at the side. Coming to the front, Richard set Johanna at their mother's feet.

Their mother's hands fell on them. Nora buried her face in the Queen's skirts.

"Mama."

"Ah." Their mother sat down, holding Johanna slightly away from her;

she slid her free arm around Nora's waist. "Ah, my dear ones. How I've missed you." She kissed them both rapidly, several times. "Johanna, you're drenched. This won't do." She beckoned, and Johanna's nurse came running. Johanna squealed but was taken.

Still holding Nora against her, Eleanor leaned forward and leveled her gaze on Richard, leaning with his arms folded on the edge of the platform in front of her.

"Well, my son, are you excited?"

He pushed away from the platform, standing taller, his face flaming, his fair hair a wild tangle from the wind. "Mother, I can't wait! When will Papa get here?"

Nora leaned on her mother. She loved Richard too, but she wished her mother would pay more heed to her. Her mother was beautiful, even though she was really old. She wore no coif, only a heavy gold ring upon her sleek red hair. Nora's hair was like old dead grass. She would never be beautiful. The Queen's arm tightened around her, but she was still tilted forward toward Richard, fixed utterly on Richard.

"He's coming. You should get ready for the ceremony." She touched the front of his coat, lifted her hand to his cheek. "Comb your hair, anyway."

He jiggled up and down, vivid. "I can't wait. I can't wait. I'm going to be Duke of Aquitaine!"

The Queen laughed. A horn blew, down the pitch. "See, now it begins. Go find your coat." She turned, beckoned to a page. "Attend the Lord Richard. Nora, now . . ." She nudged Nora back a step so that she could run her gaze over her from head to toe. Her lips curved upward and her eyes glinted. "What have you been doing, rolling in the grass? You're my big girl now; you have to be presentable."

"Mama." Nora didn't want to be the big girl. The idea reminded her that Mattie was gone, the real big girl. But she loved having her mother's attention, she cast wildly around for something to say to keep it. "Does that mean I can't play anymore?"

Eleanor laughed and hugged her again. "You will always be able to play, my girl. Just different games." Her lips brushed Nora's forehead. Nora realized she had said the right thing. Then Eleanor was turning away.

"See, here your father comes."

A ripple of excitement rose through the crowd like the wind in a dry field, turned to a rumble, and erupted into a thunderous cheer. Down the pitch came a column of riders. Nora straightened, clapping her hands together, and drew in a deep breath and held it. In the center of the horsemen, her father rode along, wearing neither crown nor royal robes, and yet it seemed that everything bowed and bent around him, as if nobody else mattered but him.

"Papa."

"Yes," Eleanor said, under her breath. "The kingly Papa." She drew her arm from Nora and sat straighter on her chair.

Nora drew back; if she got behind them, out of sight, they might forget her, and she could stay. Richard had not gone away, either, she saw, but lingered at the front of the royal stand. Her father rode up and swung directly from his saddle to the platform. He was smiling, his eyes narrow, his clothes rumpled, his beard and hair shaggy. He seemed to her like the king of the greenwood, wild and fierce, wreathed in leaves and bark. All along this side of the field, on either side of the booth, his knights rode up in a single rank, stirrup to stirrup, facing the French across the field. The king stood, throwing a quick glance that way, and then lowered his gaze to Richard, standing stiff and tall before him.

"Well, sirrah," their father said, "are you ready to shiver a lance here?"

"Oh, Papa!" Richard bounced up and down. "Can I?"

Their father barked a laugh at him, looking down on him from the height of the booth. "Not until you can pay your own ransoms when you lose."

Richard flushed pink, like a girl. "I won't lose!"

"No, of course not." The King waved him off. "Nobody ever thinks he'll lose, sirrah." He laughed again, scornful, turning away. "When you're older."

Nora bit her lip. It was mean to talk to Richard that way, and her brother drooped, kicked the ground, and then followed the page down the field. Suddenly he was just a boy again. Nora crouched down behind her mother's skirts, hoping her father did not notice her. He settled himself in the chair beside the Queen's, stretched his legs out, and for the first time turned toward Eleanor.

"You look amazingly well, considering. I'm surprised your old bones made it all the way from Poitiers."

"I would not miss this," she said. "And it's a pleasant enough ride." They didn't touch, they didn't give each other kisses, and Nora felt a little stir of worry. Her nurse had come up to the edge of the platform and Nora shrank deeper into Eleanor's shadow. Eleanor paid the king a long stare. Her attention drifted toward his front.

"Eggs for breakfast? Or was that last night's supper?"

Startled, Nora craned up a little to peer at him: his clothes were messy but she saw no yellow egg. Her father was glaring back at her mother, his face flattened with temper. He did not look down at his coat. "What a prissy old woman you are."

Nora ran her tongue over her lower lip. Her insides felt full of prickers and burrs. Her mother's hand lay on her thigh, and Nora saw how her mother was smoothing her skirt, over and over, with hard, swift, clawing fingers.

Her nurse said, "Lady Nora, come along now."

"You didn't bring your truelove," the Queen said.

The King leaned toward her a little, as if he would leap on her, pound her, maybe, with his fist. "She's afraid of you. She won't come anywhere near you."

Eleanor laughed. She was not afraid of him. Nora wondered what that was about; wasn't her mother the King's truelove? She pretended not to see her nurse beckoning her.

"Nora, come now!" the nurse said, loudly.

That caught her mother's attention, and she swung around, saw Nora there, and said, "Go on, my girl. Go get ready." Her hand dropped lightly to Nora's shoulder. "Do as you're bid, please." Nora slid off the edge of the platform and went away to be dressed and primped.

Her old nurse had gone with Mattie when Nora's big sister went to marry the Duke of Germany. Now she had this new nurse, who couldn't brush hair without hurting. They had already laced Johanna into a fresh gown, and braided her hair, and the others were waiting outside the little tent. Nora kept thinking of Mattie, who had told her stories, and sung to her when she had nightmares. Now they were all walking out onto the field for the ceremony, her brothers first, and then her and Johanna.

Johanna slipped her hand into Nora's, and Nora squeezed her fingers tight. All these people made her feel small. Out in the middle of the field everybody stood in rows, as if they were in church, and the ordinary people were all gathered closely around, to hear what went on. On either side banners hung, and a herald stood in front of them all, watching the children approach, his long shiny horn tipped down.

On big chairs in the very middle sat her father and mother and, beside them, a pale, weary-looking man in a blue velvet gown. He had a little stool for his feet. She knew that was the King of France. She and her sister and brothers went up before them, side by side, and the herald said their names, and as one they bowed, first to their parents and then to the French king.

There were only five of them now, with Mattie gone, and their baby brother still in the monastery. Henry was oldest. They called him Boy Henry because Papa's name also was Henry. Then there was Richard, and then Geoffrey. Mattie would have been between Boy Henry and Richard. After Geoffrey was Nora, and Johanna, and, back with the monks, baby John. The crowd whooped and yelled at them, and Richard suddenly raised his arm up over his head like an answer.

Then they were all shuffled around into the crowd behind their parents, where they stood in line again. The heralds were yelling in Latin. Johanna leaned on Nora's side. "I'm hungry."

Two steps in front of them on her chair, Eleanor glanced over her shoulder, and Nora whispered, "Ssssh." All the people around them were men, but behind the King of France a girl stood, who looked a little older than Nora, and now Nora caught her looking back. Nora smiled, uncertain, but the other girl only lowered her eyes.

A blast of the horn lifted her half off the ground. Johanna clutched her hand. One of Papa's men came up and began to read from a scroll, Latin again, simpler than the Latin the monks had taught her. What he read was all about Boy Henry, how noble, how good, and, at a signal, her oldest brother went up before the two kings and the Queen. He was tall and thin, with many freckles, his face sunburnt. Nora liked the dark green of the coat he wore. He knelt before his father and the French king, and the heralds spoke and the kings spoke.

They were making Boy Henry a King too. He would be King of England now, just as Papa was. In her mind suddenly she saw both Henrys trying to jam together into one chair, with one crown wrapped around their two heads, and she laughed. Her mother looked over her shoulder again, her eyes sharp and her dark brows drawn into a frown.

Johanna was shuffling from one foot to the other. Louder than before, she said, "I'm hungry."

"Sssh!"

Boy Henry got up from his knees, bowed, and came back around among the children. The herald said Richard's name and he sprang forward. They were proclaiming him Duke of Aquitaine. He would marry the daughter of the French king, Alais. Nora's eyes turned again toward the strange girl among the French. That was Alais. She had long brown hair and a sharp little nose; she was staring intently at Richard. Nora wondered what it felt like, looking for the first time on the man you knew you would marry. She imagined Alais kissing Richard and made a face.

In front of her, sitting stiff on her chair, the Queen pulled her mouth down at the corners. Her mother didn't like this, either.

Until she was old enough to marry Richard, Alais would live with them, his family. Nora felt a stir of unease: here was Alais come into a strange place, as Mattie was gone off into a strange place, and they would never see her again. She remembered how Mattie had cried when they told her. But Mama, he's so *old*. Nora pressed her lips together, her eyes stinging.

Not to her. This wouldn't happen to her. She wouldn't be sent away. Given away. She wanted something else, but she didn't know what. She had thought of being a nun, but there was so little to do.

Richard knelt and put his hands between the long, bony hands of the King of France, and rose, his head tipped forward as if he already wore a coronet. He was smiling wide as the sun. He moved back to the family and the herald spoke Geoffrey's name, who was now to be Duke of Brittany, and marry some other stranger.

Nora hunched her shoulders. This glory would never come to her, she would get nothing, just stand and watch. She glanced again at the Princess Alais and saw her looking down at her hands, sad.

Johanna suddenly yawned, pulled her hand out of Nora's, and sat down.

Now up before them all came somebody else, his hands wide, and a big, strong voice said, "My lord of England, as we have agreed, I ask you now to receive the Archbishop of Canterbury, and let you be restored to friendship, end the quarrel between you, for the good of both our kingdoms, and Holy Mother Church."

The crowd around them gave up a sudden yell, and a man came up the field toward the kings. He wore a long black cloak over a white habit with a cross hanging on his chest. The stick in his hand had a swirly top. A great cry went up from the people around them, excited. Behind her, somebody murmured, "Becket again. The man won't go away."

She knew this name, but she could not remember who Becket was. He paced up toward them, a long, gaunt man, his clothes shabby. He looked like an ordinary man but he walked like a lord. Everybody watched him. As he came up before her father, the crowd's rumbling and stirring died away into a breathless hush. In front of the King, the gaunt man knelt, set his stick down, and then lay on the ground, spreading himself like a mat upon the floor. Nora shifted a little so she could see him through the space between her mother and her father. The crowd drew in closer, leaning out to see.

"My gracious lord," he said in a churchy voice, "I beg your forgiveness for all my errors. Never was a prince more faithful than you, and never a subject more faithless than I, and I am come asking pardon not from hopes of my virtue but of yours."

Her father stood up. He looked suddenly very happy, his face flushed, his eyes bright. Face to the ground, the gaunt man spoke on, humble, beseeching, and the King went down toward him, reaching out his hands to lift him up.

Then Becket said, "I submit myself to you, my lord, henceforth and for-ever, in all things, save the honor of God."

The Queen's head snapped up. Behind Nora somebody gasped, and some-body else muttered, "Damn fool." In front of them all, halfway to Becket, his hands out, Papa stopped. A kind of pulse went through the crowd.

The King said sharply, "What is this?"

Becket was rising. Dirt smeared his robe where his knees had pressed the ground. He stood straight, his head back. "I cannot give up the rights of God, my lord, but in everything else—"

Her Papa lunged at him. "This is not what I agreed to."

Becket held his ground, tall as a steeple, as if he had God on his shoulder, and proclaimed again, "I must champion the honor of the Lord of Heaven and earth."

"*I* am your Lord!" The King wasn't happy anymore. His voice boomed across the field. Nobody else moved or spoke. He took a step toward Becket, and his fist clenched. "The kingdom is *mine*. No other authority shall rule there! God or no, kneel, Thomas, give yourself wholly to me, or go away a ruined man!"

Louis was scurrying down from the dais toward them, his frantic mur-muring unheeded. Becket stood immobile. "I am consecrated to God. I cannot wash away that duty."

Nora's father roared, "I am King, and no other, you toad, you jackass, no other than me! You owe everything to me! *Me!*"

"Papa! My lord—" Boy Henry started forward and their mother reached out and grabbed his arm and held him still. From the crowd, other voices rose. Nora stooped and tried to make Johanna stand up.

"I won't be disparaged! Honor *me,* and me alone!" Her father's voice was like a blaring horn, and the crowd fell quiet again. The King of France put one hand on her Papa's arm and mouthed something, and Papa wheeled around and cast off his touch.

"Henceforth, whatever comes that he chooses not to abide, he will call it the Honor of God. You must see this! He has given up nothing; he will pay me no respect—not even the respect of a swine for the swineherd!"

The crowd gave a yell. A voice called, "God bless the King!" Nora looked around, uneasy. The people behind her were shuffling around, drawing back, like running away slowly. Eleanor was still holding fast to Boy Henry, but now he whimpered under his breath. Richard was stiff, his whole body tipped forward, his jaw jutting like a fish's. The French king had Becket by the sleeve, was drawing him off, talking urgently into his ear. Becket's gaze never left Nora's father. His voice rang out like the archangel's trumpet.

"I am bound to the Honor of God!"

In the middle of them all, Nora's father flung up his arms as if he would take flight; he stamped his foot as if he would split the earth, and shouted, "Get him out of here before I kill him! God's Honor! God's round white backside! Get him away, get him gone!"

His rage blew back the crowd. In a sudden rush of feet, the French king and his guards and attendants bundled Thomas away. Nora's father was roaring again, oaths and threats, his arms pumping, his face red as raw meat. Boy Henry burst out of Eleanor's grasp and charged him.

"My lord—"

The King spun around toward him, his arm outstretched, and knocked him down with the back of his hand. "Stay out of this!"

Nora jumped. Even before Richard and Geoffrey started forward, Eleanor was moving; she reached Boy Henry in a few strides, and as he leapt to his feet, she hurried him off. A crowd of her retainers bustled after her.

Nora stood fast. She realized that she was holding her breath. Johanna had finally gotten up and wrapped her arms around Nora's waist, and Nora put her arms around her sister. Geoffrey was running after the Queen;

Richard paused, his hands at his sides, watching the King's temper blaze. He pivoted and ran off after his mother. Nora gasped. She and Johanna were alone, in the middle of the field, the crowd far off.

The King saw them. He quieted. He looked around, saw no one else, and stalked toward them.

"Go on—run! Everybody else is abandoning me. Run! Are you stupid?" Johanna shrank around behind Nora, who stood straight and tucked her hands behind her, the way she stood when priests talked to her. "No, Papa."

His face was red as meat. Fine sweat stood on his forehead. His breath almost made her gag. He looked her over and said, "Here to scold me, then, like your rotten mother?"

"No, Papa," she said, surprised. "You are the King."

He twitched. The high color left his face like a tide. His voice smoothed out, slower. He said, "Well, one of you is true, at least." He turned and walked off, and as he went, he lifted one arm. From all sides his men came running. One led Papa's big black horse and he mounted. Above all the men on foot surrounding him, he left the field. After he was gone, Richard trotted up across the grass to gather in Nora and Johanna.

"Why can't I—"

"Because I know you," Richard said. "If I let you run around, you'll get in trouble." He lifted her up into the cart, where already Johanna and the French girl sat. Nora plunked down, angry; they were only going up the hill. He could have let her ride his horse. With a crack of the whip, the cart began to roll, and she leaned back against the side and stared away.

Beside Nora, Alais said, suddenly, in French, "I know who you are."

Nora faced her, startled. "I know who you are too," she said.

"Your name is Eleonora and you're the second sister. I can speak French and Latin and I can read. Can you read?"

Nora said, "Yes. They make me read all the time."

Alais gave a glance over her shoulder; their attendants were walking along behind the cart, but nobody close enough to hear. Johanna was standing up in the back corner, throwing bits of straw over the side and leaning out to see where they fell. Alais said quietly, "We should be friends, because we're going to be sisters and we're almost the same age." Her gaze ran thoughtfully over Nora from head to toe, which made Nora uncomfortable; she squirmed. She thought briefly, angrily, of this girl taking Mattie's place. Alais said, "I'll be nice to you if you're nice to me."

Nora said, "All right. I—"

"But I go first, I think, because I am older."

Nora stiffened and then jumped as a cheer erupted around her. The cart was rolling up the street toward the castle on the hill, and all along the way, crowds of people stood screaming and calling. Not for her, not for Alais; it was Richard's name they shouted, over and over. Richard rode along before them, bareheaded, paying no heed to the cheers.

Alais turned to her again. "Where do you live?"

Nora said, "Well, sometimes in Poitiers, but—"

"My father says your father has everything, money and jewels and silks and sunlight, but all we have in France is piety and kindness."

Nora started. "We are kind." But she was pleased that Alais saw how great her father was. "And pious too."

The sharp little face of the French princess turned away, drawn, and for the first time her voice was uncertain. "I hope so."

Nora's heart thumped, unsteady with sympathy. Johanna was scrabbling around on the floor of the cart for more things to cast out, and Nora found a little cluster of pebbles in the corner and held them out to her. On Nora's other side, Alais was staring down at her hands now, her shoulders round, and Nora wondered if she were about to cry. She might cry, if this happened to her.

She edged closer, until she brushed against the other girl. Alais jerked her head up, her eyes wide, startled. Nora smiled at her, and between them their hands crept together and entwined.

They did not go all the way up to the castle. The cheering crowd saw them along the street and onto a pavement, with a church on one side, where the cart turned in the opposite direction from the church and went down another street and through a wooden gate. Over them now a house loomed, with wooden walls, two rows of windows, a heavy overhang of roof. Here the cart stopped and they all got out. Richard herded them along through the wide front door.

"Mama is upstairs," he said.

They had come into a dark hall, full of servants and baggage. A servant led Alais away. Nora climbed the steep, uneven stairs, tugging Johanna along by the hand. Johanna was still hungry and said so every step. At the top of the stairs was one room on one side and another on the other side, and Nora heard her mother's voice.

"Not yet," the Queen was saying; Nora went into the big room and saw her mother and Boy Henry at the far side; the Queen had her hand on his arm. "The time is not yet. Don't be precipitous. We must seem to be loyal." She saw the girls, and a smile twitched over her face like a mask. "Come, girls!" But her hand on Boy Henry's arm gave him a push away. "Go," she said to him. "He will send for you; better you not be here. Take Geoffrey with you." Boy Henry turned on his heel and went out.

Nora wondered what "precipitous" meant; briefly she imagined a cliff, and people falling off. She went up to her mother and Eleanor hugged her.

"I'm sorry," her mama said. "I'm sorry about your father."

"Mama."

"Don't be afraid of him." The Queen took Johanna's hands and spoke from one to the other. "I'll protect you."

"I'm not—"

Her mother's gaze lifted, aimed over Nora's head. "What is it?"

"The King wants to see me," Richard said, behind Nora. She felt his hand drop onto her shoulder.

"Just you?"

"No, Boy and Geoffrey too. Where are they?"

Nora's mother shrugged, her whole body moving, shoulders, head, hands. "I have no notion," she said. "You should go, though."

"Yes, Mama." Richard squeezed Nora's shoulder and he went away.

"Very well." Eleanor sat back, still holding Johanna by one hand. "Now, my girls." Nora frowned, puzzled; her mother did know where her other brothers were, she had just sent them out. Her mother turned to her again. "Don't be afraid."

"Mama, I'm not afraid." But then she thought, somehow, that her mother wanted her to be.

Johanna was already asleep, curled heavy against Nora's back. Nora cradled her head on her arm, not sleepy at all. She was thinking about the day, about her splendid father and her beautiful mother, and how her family ruled everything, and she was one of them. She imagined herself on a big horse, galloping, and everybody cheering her name. Carrying a lance with a pennon on the tip, and fighting for the glory of something. Or to save somebody. Something proud, but virtuous. She caught herself rocking back and forth on her imaginary horse.

A candle at the far end cast a sort of twilight through the long narrow room; she could see the planks of the wall opposite and hear the rumbling snore of the woman asleep by the door. The other servants had gone down to the hall. She wondered what happened there that they all wanted to go. Then, to her surprise, someone hurried through the dark and knelt by her bed.

"Nora?"

It was Alais. Nora pushed herself up, startled, but even as she moved, Alais was crawling into the bed.

"Let me in, please. Please, Nora. They made me sleep alone."

She could not move to make room because of Johanna, but she said anyway, "All right." She didn't like sleeping alone, either: it got cold, sometimes, and lonely. She pulled the cover back, and Alais crept into the space beside her.

"This is an ugly place. I thought you all lived in beautiful places."

Nora said, "We don't live here." She snuggled back against Johanna, and without waking, her little sister murmured and shifted away, giving her more room, but Alais was still jammed up against her. She could smell the French girl's breath, meaty and sour. Rigid, she lay there wide awake. She would never fall asleep now.

Alais snuggled into the mattress; the ropes underneath creaked. In a whisper she said, "Do you have boobies yet?"

Nora twitched. "What?" She didn't know what Alais meant.

"Bumps, silly." Alais shifted, pulling on the covers, banging into her. "Breastses. Like this." Her hand closed on Nora's wrist and she pulled, brushing Nora's hand against Alais' chest. For an instant, Nora felt a soft roundness under her fingers.

"No." She tried to draw her hand out of Alais' grip, but Alais had her fast.

"You're just a baby."

Nora got her hand free, and squirmed fiercely against Johanna, trying to get more room. "I'm a big girl!" *Johanna* was the baby. She struggled to get back the feeling of galloping on the big horse, of glory, pride, and greatness. She blurted out, "Someday I'm going to be king."

Alais hooted. "Girls aren't kings, silly! Girls are only women."

"I mean, like my mother. My mother is as high as a king."

"Your mother is wicked."

Nora pushed away, angry. "My mother is *not*—"

"Sssh. You'll wake everybody up. I'm sorry. I'm sorry. It's just everybody says so. I didn't mean it. You aren't a baby." Alais touched her, pleading. "Are you still my friend?"

Nora thought the whole matter of being friends to be harder than she had expected. Surreptitiously, she pressed her palm against her own bony chest.

Alais snuggled in beside her. "If we're to be friends, we have to stay close together. Where are we going next?"

Nora pulled the cover around her, the thickness of cloth between her and Alais. "I hope to Poitiers, with Mama. I hope I will go there, the happiest court in the whole world." In a flash of temper she blurted out, "Any place would be better than Fontrevault. My knees are so sore."

Alais laughed. "A convent? They put me in convents. They even made me wear nun clothes."

Nora said, "Oh, I hate that! They're so scratchy."

"And they smell."

"*Nuns* smell," Nora said. She remembered something her mother said. "Like old eggs."

Alais giggled. "You're funny, Nora. I like you a lot."

"Well, you have to like my mother too, if you want to go to Poitiers."

Again, Alais' hand came up and touched Nora, stroking her. "I will. I promise."

Nora cradled her head on her arm, pleased, and drowsy. Maybe Alais was not so bad after all. She was a helpless maiden, and Nora could defend her, like a real knight. Her eyelids drooped; for an instant, before she fell asleep, she felt the horse under her again, galloping.

Nora had saved bread crumbs from her breakfast; she was scattering them on the windowsill when the nurse called. She kept on scattering. The little birds were hungry in the winter. The nurse grabbed her by the arm and towed her away.

"Come here when I call you!" The nurse briskly stuffed her headfirst into a gown. Nora struggled up through the mass of cloth until she got her head out. "Now sit down so I can brush your hair."

Nora sat; she looked toward the window again, and the nurse pinched her arm. "Sit still!"

She bit her lips together, angry and sad. She wished the nurse off to Germany. Hunched on the stool, she tried to see the window through the corner of her eye.

The brush dragged through her hair. "How do you get your hair so snarled?"

"Ooow!" Nora twisted away from the pull of the brush, and the nurse wrestled her back onto the stool.

"Sit! This child is a devil." The brush smacked her hard on the shoulder. "Wait until we get you back to the convent, little devil."

Nora stiffened all over. On the next stool, Alais turned suddenly toward her, wide-eyed. Nora slid off the stool.

"I'm going to find my Mama!" She started toward the door. The nurse snatched at her and she sidestepped out of reach and moved faster.

"Come back here!"

"I'm going to find my Mama," Nora said, and gave the nurse a hard look, and pulled the door open.

"Wait for me," said Alais.

The servingwomen came after them; Nora went on down the stairs, hurrying, just out of reach. She hoped her Mama was down in the hall. On the stairs, she slipped by some servants coming up from below and they got in the nurses' way and held them back. Alais was right behind her, wild-eyed.

"Is this all right? Nora?"

"Come on." Gratefully she saw that the hall was full of people; that meant her mother was there, and she went in past men in long stately robes, standing around waiting, and pushed in past them all the way up to the front.

There her mother sat, and Richard also, standing beside her; the Queen was reading a letter. A strange man stood humbly before her, his hands clasped, while she read. Nora went by him.

"Mama."

Eleanor lifted her head, her brows arched. "What are you doing here?" She looked past Nora and Alais, into the crowd, brought her gaze back to Nora, and said, "Come sit down and wait; I'm busy." She went back to the letter in her hand. Richard gave Nora a quick, cheerful grin. She went on past him, behind her Mama's chair, and turned toward the room. The nurses were squeezing in past the crowd of courtiers, but they could not reach her now. Alais leaned against her, pale, her eyes blinking.

In front of them, her back to them, Eleanor in her heavy chair laid the letter aside. "I'll give it thought."

"Your Grace." The humble man bowed and backed away. Another, in a red coat, stepped forward, a letter in his hand. Reaching for it, the Queen glanced at Richard beside her.

"Why did your father want to see you last night?"

Alais whispered, "What are you going to do?" Nora bumped her with her elbow; she wanted to listen to her brother.

Richard was saying, "He asked me where Boy was." He shifted his weight from foot to foot. "He was drunk."

The Queen was reading the new letter. She turned toward the table on her other hand, picked up a quill, and dipped it into the pot of ink. "You should sign this also, since you are Duke now."

At that, Richard puffed up, making himself bigger, and his shoulders straightened. The Queen turned toward Nora.

"What is this now?"

"Mama." Nora went up closer to the Queen. "Where are we going? After here."

Her mother's green eyes regarded her; a little smile curved her lips. "Well, to Poitiers, I thought."

"I want to go to Poitiers."

"Well, of course," her Mama said.

"And Alais too?"

The Queen's eyes shifted toward Alais, back by the wall. The smile flattened out. "Yes, of course. Good day, Princess Alais."

"Good day, your Grace." Alais dipped into a little bow. "Thank you, your Grace." She turned a bright happy look at Nora, who cast her a broad look of triumph. She looked up at her mother, glad of her, who could do anything.

"You said you'd protect us, remember?"

The Queen's smile widened, and her head tipped slightly to one side. "Yes, of course. I'm your mother."

"And Alais too?"

Now the Queen actually laughed. "Nora, you will be dangerous when you're older. Yes, Alais too, of course."

On the other side of the chair, Richard straightened from writing, and Eleanor took the letter from him and the quill also. Nora lingered where she was, in the middle of everything, wanting her mother to notice her again. Richard said, "If I'm really Duke, do I give orders?"

The Queen's smile returned; she looked at him the way she looked at no one else. "Of course. Since you are Duke now." She seemed to be about to laugh again; Nora wondered what her Mama thought was funny. Eleanor laid the letter on the table and the quill jigged busily across it.

"I want to be knighted," her brother said. "And I want a new sword."

"As you will, your Grace," her mother said, still with that little laugh in her voice, and gave him a slow nod of her head, like bowing. She handed the letter back to the man in the red coat. "You may begin this at once."

"God's blessing on your Grace. Thank you." The man bobbed up and down like a duck. Someone else was coming forward, another paper in his hand. Nora bounced on her toes, not wanting to go; the nurses were still waiting, standing grimly to the side, their eyes fixed on the girls as if a stare could pull them within reach. She wished her mother would look at her, talk to her again. Then, at the back of the hall, a hard, loud voice rose.

"Way for the King of England!"

Eleanor sat straight up, and Richard swung back to his place by her side. The whole room was suddenly moving, shifting, men shuffling out of the way, flexing and bending, and up through the suddenly empty space came Nora's Papa. Nora went quickly back behind the Queen's chair to Alais, standing there by the wall.

Only the Queen stayed in her chair, the smile gone now. Everybody else was bent down over his shoes. The King strode up before Eleanor, and behind him the hall quickly emptied. Even the nurses went out. Two of her father's men stood on either side of the door, like guards.

"My lord," the Queen said, "you should send ahead; we would be more ready for you."

Nora's Papa stood looking down at her. He wore the same clothes he had the day before. His big hands rested on his belt. His voice grated, like walking on gravel. "I thought I might see more if I came unannounced. Where are the boys?" His gaze flicked toward Richard. "The other boys."

The Queen shrugged. "Will you sit, my lord?" A servant hurried up with a chair for him. "Bring my lord the King a cup of wine."

The King flung himself into the chair. "Don't think I don't know what you're doing." His head turned; he had seen Nora, just behind the Queen, and his eyes prodded at her. Nora twitched, uncomfortable.

"My lord," Eleanor said, "I am uncertain what you mean."

"You're such a bad liar, Eleanor." The King twisted in the chair, caught Nora by the hand, and dragged her up between their two chairs, in front of them both. "This little girl, now, she spoke very well yesterday, when the rest of you ran off. I think she tells the truth."

Standing in front of them, Nora slid her hands behind her back. Her mouth was dry and she swallowed once. Her mother smiled at her. "Nora has a mind. Greet your father, dear."

Nora said, "God be with you, Papa."

He stared at her. Around the black centers, his eyes were blue like plates of sky. One hand rose and picked delicately at the front of her dress. Inside the case of cloth, her body shrank away from his touch. He smoothed the front of her dress. Her mother was twisted in her chair to watch. Behind her, Richard stood, his face gripped in a frown.

"So. Just out of the convent, are you? Like it there?"

She wondered what she was supposed to say. Instead, she said the truth. "No, Papa."

He laughed. The black holes got bigger and then smaller. "What, you don't want to be a nun?"

"No, Papa, I want—" To her surprise, the story had changed. She found a sudden, eager courage. "I want to be a hero."

Eleanor gave a little chuckle, and the King snorted. "Well, God gave you the wrong stature." His gaze went beyond her. "Where are you going?"

"Nowhere, my lord," Richard said in a cool voice.

The King laughed again, so that his teeth showed. He smelled sour, like old beer and dirty clothes. His eyes watched Nora, but he spoke to her mother.

"I want to see my sons."

"They are alarmed," the Queen said, "because of what happened with Becket."

"I'll deal with Becket. Keep out of that." The servant came with the cup of wine and he took it. Nora shifted her feet, wanting to get away from them, the edges of their words like knives in the air.

"Yes, well, how you deal with Becket is getting us all into some strange places," her mother said.

"God's death!" He lifted the cup and drained it. "I never knew he had such a hunger for martyrdom. You saw him. He looks like an old man already. This is a caution against virtue, if it turns you into such a stork."

Her mother looked off across the room. "No, you are right. It does no service to your justice when half the men in the kingdom can go around you."

He twisted toward her, his face clenched. "Nobody goes around me."

"Well," she said, and faced him, her mouth smiling, but not in a good way. "It seems they do."

"Mama," Nora said, remembering how to do this. "With your leave—"

"Stay," her father said, and, reaching out, took her arm and dragged her forward, into his lap.

"Nora," her mother said. Beyond her, Richard took a step forward, his eyes wide. Nora squirmed, trying to get upright on her father's knees; his arms surrounded her like a cage. The look on her mother's face scared her. She tried to wiggle free, and his arms closed around her.

"Mama—"

The Queen said, her voice suddenly harsh, "Let go of her, sir."

"What?" the King said, with a little laugh. "Aren't you my sweetheart, Nora?" He planted a kiss on Nora's cheek. His arms draped around Nora; one hand stroked her arm. "I want my sons. Get my sons back here, woman." Abruptly, he was thrusting Nora away, off his lap, back onto her feet, and he stood up. He crooked his finger at Richard. "Attend me." His feet scraped loud on the floor. Everybody was staring at him, mute. Heavily, he went out the door, Richard on his heels.

Nora rubbed her cheek, still damp where her father's mouth had pressed; her gaze went to her mother. The Queen reached out her arms and Nora went to her and the Queen held her tight. She said, "Don't be afraid. I'll protect you." Her voice was ragged. She let Nora go and clapped her hands. "Now we'll have some music."

Feathers of steam rose from the tray of almond buns on the long wooden table. Nora crept down the kitchen steps, staying close by the wall, and swiftly ducked down under the table's edge. Deeper in the kitchen, someone was singing, and someone else laughed; nobody had noticed her. She reached up over the side of the table and gathered handfuls of buns, dumping them into the fold of her skirt and, when her skirt was full, swiftly turned and scurried back up the steps and out the door.

Just beyond the threshold, Alais hopped up and down with delight, her eyes sparkling, her hands clasped together. Nora handed her a bun. "Quick!" She started toward the garden gate.

"Hey! You girls!"

Alais shrieked and ran. Nora wheeled, knowing that voice, and looked up into Richard's merry eyes.

"Share those?"

They went into the garden and sat on a bench by the wall, and ate the buns. Richard licked the sweet dust from his fingers.

"Nora, I'm going away."

"Away," she said, startled. "Where?"

"Mama wants me to go find Boy and Geoffrey. I think she's just getting me away from Papa. Then I'm going to look for some knights to follow me. I'm duke now, I need an army." He hugged her, laid his cheek against her hair. "I'll be back."

"You're so lucky," she burst out. "To be duke. I'm nobody! Why am I a girl?"

He laughed, his arm warm around her, his cheek against her hair. "You won't always be a little girl. You'll marry someday, and then you'll be a queen, like Mama, or at least a princess. I heard them say they want you to marry somebody in Castile."

"Castile. Where's that?" A twinge of alarm went through her. She looked up into his face. She thought that nobody was as handsome as Richard.

"Somewhere in the Spanish Marches." He reached for the last of the buns, and she caught his hand and held on. His fingers were all sticky.

"I don't want to go away," she said. "I'll miss you. I won't know anybody."

"You won't go for a while. Castile—that means castles. They fight the Moors down there. You'll be a Crusader."

She frowned, puzzled. "In Jerusalem?" In the convent, they had always been praying for the Crusade. Jerusalem was on the other side of the world, and she had never heard it called Castile.

"No, there's a Crusade in Spain too. El Cid, you know, and Roland. Like them."

"Roland," she said, with a leap of excitement. There was a song about

Roland, full of thrilling passages. She tilted her face toward him again. "Will I have a sword?"

"Maybe." He kissed her hair again. "Women don't usually need swords. I have to go. I just wanted to say good-bye. You're the oldest one left at home now, so take care of Johanna."

"And Alais," she said.

"Oh, Alais," he said. He took her hand. "Nora, listen, something is going on between Mama and Papa, I don't know what, but something. Be brave, Nora. Brave and good." His arm tightened a moment and then he stood and walked away.

"When will we be in Poitiers?" Alais said happily. She sat on a chest in the back of the wagon and spread her skirts out.

Nora shrugged. The carts went very slowly and would make the journey much longer. She wished they would let her ride a horse. Her nurse climbed in over the wagon's front, turned, and lifted Johanna after her. The drover led the team up, the reins bunched in his hands, turned the horses' rumps to the cart, and backed them into the shafts. Maybe he would let her hold the reins. She hung over the edge of the wagon, looking around at the courtyard, full of other wagons, people packing up her mother's goods, a line of saddled horses waiting.

The nurse said, "Lady Nora, sit down."

Nora kept her back to her, to show she didn't hear. Her mother had come out of the hall door, and at the sight of her everybody else in the whole courtyard turned toward her as if she were the sun; everybody warmed in that light. Nora called, "Mama!" and waved, and her mother waved back.

"Lady Nora! Sit!"

She leaned on the side of the wagon. Beside her, Alais giggled and poked her with her elbow. A groom was bringing the Queen's horse; she waved away someone waiting to help her and mounted by herself. Nora watched how she did that, how she kept her skirts over her legs but got her legs across the saddle anyway. Her Mama rode like a man. She would ride like that. Then, from the gate, a yell went up.

"The King!"

Alais on the chest twisted around to look. Nora straightened. Her father on his big black horse was riding in the gate, a line of knights behind him, mailed and armed. She looked for Richard, but he wasn't with them. Most of the knights had to stay outside the wall because there was no room in the yard.

Eleanor reined her horse around, coming up beside the wagon, close enough that Nora could have reached out and touched her. The horse side-stepped, tossing its head up. His face dark, the King forced his way through the crowd toward her.

She said, "My lord, what is this?"

He threw one wide look all around the courtyard. His face was blurry with beard and his eyes were rimmed in red. Nora sat quickly down on the chest. Her father spurred his horse up head to tail with her mother's.

"Where are my sons?"

"My lord, I have no notion, really."

He stared at her, furious. "Then I'll take hostages." He twisted in his saddle, looking back toward his men. "Get these girls!"

Nora shot to her feet again. "No," the Queen said, forcing her way between him and the wagon, almost nose to nose with him, her fist clenched. "Keep your hands off my daughters." Alais reached out and gripped Nora's skirt in her fist.

He thrust his face at her. "Try to stop me, Eleanor!"

"Papa, wait." Nora leaned over the side of the wagon. "We want to go to Poitiers."

The King said evilly, "What *you* want." Two men had dismounted, were coming briskly toward the wagon. He never took his gaze off her mother.

The Queen's horse bounded up between the men and the cart. Leaning closer to the King, she spoke in a quick low voice. "Don't be foolish, my lord, on such a small matter. If you push this too hastily, you will never get them back. Alais has that handsome dowry; take her."

"Mama, no!" Nora stretched her arm out. Alais flung her arms around her waist.

"Please—please—"

The Queen never even looked at them. "Be still, Nora. I will deal with this."

"Mama!" Nora tried to catch hold of her, to make her turn and look. "You promised. Mama, you promised she would come with us!" Her fingers grazed the smooth fabric of her mother's sleeve.

Eleanor struck at her, hard, knocking her down inside the wagon. Alais gave a sob. The King's men were coming on again, climbing up toward them. Nora lunged at them, her fists raised.

"Get away! Don't you dare touch her!"

From behind, someone got hold of her and dragged her out of the way. The two men scrambled up over the side of the wagon and fastened on the little French princess. They were dragging her up over the side. She cried out once and then was limp, helpless in their arms. Nora wrenched at the arm around her waist, and only then she saw it was her mother holding her.

"Mama!" She twisted toward Eleanor. "You promised. She doesn't want to go."

Eleanor thrust her face down toward Nora's. "Be still, girl. You don't know what you're doing."

Behind her, the King was swinging his horse away. "You can keep that one. Maybe she'll poison you." He rode off after his men, who had Alais clutched in their grip. Other men were lifting out Alais' baggage. They were hauling her off like baggage. Nora gave a wordless cry. With a sharp command, her father led his men on out the gate again, taking Alais like a trophy.

Her arm still around Nora's waist, Eleanor was scowling after the King. Nora wrenched herself free and her mother turned to face her.

"Well, now, Nora. That was unseemly, wasn't it."

"Why did you do that, Mama?" Nora's voice rang out, high-pitched and furious, careless who heard.

"Come, girl," her mother said, and gave her a shake. "Settle yourself. You don't understand."

With a violent jerk of her whole body, Nora wrenched away from her mother. "You said Alais could come." Something deep and hard was gathering in her, as if she had swallowed a stone. She began to cry. "Mama, why did you lie to me?"

Her mother blinked at her, her forehead crumpled. "I can't do everything." She held out her hand, as if asking for something. "Come, be reasonable. Do you want to be like your father?"

Tears were squirting from Nora's eyes. "No, and not like *you*, either, Mama. You promised me, and you lied." She knocked aside the outstretched hand.

Eleanor recoiled; her arm rose and she slapped Nora across the face. "Cruel, ungrateful child!"

Nora sat down hard. She poked her fists into her lap, her shoulders hunched. Alais was gone; she couldn't save her after all. It didn't matter that she hadn't really liked Alais much. She wanted to be a hero, but she was just a little girl, and nobody cared. She turned to the chest and folded her arms on it, put her head down, and wept.

Later, she leaned up against the side of the wagon, looking down the road ahead.

She felt stupid. Alais was right: she couldn't be a king, and now she couldn't even be a hero.

The nurses were dozing in the back of the wagon. Her mother had taken Johanna away to ride on her saddle in front of her, to show Nora how bad she had been. The drover on his bench had his back to her. She felt as if nobody could see her, as if she weren't even there.

She didn't want to be a king anyway if it meant being mean and yelling and carrying people off by force. She wanted to be like her mother, but her *old* mother, the good mother, not this new one, who lied and broke promises, who hit and called names. Alais had said, "Your mother is wicked," and she almost cried again, because it was true.

She would tell Richard when he came back. But then in her stomach something tightened like a knot: *if* he came back. Somehow the whole world had changed. Maybe even Richard would be false now.

"You'll be a Crusader," he had said to her.

She didn't know if she wanted that. Being a Crusader meant going a long, long way and then dying. "Be good," Richard had said. "Be brave." But she was just a little girl. Under the whole broad blue sky, she was just a speck.

The wagon jolted along the road, part of the long train of freight heading down toward Poitiers. She looked all around her, at the servants walking along among the carts, the bobbing heads of horses and mules, the heaps of baggage lashed on with rope. Her mother was paying no heed to her, had gone off ahead, in the mob of riders leading the way. The nurses were sleeping. Nobody was watching her.

Nobody cared about her anymore. She waited to disappear. But she didn't.

She stood, holding on to the side to keep from falling. Carefully, she climbed up over the front of the wagon onto the bench, keeping her skirts over her legs, and sat down next to the drover, who gawked down at her, a broad, brown face in a shag of beard.

"Now, my little lady—"

She straightened her skirts, planted her feet firmly on the kickboard, and looked up at him. "Can I hold the reins?" she said.

Jim Butcher

New York Times bestseller Jim Butcher is best known for the Dresden Files series, starring Harry Dresden, a wizard for hire who goes down some very mean streets indeed to do battle against the dark creatures of the supernatural world, and who is one of the most popular fictional characters of the twenty-first century to date; he even had his own TV show. The Dresden Files books include *Storm Front, Fool Moon, Grave Peril, Summer Knight, Death Masks, Blood Rites, Dead Beat, Proven Guilty, White Night, Small Favor, Turn Coat,* and *Changes.* Butcher is also the author of the swashbuckling sword and sorcery Codex Alera series, consisting of *Furies of Calderon, Academ's Fury, Cursor's Fury, Captain's Fury,* and *Princeps' Fury.* His most recent books are *First Lord's Fury,* the new Codex Alera novel, and *Ghost Story,* a Dresden Files novel. There's also a collection of stories featuring Harry Dresden, *Side Jobs: Stories from the Dresden Files.* Coming up is a new Dresden Files novel, *Cold Days.* Butcher lives in Missouri with his wife, his son, and a ferocious guard dog.

Butcher flabbergasted everyone by killing Harry Dresden off at the end of *Changes.* (The next novel, *Ghost Story,* was told from the point of view of Harry's ghost!) Here Harry's young protégé, trying to carry on the fight against the forces of darkness *without* Harry, finds that she has some very big shoes to fill, and that she'd better fill them *fast*—or die.

BOMBSHELLS

I miss my boss.

It's been most of a year since I helped him die, and ever since then I've been the only professional wizard in the city of Chicago.

Well, okay. I'm not, like, officially a wizard. I'm still sort of an apprentice. And no one really pays me, unless you count the wallets and valuables I lift from bodies sometimes, so I guess I'm more amateur than professional. And I don't have a PI license like my boss did, or an ad in the phone book.

But I'm all there is. I'm not as strong as he was, and I'm not as good as he was. I'm just going to have to be enough.

So anyway, there I was, washing the blood off in Waldo Butters' shower.

I did a lot of living outdoors these days, which didn't seem nearly as horrible during the summer and early autumn as it had during the arctic chill of the previous superwinter. It was like sleeping on a tropical beach by comparison. Still, I missed things like regular access to plumbing, and Waldo let me clean up whenever I needed to. I had the shower heat turned all the way up, and it was heaven. It was kind of a scourgey, scoury heaven, but heaven nonetheless.

The floor of the shower turned red for a few seconds, then faded to pink for a while as I sluiced the blood off. It wasn't mine. A gang of Fomor servitors had been carrying a fifteen-year-old boy down an alley toward Lake Michigan. If they'd gotten him there, he'd have been facing a fate worse than death. I intervened, but that bastard Listen cut his throat rather than give him up. I tried to save him while Listen and his buddies ran. I failed. And I'd been right there with him, feeling everything he did, feeling his confusion and pain and terror as he died.

Harry wouldn't have felt that. Harry would have saved the day. He would have smashed the Fomor goons around like bowling pins, picked the kid up like some kind of serial-movie action hero, and taken him to safety.

I missed my boss.

I used a lot of soap. I probably cried. I had begun ignoring tears months ago, and at times I honestly didn't know when they were falling. Once I was clean—physically, anyway—I just stood there soaking up the heat, letting the water course all over me. The scar on my leg where I'd been shot was still wrinkled, but the color had changed from purple and red to angry pink. Butters said it would be gone in a couple of years. I was walking normally again, unless I pushed myself too hard. But yikes, my legs and various pieces needed to get reacquainted with a razor, even with medium-blond hair.

I was going to ignore them, but . . . grooming is important for keeping one's spirits up. A well-kept body for a well-kept mind and all that. I wasn't a fool. I knew I wasn't exactly flying level lately. My morale needed all the boost it could get. I leaned out of the shower and swiped Andi's pink plastic razor. I'd pay Waldo's werewolf girlfriend back for it later.

I wrapped up about the same time as the hot water ran out, got out of the shower, and toweled off. My things were in a pile by the door—some garage-sale Birkenstocks, an old nylon hiker's backpack, and my bloodied clothes. Another set gone. And the sandals had left partial tracks in blood at the scene, so I'd have to get rid of them, too. I was going to have to hit another thrift store at this rate. Normally, that would have cheered me up, but shopping just wasn't what it used to be.

I was carefully going over the tub and floor for fallen hairs and so on when someone knocked. I didn't stop scanning the floor. In my line of work, people can and will do awful things to you with discarded bits of your body. Not cleaning up after yourself is like asking for someone to boil your blood from twenty blocks away. No, thank you.

"Yes?" I called.

"Hey, Molly," Waldo said. "There's, uh . . . there's someone here to talk to you."

We'd prearranged a lot of things. If he'd used the word "feeling" at any point in his sentence, I would have known there was trouble outside the door. Not using it meant that there wasn't—or that he couldn't see it. I slipped on my bracelets and my ring and set both of my wands down where I could snatch them up instantly. Only then did I start putting clothes on.

"Who?" I called.

He was working hard not to sound nervous around me. I appreciated the effort. It was sweet. "Says her name is Justine. Says you know her."

I did know Justine. She was a thrall of the vampires of the White Court. Or at least a personal assistant to one and the girlfriend of another. Harry always thought well of her, though he was a big goofy idiot when it came to women who might show the potential to become damsels in distress.

"But if he was here," I muttered to myself, "he'd help her."

I didn't wipe the steam off the mirror before I left the bathroom. I didn't want to look at anything in there.

Justine was a handful of years older than me, but her hair had turned pure white. She was a knockout, one of those girls all the boys assume are too pretty to approach. She had on jeans and a button-down shirt several sizes too large for her. The shirt was Thomas's, I was certain. Her body language was poised, very neutral. Justine was as good at hiding her emotions as anyone I'd ever seen, but I could sense leashed tension and quiet fear beneath the calm surface.

I'm a wizard, or damned close to it, and I work with the mind. People don't really get to hide things from me.

If Justine was afraid, it was because she feared for Thomas. If she'd come to me for help, it was because she couldn't get help from the White Court. We could have had a polite conversation that led up to that revelation, but I had less and less patience for the amenities lately, so I cut to the chase.

"Hello, Justine. Why should I help you with Thomas when his own family won't?"

Justine's eyes bugged out. So did Waldo's.

I was getting used to that reaction.

"How did you know?" Justine asked quietly.

When you're into magic, people always assume anything you do must be connected to it. Harry always thought that was funny. To him, magic was just one more set of tools that the mind could use to solve problems. The mind was the more important part of that pairing. "Does that matter?"

She frowned and looked away from me. She shook her head. "He's missing. I know he left on some kind of errand for Lara, but she says she doesn't know anything about it. She's lying."

"She's a vampire. And you didn't answer my first question." The words came out a little harsher and harder than they'd sounded in my head. I tried to relax a little. I folded my arms and leaned against a wall. "Why should I help you?"

It's not like I wasn't planning to help her. But I knew a secret about Harry and Thomas few others did. I had to know if Justine knew the secret, too, or if I'd have to keep it hidden around her.

Justine met my eyes with hers for a moment. The look was penetrating. "If you can't go to family for help," she said, "who can you turn to?"

I averted my eyes before it could turn into an actual soulgaze, but her words and the cumulative impression of her posture, her presence, her *self*, answered the question for me.

She knew.

Thomas and Harry were half brothers. She'd have gone to Harry for help if he was alive. I was the only thing vaguely like an heir to his power around these parts, and she hoped I would be willing to step into his shoes. His huge, stompy, terrifying shoes.

"You go to friends," I said quietly. "I'll need something of Thomas's. Hair or fingernail clippings would be . . ."

She produced a zip-closed plastic bag from the breast pocket of the shirt and offered it to me without a word. I went over and picked it up. It had a number of dark hairs in it.

"You're sure they're his?"

Justine gestured toward her own snow-white mane. "It's not like they're easy to confuse."

I looked up to find Butters watching me silently from the other side of the room. He was a beaky little guy, wiry and quick. His hair had been electrocuted and then frozen that way. His eyes were steady and worried. He cut up corpses for the government, professionally, but he was one of the more savvy people in town when it came to the supernatural.

"What?" I asked him.

He considered his words before he spoke—less because he was afraid of me than because he cared about not hurting my feelings. That was the reverse of most people these days. "Is this something you should get involved in, Molly?"

What he really wanted to ask me was if I was sane. If I was going to help or just make things a lot worse.

"I don't know," I said honestly. I looked at Justine and said, "Wait here."
Then I got my stuff, took the hairs, and left.

The first thing Harry Dresden ever taught me about magic was a tracking spell.

"It's a simple principle, kid," he told me. "We're creating a link between two similar things out of energy. Then we make the energy give us an indicator of some kind, so that we can tell which way it's flowing."

"What are we going to find?" I asked.

He held up a rather thick grey hair and nodded back toward his dog, Mouse. He should have been named Moose. The giant, shaggy temple dog was pony-sized. "Mouse," Harry said, "go get lost and we'll see if we can find you."

The big dog yawned and padded agreeably toward the door. Harry let him out and then came over to sit down next to me. We were in his living room. A couple of nights before, I had thrown myself at him. Naked. And he'd dumped a pitcher of ice water over my head. I was still mortified—but he was probably right. It was the right thing for him to do. He always did the right thing, even if it meant he lost out. I still wanted to be with him so much, but maybe the time wasn't right yet.

That was okay. I could be patient. And I still got to be with him in a different way almost every day.

"All right," I said when he sat back down. "What do I do?"

In the years since that day, the spell had become routine. I'd used it to find lost people, secret places, missing socks, and generally to poke my nose where it probably didn't belong. Harry would have said that went with the territory of being a wizard. Harry was right.

I stopped in the alley outside Butters's apartment and sketched a circle on the concrete with a small piece of pink chalk. I closed the circle with a tiny effort of will, drew out one of the hairs from the plastic bag, and held it up. I focused the energy of the spell, bringing its different elements together in my head. When we'd started, Harry had let me use four different objects, teaching me how to attach ideas to them, to represent the different pieces of the spell, but that kind of thing wasn't necessary. Magic all happens inside the head of the wizard. You can use props to make things simpler, and in truly complex spells they make the difference between impossible and merely almost impossible. For this one, though, I didn't need the props anymore.

I gathered the different pieces of the spell in my head, linked them together, infused them with a moderate effort of will, and then with a murmured word released that energy down into the hair in my fingers. Then I popped the hair into my mouth, broke the chalk circle with a brush of my foot, and rose.

Harry always used an object as the indicator for his tracking spells—his amulet, a compass, or some kind of pendulum. I hadn't wanted to hurt his feelings, but that kind of thing really wasn't necessary, either. I could feel the magic coursing through the hair, making my lips tingle gently. I got out a cheap little plastic compass and a ten-foot length of chalk line. I set it up and snapped it to mark out magnetic north.

Then I took the free end of the line and turned slowly, until the tingling sensation was centered on my lips. Lips are extremely sensitive parts of the body, generally, and I've found that they give you the best tactile feedback for this sort of thing. Once I knew which direction Thomas was, I oriented the chalk line that way, made sure it was tight, and snapped it again, resulting in an extremely elongated V shape, like the tip of a giant needle. I measured the distance at the base of the V.

Then I turned ninety degrees, walked five hundred paces, and repeated the process.

Promise me you won't tell my high school math teacher about it, but after that I sat down and applied trigonometry to real life.

The math wasn't hard. I had the two angles measured against magnetic north. I had the distance between them in units of Molly-paces. Molly-paces aren't terribly scientific, but for purposes of this particular application, they were practical enough to calculate the distance to Thomas.

Using such simple tools, I couldn't get a measurement precise enough to know which door to kick down, but I now knew that he was relatively nearby—within four or five miles, as opposed to being at the North Pole or something. I move around the city a lot, because a moving target is a lot harder to hit. I probably covered three or four times that on an average day.

I'd have to get a lot closer before I could pinpoint his location any more precisely than that. So I turned my lips toward the tingle and started walking.

Thomas was in a small office building on a big lot.

The building was three stories, not huge, though it sat amidst several much larger structures. The lot it stood upon was big enough to hold something a lot bigger. Instead, most of it was landscaped into a manicured lawn and garden, complete with water features and a very small, very modest wrought-iron fence. The building itself showed a lot of stone and marble in its design, and it had more class in its cornices than the towers nearby had in their whole structures. It was gorgeous and understated at the same time; on that block, it looked like a single, small, perfect diamond being displayed amidst giant jars of rhinestones.

There were no signs outside it. There was no obvious way in, beyond a set of gates guarded by competent-looking men in dark suits. Expensive dark suits. If the guards could afford to wear those to work, it meant that whoever owned that building had money. Serious money.

I circled the building to be sure, and felt the tingling energy of the tracking spell confirming Thomas's location; but even though I'd been careful to stay on the far side of the street, someone inside noticed me. I could feel one guard's eyes tracking me, even behind his sunglasses. Maybe I should have done the initial approach under a veil—but Harry had always been against using magic except when it was truly necessary, and it was way too easy to start using it for every little thing if you let yourself.

In some ways, I'm better at the "how" of magic than Harry was. But I've come to learn that I might never be as smart as him when it came to the "why."

I went into a nearby Starbucks and got myself a cup of liquid life and started thinking about how to get in. My tongue was telling me all about what great judgment I had when I sensed the presence of supernatural power rapidly coming nearer.

I didn't panic. Panic gets you killed. Instead I turned smoothly on one heel and slipped into a short hallway leading to a small restroom. I went inside, shut the door behind me, and drew my wands from my hip pocket. I checked the energy level on my bracelets. Both of them were ready to go. My rings were all full up, too, which was about as ideal as things could get.

So I ordered my thoughts, made a small effort of will, whispered a word, and vanished.

Veils were complex magic, but I had a knack for them. Becoming truly and completely invisible was a real pain in the neck: passing light completely through you was a literal stone-cold bitch, because it left you freezing cold and blind as a bat to boot. Becoming unseen, though, was a different proposition entirely. A good veil would reduce your visibility to little more than a few flickers in the air, to a few vague shadows where they shouldn't be, but it did more than that. It created a sense of ordinariness in the air around you, an aura of boring unremarkability that you usually only felt in a job you didn't like, around three thirty in the afternoon. Once you combined that suggestion with a greatly reduced visible profile, remaining unnoticed was at least as easy as breathing.

As I vanished into that veil, I also called up an image, another combination of illusion and suggestion. This one was simple: me, as I'd appeared in the mirror a moment before, clean and seemingly perky and toting a fresh cup of creamy goodness. The sensation that went with it was just a kind of heavy dose of me: the sound of my steps and movement, the scent of Butters's shampoo, the aroma of my cup of coffee. I tied the image to one of the rings on my fingers and left it there, drawing from the energy I'd stored in a moonstone. Then I turned around, with my image layered over my actual body like a suit made of light, and walked out of the coffee shop.

Once outside, the evasion was a simple maneuver, the way all the good ones are. My image turned left and I turned right.

To anyone watching, a young woman had just come out of the store and gone sauntering down the street with her coffee. She was obviously enjoying her day. I'd put a little extra bounce and sway into the image's movements, to make her that much more noticeable (and therefore a better distraction). She'd go on walking down that street for a mile or more before she simply vanished.

Meanwhile, the real me moved silently into an alleyway and watched.

My image hadn't gone a hundred yards before a man in a black turtleneck sweater stepped out of an alley and began following it—a servitor of the Fomor. Those jerks were everywhere these days, like roaches, only more disgusting and harder to kill.

Only . . . that was just too easy. One servitor wouldn't have set my instinct alarms to jingling. They were strong, fast, and tough, sure, but no more so than any number of creatures. They didn't possess mounds of magical power; if they had, the Fomor would never have let them leave in the first place.

Something else was out there. Something that had wanted me to be distracted, watching the apparent servitor follow the apparent Molly. And if something knew me well enough to set up this sort of diversion to ensnare my attention, then it knew me well enough to find me, even beneath my veil. There were a really limited number of people who could do that.

I slipped a hand into my nylon backpack and drew out my knife, the M9 bayonet my brother had brought home from Afghanistan. I drew the heavy blade out, closed my eyes, and turned quickly with the knife in one hand and my coffee in the other. I flicked the lid off the coffee with my thumb and slewed the liquid into a wide arc at about chest level.

I heard a gasp and oriented on it, opened my eyes, and stepped toward the source of the sound, driving the knife into the air before me at slightly higher than the level of my own heart.

The steel of the blade suddenly erupted with a coruscation of light as it pierced a veil that hung in the air only inches away from me. I stepped forward rapidly through the veil, pushing the point of the knife before me toward the suddenly revealed form behind the veil. She was a woman, taller than me, dressed in ragged (coffee-stained) clothes, but with her long, fiery autumn hair unbound and wind tossed. She twisted to one side, off balance, until her shoulders touched the brick wall of the alley.

I did not relent, driving the blade toward her throat—until at the last second, one pale, slender hand snapped up and grasped my wrist, quick as a serpent but stronger and colder. My face wound up only a few inches from hers as I put the heel of one hand against the knife and leaned against it slightly—enough to push against her strength, but not enough to throw me off balance if she made a quick move. She was lean and lovely, even in the rags, with wide, oblique green eyes and perfect bone structure that could only be found in half a dozen supermodels—and in every single one of the Sidhe.

"Hello, Auntie," I said in a level voice. "It isn't nice to sneak up behind me. Especially lately."

She held my weight off of her with one arm, though it wasn't easy for her. There was a quality of strain to her melodic voice. "Child," she breathed. "You anticipated my approach. Had I not stopped thee, thou wouldst have driven cold iron into my flesh, causing me agonies untold. Thou wouldst have spilled my life's blood upon the ground." Her eyes widened. "Thou wouldst have killed me."

"I wouldst," I agreed pleasantly.

Her mouth spread into a wide smile, and her teeth were daintily pointed. "I have taught thee well."

Then she twisted with a lithe and fluid grace, away from the blade and to her feet a good long step away from me. I watched her and lowered the knife—but I didn't put it away. "I don't have time for lessons right now, Auntie Lea."

"I am not here to teach thee, child."

"I don't have time for games, either."

"Nor did I come to play with thee," the Leanansidhe said, "but to give thee warning: thou art not safe here."

I quirked an eyebrow at her. "Wow. Gosh."

She tilted her head at me in reproof, and her mouth thinned. Her eyes moved past me to look down the alley, and she shot a quick glance behind her. Her expression changed. She didn't quite lose the smug superiority that always colored her features, but she toned it down a good deal, and she lowered her voice. "Thou makest jests, child, but thou art in grave peril—as am I. We should not linger here." She shifted her eyes to mine. "If thou dost wish to brace this foe, if thou wouldst recover my Godson's brother, there are things I must tell thee."

I narrowed my eyes. Harry's Faerie Godmother had taken over as my mentor when Harry died, but she wasn't exactly one of the good faeries. In fact, she was the second in command to Mab, the Queen of Air and Darkness, and she was a bloodthirsty, dangerous being who divided her enemies into two categories: those who were dead, and those in which she had not yet taken pleasure. I hadn't known that she knew about Harry and Thomas—but it didn't shock me.

Lea was a murderous, cruel creature—but as far as I knew, she had never lied to me. Technically.

"Come," said the Leanansidhe. She turned and walked briskly toward the far end of the alley, gathering a seeming and a veil around her as she went, to hide herself from notice.

I glanced back toward the building where Thomas was being held, ground my teeth, and followed her, merging my veil with hers as we left.

———

We walked Chicago's streets unseen by thousands of eyes. The people we passed all took a few extra steps to avoid us, without really thinking about it. It's important to lay out an avoidance suggestion like that when you're in a crowd. Being unseen is kind of pointless if dozens of people keep bumping into you.

"Tell me, child," Lea said, shifting abruptly out of her archaic dialect. She did that sometimes, when we were alone. "What do you know of svartalves?"

"A little," I said. "They're from northern Europe, originally. They're small and they live underground. They're the best magical craftsmen on earth; Harry bought things from them whenever he could afford it, but they weren't cheap."

"How dry," the faerie sorceress said. "You sound like a book, child. Books frequently bear little resemblance to life." Her intense green eyes glittered as she turned to watch a young woman with an infant walk by us. "What do you *know* of them?"

"They're dangerous," I said quietly. "Very dangerous. The old Norse gods used to go to them for weapons and armor and they didn't try to fight them. Harry said he was glad he never had to fight a svartalf. They're also honorable. They signed the Unseelie Accords and they uphold them. They have a reputation for being savage about protecting their own. They aren't human, they aren't kind, and only a fool crosses them."

"Better," the Leanansidhe said. Then she added, in an offhand tone, "Fool."

I glanced back toward the building I'd found. "That's their property?"

"Their fortress," Lea replied, "the center of their mortal affairs, here at the great crossroads. What else do you recall of them?"

I shook my head. "Um. One of the Norse goddesses got jacked for her jewelry—"

"Freya," Lea said.

"And the thief—"

"Loki."

"Yeah, him. He pawned it with the svartalves or something, and there was a big to-do about getting it back."

"One wonders how it is possible to be so vague and so accurate at the same time," Lea said.

I smirked.

Lea frowned at me. "You knew the story perfectly well. You were . . . tweaking my nose, I believe is the saying."

"I had a good teacher in snark class," I said. "Freya went to get her necklace back, and the svartalves were willing to do it—but only if she agreed to kiss each and every one of them."

Lea threw her head back and laughed. "Child," she said, a wicked edge to her voice, "remember that many of the old tales were translated and transcribed by rather prudish scholars."

"What do you mean?" I asked.

"That the svartalves most certainly did not agree to give up one of the most valuable jewels in the universe for a society-wide trip to first base."

I blinked a couple of times and felt my cheeks heat up. "You mean she had to . . ."

"Precisely."

"*All* of them?"

"Indeed."

"Wow," I said. "I like to accessorize as much as the next girl, but that's over the line. Way over. I mean, you can't even *see* the line from there."

"Perhaps," Lea said. "I suppose it depends upon how badly one needs to recover something from the svartalves."

"Uh. You're saying I need to pull a train to get Thomas out of there? 'Cause . . . that just isn't going to happen."

Lea showed her teeth in another smile. "Morality is amusing."

"Would you do it?"

Lea looked offended. "For the sake of another? Certainly not. Have you any idea of the obligation that would incur?"

"Um. Not exactly."

"This is not my choice to make. You must ask yourself this question: Is your untroubled conscience more valuable to you than the vampire's life?"

"No. But there's got to be another way."

Lea seemed to consider that for a moment. "Svartalves love beauty. They covet it the way a dragon lusts for gold. You are young, lovely, and . . . I believe the phrase is 'smoking hot.' The exchange of your favors for the vampire, a straightforward transaction, is almost certain to succeed, assuming he still lives."

"We'll call that one plan B," I said. "Or maybe plan X. Or plan XXX. Why not just break in and burgle him out?"

"Child," the Leanansidhe chided me. "The svartalves are quite skilled in the Art, and this is one of their strongholds. *I* could not attempt such a thing and leave with my life." Lea tilted her head to one side and gave me one of those alien looks that made my skin crawl. "Do you wish to recover Thomas or not?"

"I wish to explore my options," I said.

The faerie sorceress shrugged. "Then I advise you to do so as rapidly as possible. If he yet lives, Thomas Raith might count the remainder of his life in hours."

I opened the door to Waldo's apartment, shut and locked it behind me, and said, "Found him."

As I turned toward the room, someone slapped me hard across the face.

This wasn't a "Hey, wake up" kind of slap. It was an openhanded blow, one that would have really hurt if it was delivered with a closed fist. I staggered to one side, stunned.

Waldo's girlfriend, Andi, folded her arms and stared at me through narrowed eyes for a moment. She was a girl of medium height, but she was a werewolf and she was built like a pinup model who was thinking about going into professional wrestling. "Hi, Molly," she said.

"Hi," I said. "And . . . ow."

She held up a pink plastic razor. "Let's have a talk about boundaries."

Something ugly way down deep inside me somewhere unsheathed its claws and tensed up. That was the part of me that wanted to catch up to Listen and do things involving railroad spikes and drains in the floor. Everyone has that inside them, somewhere. It takes fairly horrible things to awaken that kind of savagery, but it's in all of us. It's the part of us that causes senseless atrocities, that makes war hell.

No one wants to talk about it or think about it, but I couldn't afford that kind of willing ignorance. I hadn't always been this way, but after a year fighting the Fomor and the dark underside of Chicago's supernatural scene, I was somebody else. That part of me was awake and active and constantly pushing my emotions into conflict with my rationality.

I told that part of me to shut up and sit its ass down.

"Okay," I said. "But later. I'm kind of busy."

I started to brush past her into the room, but she stopped me short by placing a hand against my sternum and shoved me back against the door. It didn't look like she was trying but I hit the wood firmly.

"Now's good," she said.

In my imagination, I clenched my fists and counted to five in an enraged scream. I was sure Harry had never had to deal with this kind of nonsense. I didn't have time to lose, but I didn't want to start something violent with Andi, either. I'd catch all kinds of hell if I threw down. I allowed myself the pleasure of gritting my teeth, took a deep breath, and nodded. "Okay. What's on your mind, Andi?"

I didn't add the words "you bitch" but I thought them really loud. I should probably be a nicer person.

"This is not your apartment," Andi said. "You don't get to roll in and out of here whenever you damned well please, no matter the hour, no matter what's going on. Have you even stopped to think about what you're doing to Butters?"

"I'm not doing anything to Butters," I said. "I'm just borrowing the shower."

Andi's voice sharpened. "You came here today covered in blood. I don't know what happened, but you know what? I don't care. All I care about is what kind of trouble you might draw down onto other people."

"There was no trouble," I said. "Look, I'll buy you a new razor."

"This isn't about property or money, Christ," Andi said. "This is about respect. Butters is there for you whenever you need help, and you barely do so much as to thank him for it. What if you'd been followed here? Do you have any idea how much trouble he could get into for helping you out?"

"I wasn't followed," I said.

"Today," Andi said. "But what about next time? You have power. You can fight. I don't have what you do, but even I can fight. Butters can't. Whose shower are you going to use if it's his blood all over you?"

I folded my arms and looked carefully away from Andi. In some part of my brain I knew that she had a point, but that reasoning was coming in a distant second to my sudden urge to slap her.

"Look, Molly," she said, her voice becoming more gentle. "I know things haven't been easy for you lately. Ever since Harry died. When his ghost showed up. I know it wasn't fun."

I just looked at her without speaking. Not easy or fun. That was one way to describe it.

"There's something I think you need to hear."

"What's that?"

Andi leaned forward slightly and sharpened her words. "Get over it."

The apartment was very quiet for a moment, and the inside of me wasn't. That ugly part of me started getting louder and louder. I closed my eyes.

"People die, Molly," Andi continued. "They leave. And life goes on. Harry may have been the first friend you lost, but he won't be the last. I get that you're hurting. I get that you're trying to step into some really big shoes. But that doesn't give you the right to abuse people's better natures. A *lot* of people are hurting lately, if you didn't notice."

If I didn't notice. God, I would absolutely *kill* to be able not to notice people's pain. Not to live it beside them. Not to sense its echoes hours or days later. The ugly part of me, the black part of my heart, wanted to open a psychic channel to Andi and *show* her the kind of thing I went through on a regular basis. Let *her* see how she would like my life. And we'd see if she was so righteous afterward. It would be wrong, but . . .

I took a slow breath. No. Harry told me once that you can always tell when you're about to rationalize your way to a bad decision. It's when you start using phrases such as "It would be wrong, but . . ." His advice was to leave the conjunction out of the sentence: "It would be wrong." Period.

So I didn't do anything rash. I didn't let the rising tumult inside me come out. I spoke softly. "What is it you'd like me to do, exactly?"

Andi huffed out a little breath and waved a vague hand. "Just . . . get your head out of your ass, girl. I am not being unreasonable here, given that my boyfriend gave you a key to his freaking apartment."

I blinked once at that. Wow. I hadn't even really considered that aspect of what Butters had done. Romance and romantic conflict hadn't exactly been high on my list lately. Andi had nothing to worry about on that front . . . but I guess she didn't have way too much awareness of people's emotions to tip her off to that fact. Now I could put a name to some of the worry in her. She wasn't jealous, exactly, but she was certainly aware of the fact that I was a young woman a lot of men found attractive, and that Waldo was a man.

And she loved him. I could feel that, too.

"Think about him," Andi said quietly. "Please. Just . . . try to take care of him the way he takes care of you. Call ahead. If you'd just walked in covered with blood next Saturday night, he would have had something very awkward to explain to his parents."

I most likely would have sensed the unfamiliar presences inside the apartment before I got close enough to touch the door. But there was no point in telling Andi that. It wasn't her fault that she didn't really understand the kind of life I lived. Certainly, she didn't deserve to die for it, no matter what the opinion of my inner Sith.

I had to make my choices with my head. My heart was too broken to be trusted.

"I'll try," I said.

"Okay," Andi said.

For a second, the fingers of my right hand quivered, and I found the ugly part of me about to hurl power at the other woman, blind her, deafen her, drown her in vertigo. Lea had shown me how. But I reeled the urge to attack back under control. "Andi," I said instead.

"Yes?"

"Don't hit me again unless you intend to kill me."

I didn't mean it as a threat, exactly. It was just that I tended to react with my instincts when things started getting violent. The psychic turbulence of that kind of conflict didn't make me fall over screaming in pain anymore, but it did make it really hard to think clearly over the furious roaring of ugly me. If Andi hit me like that again . . . well. I wasn't completely sure how I would react.

I'm not Mad Hatter insane. I'm pretty sure. But studying survival under someone like Auntie Lea leaves you ready to protect yourself, not to play well with others.

Threat or not, Andi had seen her share of conflict, and she didn't back down. "If I don't think you need a good smack in the face, I won't give you one."

Waldo and Justine had gone out to pick up some dinner, and got back about ten minutes later. We all sat down to eat while I reported on the situation.

"Svartalfheim," Justine breathed. "That's . . . that's not good."

"Those are the Norse guys, right?" Butters asked.

I filled them in between bites of orange chicken, relaying what I had learned from the Leanansidhe. There was a little silence after I did.

"So . . ." Andi said after a moment. "The plan is to . . . boink him free?"

I gave her a look.

"I'm just asking," Andi said in a mild voice.

"They'd never sell," Justine said, her voice low, tight. "Not tonight."

I eyed her. "Why not?"

"They concluded an alliance today," she said. "There's a celebration tonight. Lara was invited."

"What alliance?" I asked.

"A nonaggression pact," Justine said, "with the Fomor."

I felt my eyes widen.

The Fomor situation just kept getting worse and worse. Chicago was far from the most preyed-upon city in the world, and they had still made the streets a nightmare for those of even modest magical talent. I didn't have access to the kind of information I had when I was working with Harry and the White Council, but I'd heard things through the Paranet and other sources. The Fomor were kind of an all-star team of bad guys, the survivors and outcasts and villains of a dozen different pantheons that had gone down a long time ago. They'd banded together under the banner of a group of beings known as the Fomor, and had been laying quiet for a long time—for thousands of years, in fact.

Now they were on the move—and even powerful interests like Svartalfheim, the nation of the svartalves, were getting out of the way.

Wow, I was so not wizard enough to deal with this.

"Lara must have sent Thomas in for something," Justine said. "To steal information, to disrupt the alliance somehow. Something. Trespassing would be bad enough. If he was captured spying on them . . ."

"They'll have a demonstration," I said quietly. "They'll make an example."

"Couldn't the White Court get him out?" Waldo asked.

"If the White Court seeks the return of one of their own, it would be like admitting they sent an agent in to screw around with Svartalfheim," I said. "Lara can't do that without serious repercussions. She'll deny that Thomas's intrusion had anything to do with her."

Justine rose and paced the room, her body tight. "We have to go. We have to do something. I'll pay the price; I'll pay it ten times. We have to *do* something!"

I took a few more bites of orange chicken, frowning and thinking.

"Molly!" Justine said.

I looked at the chicken. I liked the way the orange sauce contrasted with the deep green of the broccoli and the soft white contours of the rice. The three colors made a pleasant complement. It was . . . beautiful, really.

"They covet beauty like a dragon covets gold," I murmured.

Butters seemed to clue in to the fact that I was onto something. He leaned back in his chair and ate steadily from a box of noodles, his chopsticks precise. He didn't need to look to use them.

Andi picked up on it a second later and tilted her head to one side. "Molly?" she asked.

"They're having a party tonight," I said. "Right, Justine?"

"Yes."

Andi nodded impatiently. "What are we going to do?"

"We," I said, "are going shopping."

I'm kind of a tomboy. Not because I don't like being a girl or anything, because for the most part I think it's pretty sweet. But I like the outdoors, and physical activities, and learning stuff and reading things and building things. I've never really gotten very deep into the girly parts of being a girl. Andi was a little bit better at it than me. The fact that her mother hadn't brought her up the way mine had probably accounted for it. In my house, makeup was for going to church and for women with easy morals.

I know, I know: the mind boggles at the contradiction. I had issues way before I got involved with magic, believe me.

I wasn't sure how to accomplish what we needed in time to get to the party, but once I explained what we needed, I found out that when it came to being a girly girl, Justine had her shit wired tight.

Within minutes a town car picked us up and whisked us away to a private salon in the Loop, where Justine produced a completely unmarked, plain white credit card. About twenty staff members—wardrobe advisors, hairdressers, makeup artists, tailors, and accessory technicians—leapt into action and got us kitted out for the mission in a little more than an hour.

I couldn't really get away from the mirror this time. I tried to look at the young woman in it objectively, as if she was someone else, and not the one who had helped kill the man she loved and who had then failed him again by being unable to prevent even his ghost from being destroyed in its determination to protect others. That bitch deserved to be run over by a train or something.

The girl in the mirror was tall and had naturally blond hair that had been rapidly swirled up off of her neck and suspended with gleaming black chopsticks. She looked lean, probably too much so, but had a little too much muscle tone to be a meth addict. The little black dress she wore would turn heads. She looked a little tired, even with the expertly applied makeup. She was pretty—if you didn't know her, and if you didn't look too hard at what was going on in her blue eyes.

A white stretch limo pulled up to get us, and I managed to dodder out to it without falling all over myself.

"Oh my God," Andi said when we got in. The redhead stuck her feet out and wiggled them. "I love these shoes! If I have to wolf out and eat somebody's face, I am going to cry to leave these behind."

Justine smiled at her but then looked out the window, her lovely face distant, worried. "They're just shoes."

"Shoes that make my legs and my butt look awesome!" Andi said.

"Shoes that hurt," I said. My wounded leg might have healed up, but moving around in these spiky torture devices was a new motion, and a steady ache was spreading up through my leg toward my hip. The last thing I needed was for my leg to cramp up and drop me to the ground, the way it had kept doing when I first started walking on it again. Any shoes with heels that high should come with their own safety net. Or a parachute.

We'd gone with similar outfits: stylish little black dresses, black chokers, and black pumps that proclaimed us hopeful that we wouldn't spend much time on our feet. Each of us had a little Italian leather clutch, too. I'd put most of my magical gear in mine. All of us had our hair up in styles that varied only slightly. There were forged Renaissance paintings which had not had as much artist's attention as our faces.

"It just takes practice wearing them," Justine said. "Are you sure this is going to work?"

"Of course it is," I said calmly. "You've been to clubs, Justine. The three of us together would skip the line to any place in town. We're a matched set of hotness."

"Like the Robert Palmer girls," Andi said drily.

"I was going to go with Charlie's Angels," I said. "Oh, speaking of"—I opened the clutch and drew out a quartz crystal the size of my thumb—"Bosley, can you hear me?"

A second later, the crystal vibrated in my fingers and we heard Waldo's faint voice coming from it. "Loud and clear, Angels. You think these will work once you get inside?"

"Depends on how paranoid they are," I said. "If they're paranoid, they'll have defenses in place to cut off any magical communications. If they're murderously paranoid, they'll have defenses in place that let us talk so that they can listen in, and then they'll kill us."

"Fun," Butters said. "Okay, I've got the Paranet chat room up. For what it's worth, the hivemind is online."

"What have you found out?" Andi asked.

"They'll look human," Waldo replied. "Their real forms are . . . well, there's some discussion, but the basic consensus is that they look like aliens."

"Ripley or Roswell?" I asked.

"Roswell. More or less. They can wear flesh forms, though, kind of like the Red Court vampires did. So be aware that they'll be disguised."

"Got it," I said. "Anything else?"

"Not much," he said. "There's just too much lore floating around to pick out anything for sure. They might be allergic to salt. They might be supernaturally OCD and flip out if you wear your clothes inside out. They might turn to stone in sunlight."

I growled. "It was worth a shot. Okay. Keep the discussion going, and I'll get back to you if I can."

"Got it," he said. "Marci just got here. I'll bring the laptop with me and we'll be waiting for you on the east side of the building when you're ready to go. How do you look, Andi-licious?"

"Fabulous," Andi said confidently. "The hemlines on these dresses stop about an inch short of slutty nymphomaniac."

"Someone take a picture," he said cheerfully, but I could hear the worry in his voice. "I'll see you soon."

"Don't take any chances," I said. "See you soon."

I put the crystal away and tried to ignore the butterflies in my stomach.

"This isn't going to work," Justine murmured.

"It is going to work," I told her, keeping my tone confident. "We'll breeze right in. The Rack will be with us."

Justine glanced at me with an arched eyebrow. "The Rack?"

"The Rack is more than just boobs, Justine," I told her soberly. "It's an energy field created by all living boobs. It surrounds us, penetrates us, and binds the galaxy together."

Andi started giggling. "You're insane."

"But functionally so," I said, and adjusted myself to round out a little better. "Just let go your conscious self and act on instinct."

Justine stared blankly at me for a second. Then her face lightened and she let out a little laugh. "The Rack will be with us?"

I couldn't stop myself from cracking a smile. "Always."

The limo joined a line of similar vehicles dropping people off at the entrance to the svartalf stronghold. A valet opened our door, and I swung my legs out and tried to leave the car without flashing everyone in sight. Andi and Justine followed me out, and I started walking confidently toward the entrance with the other two flanking me. Our heels clicked in near unison, and I suddenly felt every eye in sight swivel toward us. A cloud of thought and emotion rolled out in response to our presence— pleasure, mostly, along with a mixed slurry of desire, outright lust, jealousy, anxiety, and surprise. It hurt to feel all of that scraping against the inside of my head, but it was necessary. I didn't sense any outright hostility or imminent violence, and the instant of warning I might get between sensing an attacker's intention and the moment of attack might save our lives.

A security guard at the door watched us intently as we approached, and I could feel the uncomplicated sexual attraction churning through him. He kept it off his face and out of his voice and body, though. "Good evening, ladies," he said. "May I see your invitations?"

I arched an eyebrow at him, gave him what I hoped was a seductive smile, and tried to arch my back a little more. Deploying the Rack had worked before. "You don't need to see our invitation."

"Um," he said. "Miss . . . I kind of do."

Andi stepped up beside me and gave him a sex-kitten smile that made me hate her a little, just for a second. "No you don't."

"Uh," he said, "yeah. Still do."

Justine stepped up on my other side. She looked more sweet than sexy, but only barely. "I'm sure it was just an oversight, sir. Couldn't you ask your supervisor if we might come to the reception?"

He stared at us for a long moment, clearly hesitant. Then one hand slowly went to the radio at his side and he lifted it to his mouth. A moment later a slight, small man in a silk suit appeared from inside the building. He took a long look at us.

The interest I'd felt from the guard was fairly normal. It had just been a spark, the instinct-level response of any male to a desirable female.

What came off of the new guy was . . . it was more like a road flare. It burned a thousand times hotter and brighter, and it kept *on* burning. I'd sensed lust and desire in others before. This went so much deeper and wider than mere lust that I didn't think there was a word for it. It was . . . a vast and inhuman yearning, blended with a fierce and jealous love, and seasoned with sexual attraction and desire. It was like standing near a tiny sun, and I suddenly understood exactly what Auntie Lea had been trying to tell me.

Fire is hot. Water is wet. And svartalves are suckers for pretty girls. They could no more change their nature than they could the course of the stars.

"Ladies," the new guy said, smiling at us. It was a charming smile, but there was something distant and disquieting in his face all the same. "Please, wait just a moment for me to alert my other staff. We would be honored if you would join us."

He turned and went inside.

Justine gave me a sidelong look.

"The Rack can have a powerful influence over the weak-minded," I said.

"I'd feel better if he hadn't left on a Darth Vader line," Andi breathed. "He smelled odd. Was he . . . ?"

"Yeah," I whispered back. "One of them."

The man in the silk suit reappeared, still smiling, and opened the door for us. "Ladies," he said, "I am Mister Etri. Please, come inside."

———

I had never in my life seen a place more opulent than the inside of the svart-alves' stronghold. Not in magazines, not in the movies. Not even on *Cribs*.

There were tons of granite and marble. There were sections of wall that had been inlaid with precious and semiprecious stones. Lighting fixtures were crafted of what looked like solid gold, and the light switches looked like they'd been carved from fine ivory. Security guards were stationed every twenty or thirty feet, standing at rigid attention like those guys outside Buckingham Palace, only without the big hats. Light came from everywhere and from nowhere, making all shadows thin and wispy things without becoming too bright for the eyes. Music drifted on the air, some old classical thing that was all strings and no drumbeat.

Etri led us down a couple of hallways to a vast cathedral of a ballroom. It was absolutely palatial in there—in fact, I was pretty sure that the room shouldn't have *fit* in the building we'd just entered—and it was filled with expensive-looking people in expensive-looking clothing.

We paused in the entry while Etri stopped to speak to yet another se-curity guy. I took the moment it offered to sweep my gaze over the room. The place wasn't close to full, but there were a lot of people there. I recog-nized a couple of celebrities, people you'd know if I told you their names. There were a number of the Sidhe in attendance, their usual awe-inspiring physical perfection muted to mere exotic beauty. I spotted Gentleman Johnnie Marcone, the head of Chicago's outfit in attendance, with his gorilla Hendricks and his personal attack witch, Gard, floating around near him. There were any number of people who I was sure weren't people; I could sense the blurring of perception in the air around them as if they were cut off from me by a thin curtain of falling water.

But I didn't see Thomas.

"Molly," Justine whispered, barely audible. "Is he . . . ?"

The tracking spell I'd focused on my lips was still functioning, a faint tingle telling me that Thomas was nearby, deeper into the interior of the building. "He's alive," I said. "He's here."

Justine shuddered and took a deep breath. She blinked slowly, once, her face showing nothing as she did. I felt the surge of simultaneous relief and terror in her presence, though, a sudden blast of emotion that cried out for her to scream or fight or burst into tears. She did none of that, and I turned my eyes away from her in order to give her the illusion that I hadn't noticed her near meltdown.

In the center of the ballroom, there was a small, raised platform of stone, with a few stairs leading up onto it. Upon the platform was a podium of the same material. Resting on the podium was a thick folio of papers and a neat row of fountain pens. There was something solemn and ceremonial about the way it was set up.

Justine was looking at it, too. "That must be it."

"The treaty?"

She nodded. "The svartalves are very methodical about business. They'll conclude the treaty precisely at midnight. They always do."

Andi tapped a finger thoughtfully on her hip. "What if something happened to their treaty first? I mean, if someone spilled a bunch of wine on it or something. That would be attention getting, I bet—maybe give a couple of us a chance to sneak further in."

I shook my head. "No. We're guests here. Do you understand?"

"Uh. Not really."

"The svartalves are old-school," I said. "*Really* old-school. If we break the peace when they've invited us into their territory, we're violating our guest right and offering them disrespect as our hosts—right out in the open, in front of the entire supernatural community. They'll react . . . badly."

Andi frowned and said, "Then what's our next move?"

Why do people keep asking me that? Is this what all wizard types go through? I'd probably asked Harry that question a hundred times, but I never realized how hard it was to hear it coming toward you. But Harry always knew what to do next. All I could do was improvise desperately and hope for the best.

"Justine," I said, "do you know any of the players here?"

As Lara Raith's personal assistant, Justine came in contact with a lot of people and not-quite-people. Lara had so many fingers in so many pies that I could barely make a joke about it, and Justine saw, heard, and thought a lot more than anyone gave her credit for. The white-haired girl scanned the room, her dark eyes flicking from face to face. "Several."

"All right. I want you to circulate and see what you can find out," I said. "Keep an eye out. If you see them sending the brute squad after us, get on the crystal and warn us."

"Okay," Justine whispered. "Careful."

Etri returned and smiled again, though his eyes remained oddly, unsettlingly without expression. He flicked one hand and a man in a tux floated over to us with a tray of drinks. We helped ourselves, and Etri did, too. He lifted his glass to us and said, "Ladies, be welcome. To beauty."

We echoed him and we all sipped. I barely let my lips touch the liquid. It was champagne, really good stuff. It fizzed and I could barely taste the alcohol. I wasn't worried about poison. Etri had quite diffidently allowed us to choose our glasses before taking one of his own.

I was actually more worried about the fact that I'd stopped to consider potential poisoning, and to watch Etri's actions carefully as he served us. Is it paranoid to worry about things like that? It seemed reasonable to me at the time.

Man, maybe I'm more messed up than I thought I was.

"Please, enjoy the reception," Etri said. "I'm afraid I must insist on a dance with each of you lovely young ladies when time and duty shall allow. Who shall be first?"

Justine gave him a Rack-infused smile and lifted her hand. If you twisted my arm, I'd tell you that Justine was definitely the prettiest girl in our little trio, and Etri evidently agreed. His eyes turned warm for an instant before he took Justine's hand and led her out onto the dance floor. They vanished into the moving crowd.

"I couldn't do this ballroom stuff anyway," Andi said. "Not nearly enough booty bouncing. Next move time?"

"Next move time," I said. "Come on."

I turned the follow the tingle in my lips and the two of us made our way to the back side of the ballroom, where doors led deeper into the facility. There were no guards on the doors, but as we got closer, Andi's steps started to slow. She glanced over to one side, where there was a refreshments table, and I saw her begin to turn toward it.

I caught her arm and said, "Hold it. Where are you going?"

"Um," she said, frowning. "Over there?"

I extended my senses and felt the subtle weaving of magic in the air around the doorway, cobweb fine. It was a kind of veil, designed to direct the attention of anyone approaching it away from the doorway and toward anything else in the room. It made the refreshment table look yummier. If Andi had spotted a guy, he would have looked a lot cuter than he actually was.

I'd been having a powerful faerie sorceress throwing veils and glamours at me for almost a year, building up my mental defenses, and a few months ago I'd gone twelve rounds in the psychic boxing ring with a heavyweight champion necromancer. I hadn't even noticed the gentle magical weaving hitting my mental shields.

"It's an enchantment," I told her. "Don't let it sway you."

"What?" she asked. "I don't feel anything. I'm just hungry."

"You wouldn't feel it," I said. "That's how it works. Take my hand and close your eyes. Trust me."

"If I had a nickel for every time a bad evening started with a line like that," she muttered. But she put her hand in mine and closed her eyes.

I walked her toward the doorway and felt her growing more tense as we went—but then we passed through it and she let out her breath explosively, blinking her eyes open. "Wow. That felt . . . like nothing at all."

"It's how you recognize quality enchantment," I said. "If you don't know it's got you, you can't fight it off." The hallway we stood in looked much like any in any office building. I tried the nearest door and found it locked. So were the next couple, but the last was an empty conference room, and I slipped inside.

I fumbled the crystal out of my little clutch and said, "Bosley, can you hear me?"

"Loud and clear, Angels," came Waldo's voice. Neither of us used real names. The crystals were probably secure, but a year with Lea's nasty trickery as a daily feature of life had taught me not to make many assumptions.

"Were you able to come up with those floor plans?"

"About ninety seconds ago. The building's owners filed everything with the city in triplicate, including electronic copies, which I am now looking at, courtesy of the hivemind."

"Advantage, nerds," I said. "Tell them they did good, Boz."

"Will do," Waldo said. "These people you're visiting are thorough, Angels. Be careful."

"When am I not careful?" I said.

Andi had taken up a guard position against the wall next to the door, where she could grab anyone who opened it. "Seriously?"

I couldn't help but smile a little. "I think our lost lamb is in the wing of the building to the west of the reception hall. What's there?"

"Um . . . offices, it looks like. Second floor, more offices. Third floor, more offi—hello there."

"What'd you find?"

"A vault," Waldo said. "Reinforced steel. Huge."

"Hah," I said. "A reinforced-steel vault? Twenty bucks says it's a dungeon. We start there."

"Whatever it is, it's in the basement. There should be a stairway leading down to it at the end of the hallway leading out of the reception hall."

"Bingo," I said. "Stay tuned, Bosley."

"Will do. Your chariot awaits."

I put the crystal away and began putting on my rings. I got them all together, then began to pick up my wands, and realized that I couldn't carry them in each hand while also carrying the little clutch. "I knew I should have gone for a messenger bag," I muttered.

"With that dress?" Andi asked. "Are you kidding?"

"True." I took the crystal out and tucked it into my décolletage, palmed one of the little wands in each hand, and nodded to Andi. "If it's a vault or a dungeon, there will be guards. I'm going to make it hard for them to see us, but we might have to move fast."

Andi looked down at her shoes and sighed mournfully. Then she stepped out of them and peeled the little black dress off. She hadn't been wearing anything underneath. She closed her eyes for a second and then her form just seemed to blur and melt. Werewolves don't do dramatic, painful transformations except right at first, I've been told. This looked as natural as a living being turning in a circle and sitting down. One moment Andi was there, and the next there was a great russet-furred wolf sitting where she'd been.

It was highly cool magic. I was going to have to figure out how that was done, one of these days.

"Don't draw blood unless it's absolutely necessary," I said, stepping out of my own torturous shoes. "I'm going to try to make this quick and painless. If there's any rough stuff, not killing anyone will go a long way with the svartalves."

Andi yawned at me.

"Ready?" I asked.

Andi bobbed her lupine head in a sharp, decisive nod. I drew the concealing magic of my top-of-the-line veil around us, and the light suddenly went dim, the colors leaching out of the world. We would be almost impossible to see. And anyone who came within fifty or sixty feet of us would develop a sudden desire for a bit of introspection, questioning their path in life so deeply that there was practically no chance we'd be detected as long as we were quiet.

With Andi walking right beside me, we stole out into the hallway. We found the stairwell Waldo had told us about, and I opened the door to it slowly. I didn't go first. You can't do much better than having a werewolf as your guide, and I'd worked with Andi and her friends often enough in the past year to make our movements routine.

Andi went through first, moving in total silence, her ears perked, her nose twitching. Wolves have incredible senses of smell. Hearing, too. If anyone was around, Andi would sense them. After a tense quarter of a minute, she gave me the signal that it was all clear by sitting down. I eased up next to her and extended my senses, feeling for any more magical defenses or enchantments. There were half a dozen on the first section of the stairwell—simple things, the sorcerous equivalent of trip wires.

Fortunately, Auntie Lea had shown me how to circumvent enchantments such as these. I made an effort of will and modified our veil, and then I nodded to Andi and we started slowly down the stairs. We slipped through the invisible fields of magic without disturbing them, and crept down to the basement.

I checked the door at the bottom of the stairs and found it unlocked.

"This seems way too easy," I muttered. "If it's a prison, shouldn't this be locked?"

Andi let out a low growl, and I could sense her agreement and suspicion.

My mouth still tingled, much more strongly now. Thomas was close. "Guess there's not a lot of choice here." I opened the door, slowly and quietly.

The door didn't open onto some kind of dungeon. It didn't open up to show us a vault, either. Instead, Andi and I found ourselves staring at a long hallway every bit as opulent as those above, with large and ornate doors spaced generously along it. Each door had a simple number on it, wrought in what looked like pure silver. Very subdued lighting was spaced strategically along its length, leaving it comfortably dim without being dark.

Andi's low growl turned into a confused little sound and she tilted her head to one side.

"Yeah," I said, perplexed. "It looks like . . . a hotel. There's even a sign showing fire escape routes on the wall."

Andi gave her head a little shake, and I sensed enough of her emotions to understand her meaning. *What the hell?*

"I know," I said. "Is this . . . living quarters for the svartalves? Guest accommodations?"

Andi glanced up at me and flicked her ears. *Why are you asking me? I can't even talk.*

"I know you can't. Just thinking out loud."

Andi blinked, her ears snapping toward me, and she gave me a sidelong glance. *You heard me?*

"I didn't so much hear you as just . . . understand you."

She leaned very slightly away from me. *Just when I thought you couldn't get any more weird and disturbing.*

I gave her a maliciously wide smile, and the crazy eyes I used to use to scare my kid brothers and sisters.

Andi snorted and then began testing the air with her nose. I watched her closely. Her hackles rose up and I saw her crouch down. *There are things here. Too many scents to sort out. Something familiar, and not in a good way.*

"Thomas is close. Come on." We started forward, and I kept my face turned directly toward the tingling signature of my tracking spell. It began to bear to the right, and as we got to the door to room 6, the tingle suddenly swung to the very corner of my mouth, until I turned to face the doorway directly. "Here, in six."

Andi looked up and down the hall, her eyes restless, her ears trying to swivel in every direction. *I don't like this.*

"Too easy," I whispered. "This is way too easy." I reached out toward the doorknob and stopped. My head told me this situation was all wrong. So did my instincts. If Thomas was a prisoner being held by Svartalfheim, then where were the cages, the chains, the locks, the bars, the guards? And if he wasn't being held against his will . . . what *was* he doing here?

When you find yourself in a situation that doesn't make any sense, it's usually for one reason: you have bad information. You can get bad information in several ways. Sometimes you're just plain wrong about what you learn. More often, and more dangerously, your information is bad because you made a faulty assumption.

Worst of all is when someone deliberately feeds it to you—and, like a sucker, you trust her and take it without hesitation.

"Auntie," I breathed. "She *tricked* me." Lea hadn't sent me into the building to rescue Thomas—or at least not only for that. It was no freaking coincidence that she'd taught me how to specifically circumvent the magical security the svartalves were using, either. She'd had another purpose in bringing me here, on this night.

I replayed our conversation in my mind and snarled. Nothing she told me was a lie, and all of it had been tailored to make me reach the wrong conclusion—that Thomas had to be rescued and that I was the only one who would do it. I didn't know why the Leanansidhe thought I needed to be where I was, but she sure as hell had made sure I would get there.

"That conniving, doublespeaking, treacherous *bitch*. When I catch up with her, I'm going to—"

Andi let out a sudden, very low growl, and I shut up in the nick of time.

The door from the upstairs opened, and that bastard Listen and several turtlenecks started walking down the hall toward us.

Listen was a lean and fit-looking man of middling height. His hair was cropped military short, his skin was pale, and his dark eyes looked hard and intelligent. The werewolves and I had tried to bring him down half a dozen different times, but he always managed to either escape or turn the tables and make us run for our lives.

Vicious bad guys are bad enough. Vicious, resourceful, ruthless, professional, *smart* bad guys are way worse. Listen was one of the latter and I hated his fishy guts.

He and his lackeys were dressed in the standard uniform of the Fomors' servitors: black slacks, black shoes, and a black turtleneck sweater. The high neck of the sweater covered up the gills on both sides of their necks, so that they could pass as mortals. They weren't, or at least they weren't anymore. The Fomor had changed them, making them stronger, faster, and all but immune to pain. I'd never managed to set up a successful ambush before, and now one had fallen right into my lap. I absolutely *ached* to avenge the blood I'd washed from my body early that very day.

But the servitors had weird minds, and they kept getting weirder. It was damned difficult to get into their heads the way I would need to do, and if that first attack failed in close quarters like these, that crew would tear Andi and me apart.

So I ground my teeth. I put my hand on Andi's neck and squeezed slightly as I crouched down beside her, focusing on the veil. I had to damp down on the introspection suggestion: Listen had nearly killed me a few months before, when he noticed a similar enchantment altering the course of his thoughts. That had been damned scary, but I'd worked on it since then. I closed my eyes and spun the lightest, finest cobwebs of suggestion that my gifts could manage while simultaneously drawing the veil even tighter around us. The light in the hallway shrunk to almost nothing, and the air just over my skin became noticeably cooler.

They came closer, Listen clearly in the lead, walking with swift and silent purpose. The son of a bitch passed within two feet of me. I could have reached out and touched him with my hand.

None of them stopped.

They went down the hall to room 8, and Listen pushed a key into a door. He opened it and he and his buddies began to enter the room.

This was an opportunity I couldn't pass up. For all the horror the Fomor had brought to the world since the extinction of the Red Court, we still didn't know why they did what they did. We didn't know what they wanted, or how they thought their current actions would get it for them.

So I moved in all the silence the past year had taught me the hard way, and stalked up to the line of servitors passing into the chamber. After a startled second, Andi joined me, just as quietly. We just barely slipped through the door before it shut.

No one looked back at us as we passed into a palatial suite, furnished as lavishly as the rest of the building. In addition to the half dozen turtlenecks in Listen's party, another five were standing around the room in a guard position, backs straight, their arms clasped behind them.

"Where is he?" Listen asked a guard standing beside a door. The guard was the biggest turtleneck there, with a neck like a fireplug.

"Inside," the guard said.

"It is nearly time," Listen said. "Inform him."

"He left orders that he was not to be disturbed."

Listen seemed to consider that for a moment. Then he said, "A lack of punctuality will invalidate the treaty and make our mission impossible. Inform him."

The guard scowled. "The lord left orders that—"

Listen's upper body surged in a sudden motion, so fast that I could only see it *as* motion. The big guard let out a sudden hiss and a grunt, and blood abruptly fountained from his throat. He staggered a step, turned to Listen, and raised a hand.

Then he shuddered and collapsed to the floor, blood pumping rapidly from a huge and jagged wound in his neck.

Listen dropped a chunk of meat the size of a baseball from his bare, bloody fingers, and bent over to wipe them clean on the dead turtleneck's sweater. The blood didn't show against the black. He straightened up again and then knocked on the door.

"My lord. It is nearly midnight."

He did it again exactly sixty seconds later.

And he repeated it three more times before a slurred voice answered, "I left orders that I was not to be disturbed."

"Forgive me, my lord, but the time is upon us. If we do not act, our efforts are for nothing."

"It is not for you to presume what orders may or may not be ignored," said the voice. "Execute the fool who allowed my sleep to be disturbed."

"It is already done, my lord."

There was a somewhat mollified grunt from the far side of the door, and a moment later it opened, and for the first time I saw one of the lords of the Fomor.

He was a tall, extremely gaunt being, yet somehow not thin. His hands and feet were too large, and his stomach bulged as if it contained a basketball. His jowls were oversized as well, his jaws swollen as if he had the mumps. His lips were too wide, too thick, and too rubbery looking. His hair look too flattened, too limp, like strands of seaweed just washed up onto shore, and on the whole he looked like some kind of gangling, poisonous frog. He was dressed only in a blanket draped across his shoulders. Ew.

There were three women in the room behind him, naked and scattered and dead. Each had livid purple bruises around her throat and glassy, staring eyes.

The turtlenecks all dropped to the floor in supplication as the Fomor entered, though Listen only genuflected upon one knee.

"He is here?" asked the Fomor.

"Yes, my lord," Listen said, "along with both of his bodyguards."

The Fomor croaked out a little laugh and rubbed his splay-fingered hands together. "Mortal upstart. Calling himself a Baron. He will pay for what he did to my brother."

"Yes, my lord."

"No one is allowed to murder my family but me."

"Of course, my lord."

"Bring me the shell."

Listen bowed and nodded to three of the other turtlenecks. They hurried to another door and then emerged, carrying between them an oyster shell that must have weighed half a ton. The thing was monstrous and covered in a crust of coral or barnacles or whatever those things are that grow on the hulls of ships. It was probably seven feet across. The turtlenecks put it down on the floor in the middle of the room.

The Fomor crossed to the shell, touched it with one hand, and murmured a word. Instantly, light blossomed all across its surface, curling and twisting in patterns or maybe letters which I had never seen before. The Fomor stood over it for a time, one hand outstretched, bulbous eyes narrowed, saying something in a hissing, bubbling tongue.

I didn't know what he was doing, but he was moving a lot of energy around, whatever it was. I could feel it filling the air of the chamber, making it seem tighter and somehow harder to breathe.

"My lord?" asked Listen abruptly. "What are you doing?"

"Making a present for our new allies, of course," the Fomor said. "I can hardly annihilate the svartalves along with everyone else. Not yet."

"This is not according to the plans of the Empress."

"The Empress," spat the Fomor, "told me that I ought not harm our new allies. She said nothing of the puling scum attending their festivities."

"The svartalves value their honor dearly," Listen said. "You will shame them if their guests come to harm whilst under their hospitality, my lord. It could defeat the point of the alliance."

The Fomor spat. A glob of yellowy, mucus-like substance splattered the floor near Listen's feet. It hissed and crackled against the marble floor. "Once the treaty is signed, it is done. My gift will be given to them in the moments after: I will spare their miserable lives. And if the rest of the scum turn against the svartalves, they will have no choice but to turn to *us* for our strength." He smirked. "Fear not, Listen. I am not so foolish as to destroy one of the Empress' special pets, even in an accident. You and your fellows will survive."

I suddenly recognized the tenor of energy building up in the giant shell on the floor and my heart just about stopped.

Holy crap.

Lord Froggy had himself a *bomb*.

Like, right *there*.

"My life belongs to my masters, to spend as they will, my lord," Listen said. "Have you any other instruction?"

"Seize whatever treasure you might from the dead before we depart."

Listen bowed his head. "How efficacious do you anticipate your gift to be?"

"The one I made for the Red Court in the Congo was deadly enough," Lord Froggy said, a smug tone in his voice.

My heart pounded even harder. During its war with the White Council, the Red Court had used some kind of nerve gas on a hospital tending wounded wizards. The weapon had killed tens of thousands of people in a city far smaller and less crowded than Chicago.

My bare feet felt tiny and cold.

Lord Froggy grunted and fluttered his fingers, and the bomb-shell vanished, hidden by a veil as good as anything I could do. The Fomor lord abruptly lowered his hand, smiling. "Bring my robes."

The turtlenecks hurriedly dressed Lord Froggy in what might have been the tackiest robe in the history of robekind. Multiple colors wavered over it in patterns like the ripples on water, but seemed random, clashing with one another. It was beaded with pearls, some of them the size of big supermarket gumballs. They put a crown-like circlet on his head after that, and then Lord Froggy and company headed out the door.

I crouched as far to the side as I could, almost under the minibar, with Andi huddling right beside me, holding my veil in tight. Lord Froggy blew right by me, with the turtlenecks walking in two columns behind him, their movements precise and uniform—until one of the last pair stopped, his hand holding the door open.

It was Listen.

His eyes swept the room slowly, and he frowned.

"What is it?" asked the other turtleneck.

"Do you smell something?" Listen asked.

"Like what?"

"Perfume."

Oh, crap.

I closed my eyes and focused on my suggestion frantically, adding threads of anxiety to it, trying to keep it too fine for Listen to pick up on.

After a moment, the other turtleneck said, "I've never really liked perfume. We should not be so far from the lord."

Listen hesitated a moment more before he nodded and began to leave.

"Molly!" said Justine's voice quite clearly from the crystal tucked into my dress. "Miss Gard freaked out about two minutes ago and all but carried Marcone out of here. Security is mobilizing."

Sometimes I think my life is all about bad timing.

Listen whirled around toward us at once, but Andi was faster. She bounded from the floor into a ten-foot leap and slammed against the doorway, hammering it closed with the full weight of her body. In a flickering instant, she was a naked human girl again, straining against the door as she reached up and manually snapped its locks closed.

I fished the crystal out of my dress and said, "There's a bomb on the premises, down in the guest wing. I repeat, a *bomb* in the guest wing, in the Fomor Ambassador's quarters. Find Etri or one of the other svartalves and tell them that the Fomor is planning to murder the svartalves' guests."

"Oh my God," Justine said.

"Holy crap!" chimed in Butters.

Something heavy and moving fast slammed into the door from the other side, and it jumped in its frame. Andi was actually knocked back off of it a few inches, and she reset herself, pressing her shoulder against it to reinforce it. "Molly!"

This was another one of those situations in which panic can get you killed. So while I wanted to scream and run around in circles, what I did was close my eyes for a moment as I released the veil and take a slow, deep breath, ordering my thoughts.

First: if Froggy and the turtlenecks managed to get back into the room, they'd kill us. There were already at least four dead bodies in the suite. Why not add two more? And, all things considered, they'd probably be able to do it. So, priority one was to keep them out of the room, at least until the svartalves sorted things out.

Second: the bomb. If that thing went off, and it was some kind of nerve agent like the Red Court used in Africa, the casualties could be in the hundreds of thousands, and would include Andi and Thomas and Justine—plus Butters and Marci, waiting outside in the car. The bomb had to be disarmed or moved to somewhere safe. Oh, and it would probably need to be not invisible for either of those things to happen.

And three: rescue Thomas. Can't forget the mission, regardless of how complicated things got.

The door boomed again.

"Molly!" Andi screamed, her fear making her voice vibrant, piercing.

"Dammit," I growled. "What would Harry do?"

If Harry was here, he would just hold the stupid door shut. His magic talents had been, like, superhero strong when it came to being able to deliver massive amounts of energy. I'm fairly sure he could have stopped a speeding locomotive. Or at least a speeding semitrailer. But my talents just didn't run to the physical.

Harry had once told me that when you had one problem, you had a problem—but when you had several problems, you might also have several solutions.

I stood up and dropped my wands into my hands, gripping them hard. I faced the doorway and said, "Get ready."

Andi flashed me a glance. "For what?"

"To open the door," I said. "Then shut it behind me."

"What?"

"Close your eyes. Go on three," I said, and bent my knees slightly. "One!"

The door rattled again.

"Two!"

"Are you insane?" Andi demanded.

"Three!" I screamed, and sprinted for the door, lifting both wands.

Andi squeezed her eyes shut and swung the door open, and I deployed the One Woman Rave.

Channeling the strength of my will, light and sound burst from the ends of the two wands. Not light like from a flashlight—more like the light of a small nuclear explosion. The sound wasn't loud like a scream, or a small explosion, or even the howl of a passing train. It was like standing on the deck of one of those old World War II battleships when they fired their big guns—a force that could stun a full-grown man and knock him on his ass.

I charged ahead with a wall of sound and furious light leading the way, and burst into the hall among the scattered forms of the startled, dazed turtlenecks.

And then I started playing nasty.

A few seconds later, the scattered turtlenecks were all on their feet again, though they looked a little disoriented and were blinking their eyes. Down the hallway, one of the turtlenecks was helping Lord Froggy to his feet, his lank hair disheveled, his robes in disarray. His ugly face was contorted in fury. "What is happening here, Listen?" he demanded. He was screaming at the top of his lungs. I doubt his ears were working very well.

"My lord," Listen said, "I believe this is more of the work of the Ragged Lady."

"What!? Speak up, fool!"

Listen's cheek twitched once. Then he repeated himself in a shout.

Froggy made a hissing sound. "Meddling bitch," he snarled. "Break down that door and bring me her *heart*."

"Yes, my lord," Listen said, and the turtlenecks grouped up around the door to room 8 again.

They didn't use any tools. They didn't need any. They just started kicking the door, three of them at a time, working in unison, driving the heels of their shoes at the wood. In three kicks, cracks began to form and the door groaned. In five, it broke and swung in loosely on its hinges.

"Kill her!" snarled Lord Froggy, pacing closer to the broken door. "*Kill* her!"

All but two of the turtlenecks poured into the room.

From behind my renewed veil, I figured the timing was about right to discontinue my illusion just as the door bounced back after they'd rushed through it. The silver numeral 8 hanging on the door blurred and melted back into a silver numeral 6.

Lord Froggy's eyes widened in sudden, startled realization.

One of the turtlenecks flew back out the door to room 6 and smashed into the wall on the far side. He hit like a rag doll and flopped off it to the ground. There was a body-shaped outline in cracked marble and flecks of fresh blood left on the wall behind him.

And from the other side of the broken door, Thomas Raith, vampire, said, "It's Listen, right? Wow. Did you clowns ever pick the wrong room."

"We made a mistake," Listen said.

"Yes. Yes, you did."

And things started going crunch and thump in the room beyond.

Lord Froggy hissed and swiveled his bulgy head around on his gangly neck. "Ragged bitch," he hissed. "I know you are here."

This time, I knew exactly what Harry would do. I lifted my sonic wand and sent my voice down to the far end of the hall, behind him. "Hi there, Froggy. Is it as hard as it looks, holding up villain clichés, or does it come naturally to you?"

"You *dare* mock *me*?" the Fomor snarled. He threw a spiraling corkscrew of deep green energy down the hall, and it hissed and left burn marks upon everything it touched, ending at the doors. When it hit *them*, there was a snarling, crackling sound, and the green light spread across their surface in the pattern of a fisherman's net.

"Hard to do anything else to a guy with a face like yours," I said, this time from directly beside him. "Did you kill those girls, or did they volunteer once they saw you with your shirt off?"

The Fomor snarled and swatted at the air beside him. Then his eyes narrowed, and he started muttering and weaving his spatulate fingers in complicated patterns. I could feel the energy coming off of him at once, and knew exactly what he was trying to do—unravel my veil. But I'd been playing that game with Auntie Lea for months.

Lord Froggy hadn't.

As his questing threads of magic spread out, I sent out whispers of my own power to barely brush them, guiding them one by one out and around the area covered by my veil. I couldn't afford to let him find me. Not like that, anyway. He wasn't thinking, and if I didn't get him to, it was entirely possible that he'd be too stupid to fool.

I couldn't have him giving up and leaving, either, so when I was sure I'd compromised his seeking spell I used the sonic wand again, this time directly above his head. "This kind of thing really isn't for amateurs. Are you sure you shouldn't sit this one out and let Listen give it a shot?"

Lord Froggy tilted his head up and then narrowed his eyes. He lifted a hand, spat a hissing word, and fire leapt up from his fingers to engulf the ceiling above him.

It took about two seconds for the fire alarm to go off, and another two before the sprinkler system kicked in. But I was back at the door to room

8 when the falling water began to dissolve my veil. Magic is a kind of energy, and follows its own laws. One of those laws is that water tends to ground out active magical constructs, and my veil started melting away like it was made of cotton candy.

"Hah!" spat the Fomor, spotting me. I saw him send a bolt of viridian light at me. I threw myself facedown to the floor and it passed over me, splashing against the door. I whipped over onto my back, just in time to raise a shield against a second bolt and a third. My physical shields aren't great, but the Fomor's spell was pure energy, and that made it easier for me to handle. I deflected the bolts left and right, and they blasted chunks of marble the size of bricks out of the walls when they struck.

Lord Froggy's eyes flared even larger and more furious that he'd missed. "Mortal cow!"

Okay, now. That stung. I mean, maybe it's a little shallow, and maybe it's a little petty, and maybe it shows a lack of character of some kind that Froggy's insult to my appearance got under my skin more effectively than attempted murder.

"Cow?" I snarled as water from the sprinkler system started soaking me. "I *rock* this dress!"

I dropped one of my wands and thrust my palm out at him, sending out an invisible bolt of pure memory, narrowed and focused with magic, like light passing through a magnifying glass. Sometimes you don't really remember traumatic injuries, and my memory of getting shot in the leg was pretty blurry. It hadn't hurt so much when I actually got shot and I'd had a few things occupying my attention. Mostly, I'd just felt surprised and then numb—but when they were tending the wound in the helicopter, later, now *that* was pain. They'd dug the bullet out with forceps, cleaned the site with something that burned like Hell itself, and when they'd put the pressure bandage on it and tightened the straps, it hurt so bad that I'd thought I was going to die.

That's what I gave to Lord Froggy, with every bit of strength I could muster.

He wove a shield against the attack, but I guess he wasn't used to handling something so intangible as a memory. Even with the falling water weakening it, I felt the strike smash through his defense and sink home, and Froggy let out a sudden, high-pitched shriek. He staggered and fell heavily against the wall, clutching at his leg.

"Kill her!" he said, his voice two octaves higher than it had been a moment before. "Kill her, kill her, kill her!"

The remaining pair of turtlenecks in the hallway plunged toward me. A wave of fatigue from my recent efforts, especially that last one, almost held me pinned to the floor—but I scrambled to my feet, lurched to the door to room 8, and pounded against it with one fist. "Andi! Andi, it's Molly! Andi, let me—"

The door jerked open and I fell into the room. I snapped my legs up into a fetal curl, and Andi slammed the door shut behind me and hit the locks.

"What the *hell*, Molly?" she demanded. Andi was soaking wet, along with everything else in the room—including the Fomor's bomb.

I got up and scrambled toward it. "I couldn't take apart the veil over the bomb from the outside," I panted. "We didn't have time to build up a fire, and I can't call up enough of my own to set off the alarms. I had to get Froggy to do it for me."

The door shuddered under more blows from the turtlenecks.

"Hold them off," I told her. "I'll disarm the bomb."

"Can you *do* that?" Andi asked.

"Piece of cake," I lied.

"Okay," Andi said. She grimaced. "I'm going to smell like wet dog all night."

She turned to face the door in a ready position as I reached the giant shell. I forced the battering enemies at the door out of my thoughts and focused my complete attention on the shell before me. Then I extended my senses toward it and began feeling out the energy moving through it.

There was a *lot* of energy involved in this thing, power stored up inside and ready to explode. A thin coating of enchantment lined the shell's exterior, kind of the magical equivalent of a control panel. The water was eroding it slowly, but not fast enough to start melting the core enchantment and dispersing the stored energy. But if I didn't move fast, the water *would* destroy the surface enchantment and make it impossible for *anyone* to disarm the bomb.

I closed my eyes and put one hand out over the shell like Froggy had done. I could feel the energy of the shell reaching up to my fingers, ready to respond, and I began pouring my own energy down into it, trying to feel it out. It was a straightforward spell, nothing complicated, but I didn't know what anything did—it was like having a remote control for the TV, if someone had forgotten to label any of the buttons. I couldn't just start pushing them randomly.

On the other hand, I couldn't *not* do it, either.

It would have to be an educated guess.

On a TV remote, the power button is almost always a little apart from the others, or else somehow centered. That's what I was looking for—to turn the bomb off. I started eliminating all the portions of the spell that seemed too complex or too small, narrowing my choices bit by bit. It came down to two. If I guessed wrong . . .

I burst out into a nervous giggle. "Hey, Andi. Blue wire or red wire?"

A turtleneck's foot smashed a hole in the door, and Andi whipped her head around to give me an incredulous look. "Are you fucking *kidding* me?" she shouted. "Blue, you *always* cut the blue!"

Half of the door broke down and crashed to the floor. Andi blurred into her wolf form and surged forward, ripping at the first turtleneck as he tried to come in.

I turned my attention back to the bomb and picked the second option. I focused my will on it. It took me a couple of tries, because I was freaking terrified, and pants-wetting fear is generally not conducive to lucidity.

"Hey, God," I whispered. "I know I haven't been around much lately, but if you could do me a solid here, it would be really awesome for a lot of people. Please let me be right."

I cut the blue wire.

Nothing happened.

I felt a heavy, almost paralytic surge of relief—and then Lord Froggy hopped over the two turtlenecks struggling with Andi and smashed into me.

I went down hard on the marble floor, and Froggy rode me down, pinning me beneath his too-gaunt body. He wrapped the fingers of one hand all the way around my neck with room enough for them to overlap his thumb, and squeezed. He was hideously strong. My breath stopped instantly and my head began to pound, and my vision to darken.

"Little *bitch*," he hissed. He started punching me with his other hand. The blows landed on my left cheekbone. They should have hurt, but I think something was wrong with my brain. I registered the impact but everything else was swallowed by the growing darkness. I could feel myself struggling, but I didn't get anywhere. Froggy was way, way stronger than he looked. My eyes weren't focusing very well, but I found myself staring down a dark tunnel toward one of the dead girls on the bedroom floor, and the dark purple band of bruising around her throat.

Then the floor a few feet away rippled, and an odd-looking grey creature popped up out of it.

The svartalf was maybe four-six and entirely naked. His skin was a mottled shade of grey, and his eyes were huge and entirely black. His head was a little larger than most people's and he was bald, though his eyebrows were silvery-white. He did look kind of Roswellian, only instead of being super-skinny he was built like a professional boxer, lean and strong—and he carried a short, simple sword in his hand.

"Fomor," said the svartalf calmly. I recognized Mister Etri's voice. "One should not strike ladies."

Froggy started to say something, but then Etri's sword went snicker-snack, and the hand that was choking the life out of me was severed cleanly from the Fomor's wrist. Froggy screamed and fell away from me, spitting words and trying to summon power as he scrambled away on three limbs.

"You have violated guest right," Etri continued calmly. He made a gesture and the marble beneath Lord Froggy turned suddenly liquid. Froggy sank about three inches, and then the floor hardened around him again. The Fomor screamed.

"You have attacked a guest under the hospitality and protection of Svartalfheim," he said, his tone of voice never changing. The sword swept out again and struck the nose from Froggy's face, spewing ichor everywhere and drawing even more howling. Etri stood over the fallen Fomor and looked down at him with absolutely no expression on his face. "Have you anything to say on your own behalf?"

"No!" Froggy screamed. "You cannot do this! I have harmed none of your people!"

There was a pulse of rage from Etri so hot that I thought the falling water would burst into steam when it struck him. "Harmed us?" he said quietly. He glanced at the shell and then back at Froggy with pure contempt. "You would have used our alliance as a pretext to murder innocent thousands, making us your accomplices." He crouched down to put his face inches from Froggy's, and said in a calm, quiet, pitiless voice, "You have stained the honor of Svartalfheim."

"I will make payment!" Froggy gabbled. "You will be compensated for your pains!"

"There is but one price for your actions, Fomor. And there are no negotiations."

"No," Froggy protested. "No. NO!"

Etri turned away from him and surveyed the room. Andi was still in wolf form. One of the turtlenecks was bleeding out onto the marble floor, the sprinklers spreading the blood into a huge pool. The other was crouched in a corner with his arms curled around his head, covered in bleeding wounds. Andi faced him, panting, blood dripping from her reddened fangs, a steady growl bubbling in her chest.

Etri turned to me and offered me his hand. I thanked him and let him pull me up to a sitting position. My throat hurt. My head hurt. My face hurt. It's killing me, nyuk, nyuk, nyuk. C'mere, you.

You know you've been punched loopy when you're doing a one-person Three Stooges routine in your internal monologue.

"I apologize," Etri said, "for interfering in your struggle. Please do not presume that I did so because I thought you unable to protect yourself."

My voice came out in a croak. "It's your house, and your honor that was at stake. You had the right."

The answer seemed to please him and he inclined his head slightly. "I further apologize for not handling this matter myself. It was not your responsibility to discover or take action against this scum's behavior."

"It was presumptuous of me," I said. "But there was little time to act."

"Your ally alerted us to the danger. You did nothing improper. Svartalfheim thanks you for your assistance in this matter. You are owed a favor."

I was about to tell him that no such thing was necessary, but I stopped myself. Etri wasn't uttering social pleasantries. This wasn't a friendly exchange. It was an audit, an accounting. I just inclined my head to him. "Thank you, Mister Etri."

"Of course, Miss Carpenter."

Svartalves in security uniforms, mixed with mortal security guards, came into the room. Etri went to them and quietly gave instructions. The Fomor and his servitors were trussed up and taken from the room.

"What will happen to them?" I asked Etri.

"We will make an example of the Fomor," Etri said.

"What of your treaty?" I asked.

"It was never signed," he said. "Mostly because of you, Miss Carpenter. While Svartalfheim does not pay debts which were never incurred, we appreciate your role in this matter. It will be considered in the future."

"The Fomor don't deserve an honorable ally."

"It would seem not," he said.

"What about the turtlenecks?" I asked.

"What of them?"

"Will you . . . deal with them?"

Etri just looked at me. "Why would we?"

"They were sort of in on it," I said.

"They were property," said the svartalf. "If a man strikes you with a hammer, it is the man who is punished. There is no reason to destroy the hammer. We care nothing for them."

"What about them?" I asked, and nodded toward the dead girls in the Fomor's chamber. "Do you care what happened to them?"

Etri looked at them and sighed. "Beautiful things ought not be destroyed," he said. "But they were not our guests. We owe no one for their end and will not answer for it."

"There is a vampire in your custody," I said, "is there not?"

Etri regarded me for a moment and then said, "Yes."

"You owe me a favor. I wish to secure his release."

He arched an eyebrow. Then he bowed slightly and said, "Come with me."

I followed Etri out of the suite and across the hall to room 6. Though the door was shattered, Etri stopped outside of it respectfully and knocked. A moment later, a female voice said, "You may enter."

We went in. It was a suite much like the Fomor's, only with way more throw pillows and plush furniture. It was a wreck. The floor was literally covered with shattered furniture, broken décor, and broken turtlenecks. Svartalf security was already binding them and carrying them from the room.

Listen walked out on his own power, his hands behind his back, one of his eyes swollen halfway shut. He gave me a steady look as he went by, and said nothing.

Bastard.

Etri turned toward the curtained door to the suite's bedroom and spoke.

"The mortal apprentice who warned us has earned a favor. She asks for the release of the vampire."

"Impossible," answered the female voice. "That account has been settled."

Etri turned to me and shrugged. "I am sorry."

"Wait," I said. "May I speak to him?"

"In a moment."

We waited. Thomas appeared from the doorway to the bedroom dressed in a black terry-cloth bathrobe. He'd just gotten out of the shower. Thomas was maybe half an inch under six feet tall, and there wasn't an inch of his body that didn't scream sex symbol. His eyes were a shade of deep crystalline blue, and his dark hair hung to his wide shoulders. My body did what it always did around him, and started screaming at me to make babies. I ignored it. Mostly.

"Molly," he said. "Are you all right?"

"Nothing a bucket of aspirin won't help," I said. "Um. Are you okay?"

He blinked. "Why wouldn't I be?"

"I thought . . . you know. You'd been captured as a spy."

"Well, sure," he said.

"I thought they would, uh. Make an example of you?"

He blinked again. "Why would they do that?"

The door to the bedroom opened again, and a female svartalf appeared. She looked a lot like Etri—tiny and beautiful, though she had long silver hair instead of a cueball. She was wearing what might have been Thomas's shirt, and it hung down almost to her ankles. She had a decidedly . . . smug look about her. Behind her, I saw several other sets of wide, dark eyes peer out of the shadowy bedchamber.

"Oh," I said. "*Oh*. You, uh. You made a deal."

Thomas smirked. "It's a tough, dirty job. . . ."

"And one that is not yet finished," said the female svartalf. "You are ours until dawn."

Thomas looked from me to the bedroom and back and spread his hands. "You know how it is, Molly. Duty calls."

"Um," I said. "What do you want me to tell Justine?"

Again he gave me a look of near incomprehension. "The truth. What else?"

———

"Oh, thank goodness," Justine said as we were walking out. "I was afraid they'd have starved him."

I blinked. "Your boyfriend is banging a roomful of elfgirls and you're *happy* about it?"

Justine tilted her head back and laughed. "When you're in love with an incubus, it changes your viewpoint a little, I think. It isn't as though this is something new. I know how he feels about me, and he needs to feed to be healthy. So what's the harm?" She smirked. "And besides. He's *always* ready for more."

"You're a very weird person, Justine."

Andi snorted, and nudged me with her shoulder in a friendly way. She'd recovered her dress and the shoes she liked. "Look who's talking."

After everyone was safe home, I walked from Waldo's apartment to the nearest parking garage. I found a dark corner, sat down, and waited. Lea shimmered into being about two hours later and sat down beside me.

"You tricked me," I said. "You sent me in there blind."

"Indeed. Just as Lara did her brother—except that my agent succeeded where hers failed."

"But why? Why send us in there?"

"The treaty with the Fomor could not be allowed to conclude," she said. "If one nation agreed to neutrality with them, a dozen more would follow. The Fomor would be able to divide the others and contend with them one by one. The situation was delicate. The presence of active agents was intended to disrupt its equilibrium—to show the Fomor's true nature in a test of fire."

"Why didn't you just tell me that?" I asked.

"Because you would neither have trusted nor believed me, obviously," she said.

I frowned at her. "You should have told me anyway."

"Do not be ridiculous, child." Lea sniffed. "There was no time to humor your doubts and suspicions and theories and endless questions. Better to give you a simple prize upon which to focus—Thomas."

"How did you know I would find the bomb?"

She arched an eyebrow. "Bomb?" She shook her head. "I did not know what was happening in any specific sense. But the Fomor are betrayers. Ever have they been, ever will they be. The only question is what form their treachery will take. The svartalves had to be shown."

"How did you know I would discover it?"

"I did not," she said. "But I know your mentor. When it comes to meddling, to unearthing awkward truths, he has taught you exceedingly well." She smiled. "You have also learned his aptitude for taking orderly situations and reducing them to elemental chaos."

"Meaning what?" I demanded.

Her smile was maddeningly smug. "Meaning that I was confident that whatever happened, it would not include the smooth completion of the treaty."

"But you could have done everything I did."

"No, child," Lea said. "The svartalves would never have asked me to be their guest at the reception. They love neatness and order. They would have known my purposes were not orderly ones."

"And they didn't know that about me?"

"They cannot judge others except by their actions," Lea said. "Hence their treaty with the Fomor, who had not yet crossed their paths. My actions have shown me to be someone who must be treated with caution. You had . . . a clean record with them. And you are smoking hot. All is well, your city saved, and now a group of wealthy, skilled, and influential beings owes you a favor." She paused for a moment and then leaned toward me slightly. "Perhaps some expression of gratitude is in order."

"From me, to you?" I asked. "For that?"

"I think your evening turned out quite well," Lea said her eyebrows raised. "Goodness, but you are a difficult child. How he manages to endure your insolence I will never know. You probably think you have earned some sort of reward from me." She rose and turned to go.

"Wait!" I said suddenly.

She paused.

I think my heart had stopped beating. I started shaking, everywhere. "You said that you know Harry. Not knew him. Know. Present tense."

"Did I?"

"You said you don't know how he manages to put up with me. Manages. Present tense."

"Did I?"

"Auntie," I asked her, and I could barely whisper. "Auntie . . . is Harry . . . is he alive?"

Lea turned to me very slowly, and her eyes glinted with green, wicked knowledge. "I did not say that he was alive, child. And neither should you. Not yet."

I bowed my head and started crying. Or laughing. Or both. I couldn't tell. Lea didn't wait around for it. Emotional displays made her uncomfortable.

Harry. Alive.

I *hadn't* killed him.

Best reward ever.

"Thank you, Auntie," I whispered. "Thank you."